MEDUSA
AND
THE DEVIL

SIMON
MARLOWE

CRANTHORPE
MILLNER
PUBLISHERS

First published by Cranthorpe Millner Publishers (2023)

ISBN 978-1-80378-130-3 (Paperback)

www.cranthorpemillner.com

Cranthorpe Millner Publishers

Simon Marlowe is an author who has promised he will spend more time on his artwork once he's finished writing! Educated in the so-called "university of life" before eventually going to a few "real" universities, Simon returned to live in his hometown in Essex, after spending far too long making loud music and a nuisance of himself in South London. However, after recently captaining the Authors team on the TV quiz show *Eggheads*, he will only agree to further media appearances that guarantee cheeseburger and fries in the green room (and no pickle, limp lettuce or ketchup). He also describes his sense of humour as like a desert, or arid, which partially accounts for this short bio being highly uninformative.

Medusa and the Devil is his third novel and the second book in the darkly comic, crime and mystery thriller trilogy.

A special thanks, as all ways, to my magnificent family, known as Christine, James and Jessica. Also, many thanks to Kirsty and the team at Cranthorpe Millner, especially Lydia for her thoughtful edits, Vicky, Shannon and Sue, and anyone else who deserves a mention! Finally, for those of you who take the time to read my stories, and for those of you who review and spread the word: muchas gracias!

"He who steals a little, steals with the same wish as he who steals much, but with less power."

– Plato

We Therefore Commit This Body To The Ground

1

I'm six feet under; the only problem is, I'm not dead. When they put me down here, they told me I had five hours left to live – if I didn't move or waste my time trying to get out. Which means the only thing that's going to save my arse is a miracle. Stranger things can happen, but based on my track record, which is south of bad and more towards villain, there's no fairy godmother going to wave her magic wand, lift the curse and shack me up with Cinders.

The only good thing is they haven't gone cheap, because the coffin is mahogany – nothing but quality for my funeral.

I guess it's all over, like I've been to hospital and got told I've got cancer. Only it's not six months, or six weeks, or even six days – it's happening now.

So, I might as well just lie here in the dark until I'm dragged down to hell.

All of which means, while I'm waiting, I'm going to try and work out how I got into this hole, which is also a déjà vu kind of thing, but more of that later.

However, it all started when Grandad phoned me, which went something like this:

'Steven?'

'Yeah.'

'It's me.'

'Yeah.'

'What do yous know about Medusa?'

'Medusa?'

'Yeah.'

'A scary Greek woman who turns you into stone if you look at her face.'

'That's right, son, *Jason and the Argonauts* and all that. But that's before your time. Yous laugh at all of that now if yous saw them films, but they were good in the day. Anyways, there's someone yous need to meet and 'e 'as a Medusa. Not a real one, mind, Steven, if that's what yous wondering. A small one, which yous can put it in your pocket when you collect it for me. Tony should be sat next to yous by now, so 'e can tell yous what to do about it.'

'Yeah, he is.'

'Good lad. And don't forget, when yous out in the sun, yous need to wear an 'at. Not good for the skin if yous don't 'ave suntan and an 'at.'

Grandad had a thing about the sun because he'd had cancer.

'Good talking to yers. Be good and keep out of trouble – unless yous need to do some.'

And that was it, end of, doing something off-piste for my boss.

He also happens to be my biological dad, but trust me,

2

there is nothing about him that is fatherly, or grandfatherly; it is all transactional. The only good thing is, I'm a thousand of miles away from him, living on a small Mediterranean island. Which wasn't the case six months ago, when I was running around like a blue-arsed fly looking for his girlfriend, who in the end turned up dead. But that's another story, as is the other people who ended up dead in another kind of hole. Which is part of the reason why I'm out here investing in things for Grandad, but mainly I'm here because I need to be out of sight and out of mind, until it's safe to go back home.

Tony comes from the same part of Essex as me, which for those of you who don't know, is like the dog's arse of London, running down the east side of the Thames. He landed half an hour ago and was sitting on the sofa sipping lemonade, looking all suited and booted for a business meeting. The only thing that let himself down was his trademark white trainers, which he said kept his feet comfy. He'd also taken on board Grandad's advice about the climate and had carefully placed his short brimmed Mexican hat next to him, like it was some prized possession that he only wore on Sundays.

'Don't worry, Steven,' said Tony, holding his glass in his fat fingers out in front him, 'I know what yer going to say about me being here.'

'Yeah, you're right,' I said, sitting down opposite him in my sandals, shorts and t-shirt.

'Yeah, well, it's not a problem.'

And that was that, he thought he had solved the issue. But it's what I call a warning sign: someone from Grandad's crew flying in especially to be with me, to collect something that could easily go by parcel post.

'So, the Medusa,' said Tony. 'That's all I'm here for.'

He then put his lemonade down on the coffee table and pulled out from his inside jacket pocket a folded piece of paper.

'The gorgon, Medusa,' he said, handing me a scruffy bit of paper. 'It's a bit of an artefact – that's the picture of it. It's good and small, so you can easily put it in your pocket.'

'It looks like ivory?'

'Yeah, that's right. What you're looking at is the end of the Medusa. Perseus has beheaded her and he is going to use the head like a weapon of mass destruction.'

'Turn people to stone, you mean?'

'Yeah, I think that's pretty destructive, don't you? Then, if you look a bit closer, the things spewing out of her neck, it ain't just blood, she's also giving birth.'

'Nice.'

'Yeah, that's gorgons for you. They are Poseidon's kids. Pegasus the horse and her brother, Chrysaor.'

I could just make out the two figures, with Medusa's body on the ground and the children of the Medusa being born.

'I've heard of Pegasus,' I said, impressed by Tony's grip on all things Greek.

'Yeah, it's got wings, unlike most of the horses I bet on. Anyways, the other one, Chrysaor, is a bit of a nobody, but had a golden sword.'

'Useful in a fight then.'

'Yeah.'

'How do you know all this stuff?'

'I watched some video Grandad gave us.'

'Good memory then?'

'Yeah, I like to remember things.'

4

I grinned because there was one or two things Tony would remember about me, even if it were all in the past.

'So,' I said, stretching out and handing back his picture of the Medusa, 'how are things back on the estate?'

'Calm,' he said.

'That's good. Anyone talking about me?'

'No, people know better than that.'

Unlikely, I thought, but it meant nobody was talking to the police. There were a few people I could have mentioned that would have been handy to get intel on, like my mum and Mrs C, but that would have meant ending up talking about the other dead people I had left in a hole, like my half-brother Greg and Mrs C's son, my old mate Anthony.

'How's the lemonade?' I asked.

'Yeah, it's nice, Steven. Very refreshing.'

That's when Tony started looking around the place and taking in the villa. It was part of the property portfolio I had purchased for Grandad, which was all about getting money into the system. And I must admit, the plush white walls, artwork and furnishings was a step up, and something I was more than happy with.

'How many bedrooms you got then?' he asked.

'Three,' I said, looking at his suitcase, which he had by his feet.

'It's just you then, you ain't loved-up with somebody?'

There was someone, but she had made a swift exit for her own safety. If Grandad had found out, she would also be six feet under.

'No, it's just me,' I said. 'I like to keep things quiet.'

'That's good, nothing like a low profile, after everything that happened.'

'Well, that's why I'm here, isn't it, Tony, keeping out of the way.'

'Yeah, of course, that's all water under the bridge. None of my business really, as you know.'

He was right, it wasn't any of his business.

'So, what do I need to do to pick up the Medusa?'

Tony put his hand into his inside jacket pocket again and pulled out the same piece of paper of the Medusa. He then worked out he needed to check all his pockets before he found what he wanted. This time he had a smaller piece of paper and looked at it like he needed specs.

'You need to go and see this Russian captain,' he said, rubbing his face. 'You need to be there, down in the port where the ship is, at ten, and he'll give you the Medusa.'

He handed me the piece of paper and started scanning the room.

'The toilet is through there,' I said, pointing.

'Thanks,' he said, but he wasn't moving.

'What is it, Tony?'

'Where's your tele?'

'I haven't got one.'

Tony was in shock.

And the only time I'd seen him look like that was when a load of cows ran over him.

2

I took pity on Tony before I left the villa. I set him up on my laptop so he could watch Italian football, which was all he was going to get where I was living. Next, I needed a taxi.

These things are a bit like creatures of the night, with their neon taxi banners blazing, flashing through the lanes, running up and down the hills and zooming through the old town like they're fuelled on amphetamines laced with chip fat.

I'd hired Zammit to do all my chauffeuring. He was a young skinny guy, with a narrow dragged-out face, an earring in his left ear and a cigarette always somewhere near his mouth. And he'd done a good job at getting me around the place since I'd got here. He never asked questions and took my cash with a smile and a wink.

He came from the Arab bit of the island and moaned a lot about the big bosses who ran this place, who he said were all racists. In fact, he moaned a lot about a lot of things, and he never failed to go on about how some guy or other needed a whipping, a beating, castration or death – usually in that order.

Now, there is a lot of stuff in the world that you can get exercised about, but it was like Zammit was always on one, cursing all the usual suspects and promising a reckoning that brought a lot of stuff down on their heads. And if there was one person who Zammit hated more than all the other people he hated, and who had him spitting blood, it was the guy printed on random posters along the roads, which popped up just as much as the yellow taxis did. And they said something like this:

VOTE MARK
VOTE GRECH
VOTE MARK GRECH

These were the words that topped and tailed a picture of the biggest boss of them all, head honcho and prime minister of this little strategic island. And I had sympathy with Zammit's spit, which would go flying out of the window of his taxi, in the hope it would land on the grinning monkey head.

However, he had yet to hit the mark.

Anyway, he had the windows up and hardcore French hip-hop thumping out of his thousand-watt speakers. It meant we were flying along at a speed no one would survive if a car came towards us.

Once down from the hills we drove through the old town and across a bridge, which took us into the port. This was what made the place famous, all ramparts and fortifications, like knights of the roundtable looking out to sea. It was picture postcard stuff – lights beaming and showing off, cardboard cut-out stone walls, the whiff of cooking in the night, wafting out of bent houses, as if a giant had whacked the rooftops with a huff and a puff. That's what the tourists came to see, who stayed in all the swanky hotels that were spreading like acne all over the seafront.

We bounced up and down on the cobbles, with a high stone wall port side and the old housing looking down on us. Zammit then pulled up next to the Leninsky Komsomol. It was the only ship in town and sunk low, which meant it had cargo still on it, probably with gravels or sands for all the building work that was going on.

There was a gang plank close to the ship's bridge. Zammit told me what I was already thinking: 'You can see the way, but I wouldn't go in.'

I stayed in the back of the taxi, watching.

The thing is, unless there was someone standing there with a gun or machete, I didn't have a lot of choice. It was why I was there and not Tony.

'Just wait,' I said, as I got out and looked around.

A dog barked, a TV talked and a few shouts drifted through the warm night air.

I told Zammit to wait. I could feel the cobblestones beneath my feet as I got up close to the ship's gang plank. I looked up and there was a hand and a face waving me in. I checked on Zammit, who was singing to himself and smoking weed. That's when I realised I had been way to casual for this little job, but it was also too late to do anything else about it.

The hand and the face turned out to be a Filipino-looking guy, who said, 'Come, come.' I followed him through the ship's corridors. It was either a good way to confuse me before I got jumped or it was the way to the Russian.

As it turned out, the Russian was sitting in a swivel seat on the bridge, wearing a busted-looking captain's hat. I didn't know much about the Merchant Navy but that hat looked like it was either a gift from his nieces or he'd ordered it online from a novelty shop.

'Are you on holiday, Mr Mason?' he said, proving he was Russian, his fat pink face looking like he ate vodka on long nights at the wheel.

'No,' I said, looking behind me to see what the Filipino guy was up to, but he had gone.

'Like me then,' he said, as I stood there looking at the red and green switches on the console behind him. 'We are always working.'

Then, for whatever reason, he just stared at me, like he

was spaced out or was trying to read my mind.

Unfortunately for him, there was not a lot going on in my brain because I was waiting to see if I had to fight or run.

Anyway, this could have gone on for a lot longer, had he not snapped out of it.

'So, you are a parcel man?' he said.

'Well, I ain't UPS, if that's what you mean, but I am here to collect.'

This kicked off a bit of a nervous twitch in the old seadog, with his left eye and then his right.

'But you are familiar with the nature of the delivery process?' he said, swivelling in his captain's chair. 'There is the supplier, the transporter and the receiver.'

'You mean,' I said, sighing, 'there's a spanner in the works.'

'Yes, Mr Mason,' he said. 'A spanner has been thrown into the machinery.'

'But it's your job to fix it,' I told him.

'Perhaps...' he said.

Which didn't sound like he was going to give me a full refund.

'Do you have it?' I said, leaning back against the side of the ship's metal door.

'Had... I think... is the proper English tense,' he said, looking uneasy. 'But I have not rested on my laurels. I have a possible solution. This, I also think, is what Americans say is... proactive.'

'Yeah, well, it still sounds like BS to me.'

'I understand, but I must remind you of the process, and mine is to merely transport.'

'Are you trying to tell me it has gone walkies since you

docked?'

'Exactly, Mr Mason! You see, even with my poor English, you can still understand me.'

I wish hadn't because there were all kinds of problems for me now.

'Who's nicked it then?'

'Ah, well, it was always in the possession of one man: Max Schmidt.'

'Sounds German?'

'He is, but no friend of mine, you understand, Mr Mason, but that is not because he is German.'

'And where is he now?'

'If he is not with you, then he is a free man, no?'

'You mean, you let him leave the ship with the merchandise?'

'I cannot stop a man who has reached his destination.'

'You didn't need to stop him. You just needed to make sure you had the Medusa for me to collect.'

'If an apology means anything to you, Mr Mason, I will apologise, but I don't think that would have a lot of meaning for you.'

'You can write me a letter if you want, but right now, just tell me what you know about this Schmidt.'

'I think he is a man capable of anything, but for these purposes he is a smuggler. That is as much as I can tell you because that is as much as I care to know.'

'Now, that's what I call unhelpful.'

'Apologies again, but you must understand this has not been an easy journey for us.'

'Did something happen, between you and him, or the crew?'

He shrugged, which meant something had gone on.

'Well, did it or didn't it?'

That's when the Russian started staring again, like he had a medical condition.

Then his lips started quivering.

'You see,' he said, 'there is always more than one parcel. Otherwise, I am not maximising my cost benefit.'

'What does that mean?'

He answered by pointing down the corridor behind me.

The Filipino guy was walking towards us and herding in front of him a couple of kids and a woman.

'I'm afraid,' said the Russian, 'there can be more than one Medusa.'

I moved away from the doorway and stood next to the Russian.

In came two kids and a woman, who was dressed all in black from head to toe.

'They are from England, Mr Mason,' said the Russian, who, like me, was looking them up and down as if it was the first time he had seen them.

The woman was standing behind the two kids. All I could see was her head looking down. The two kids – a pint-sized boy and a girl who was older – wore t-shirts, shorts and trainers. They hugged each other close, afraid to let go.

'I think we will find the mother will not speak,' said the Russian. 'Or the little boy. But we have found the girl to have… how you say… plenty of mouth.'

'My name is Sonia and I am eight,' said the little girl, who had sprung to life and had a South London accent. 'And this is my brother Zain, he is four, and this is my mummy.'

The mum lifted her head. She was stony-faced, harsh

looking. And then I noticed there was sweat all over her face. She was struggling to stand up. But the girl, whose black hair had ringlets running down the side of her face, had a glow about her. But the boy looked shy and scared.

'So, Mr Mason, I am sure you are wondering what this family has to do with anything,' said the Russian, who was now going to tell me why this family had something to do with me. 'Our friend, Max Schmidt, brought two versions of the Medusa with him. One that he has in his pocket, and one that is in front of you, living and breathing, trying to turn all who gaze upon her into stone.'

'Yeah, well, I ain't immigration. I just pick up parcels.'

The Russian started to chuckle.

'The woman is a troubled soul,' he said, looking suspiciously at the mum as she put her head down.

'If you don't like her, why didn't you just throw her overboard.'

'Trust me, most of my crew wanted to.'

'So, what stopped you?'

'Because we paid for our ticket!' shouted Sonia, who clearly had the balls to stand up for herself.

It also meant, seeing as they decided to travel on a cargo ship, they were about as legal as the artefact.

'Little girl,' said the Russian, who bent down to her level, 'if it wasn't for me, your German friend, Mr Schmidt, would have done a lot worse to you.'

'OK,' I said, also bending down to the little girl's level, 'what can you tell me about this Max Schmidt?'

'He was taking us to Germany,' she said, with the hope that this still might happen.

'Yeah, but what's wrong with going back home?'

She shrugged. She wasn't going to answer that one.

'Don't you want to go back home?' I said, looking at the mum who was leaning on the little boy to keep upright.

Sonia shook her head.

'Perhaps they cannot go home,' said the Russian, 'when you have been doing things against your country.'

I eased myself back up, stretched, and then had the light bulb moment and twigged what the Russian's "proactive solution" for finding Max Schmidt was going to be.

'No,' I said to the Russian.

'Mr Mason,' he said, smiling, 'it would be a missed opportunity for you not to consider their usefulness, given your current predicament.'

'We can help you,' said Sonia.

'How's that? All I can see is your mum needs to go to a hospital.'

'No!' shouted the mum.

'The Medusa speaks,' said the Russian. 'But consider, Mr Mason, they might know where your Max Schmidt is.'

'Do you know where he is?' I asked the family.

'Yes,' said Sonia.

'Do you know where on the island?'

She nodded, but I doubted it.

'So, where is he then?'

'We will tell you if you help us.'

'But how do you know where he is?'

She wasn't telling, but she was doing her best to make it look as if she knew.

'Even if they don't know, Mr Mason,' said the Russian, 'they will know what he looks like. I have no picture of him to give you.'

This was not what I wanted. Never accept alternative goods for the ones you ordered.

But the little girl had something about her, which reminded me of myself, when I was a kid.

What did I have to lose?

Right or wrong, it was enough for me to say yes.

3

The Russian told me he'd be leaving port next week, so we did a deal: if Max Schmidt and the Medusa don't turn up, he would take the family off me, free of charge, when they ship out. True, he wasn't going to where the family wanted to go, but it would get them out of my neatly cropped hair and save me from having to join the Red Cross.

I agreed to it because I wasn't in the mood for negotiation – where a Russian captain is thrown overboard with an anchor tied around his neck. What was far better for everybody was finding Max Schmidt, getting the Medusa off him, agreeing compensation for the disruption of inconvenience, and seeing this Medusa mum and her brood on their way to another country.

Zammit didn't seem too bothered that he had a large bulging suitcase in the boot of his car and a motley crew sitting in the backseat together. But, like a pissed off parent on a rainy day out, I kept glancing in the rear-view mirror to let them know I was none too happy with having to provide adoption services.

The mum was soon out of it, eyes shut, asleep or

unconscious. The kid, Zain, looked like a load of demons had spooked him since the day he was born, or he was suffering from PTSD and he had seen enough terror and horror he would never talk again. The girl though, Sonia, she was sharp-eyed, alert, watching me as much as I was watching her. In fact, it was not the mum who could turn people to stone, but this little girl, who, at the grand old age of eight, was keeping the family together.

'Where are we going?' she said, after staring at the back of my head for a good five minutes.

'My villa,' I said, wondering why I had agreed to any of this with the Russian.

'Are you rich?' she asked.

'Heh, maybe she will marry you,' said Zammit.

'I don't want to get married,' she said. 'I want to go to Germany.'

'OK, you can marry someone in Germany,' said Zammit, laughing.

'Shut it,' I said to Zammit, as I turned around to face her. 'You don't need be afraid. I'll look after you, and there's no harm coming your way. If you guys keep your side of the bargain, that would be a big help to me. The Russian said he'd take you back, so whatever happens, you can be on your way.'

'To Germany?' asked Sonia.

'You know, there are Nazis in Germany,' said Zammit, who really couldn't help teasing the little girl.

'What's a Nazi?'

'Nothing,' I said.

'They are racists, like there are racists everywhere,' said Zammit, on his favourite topic.

'What's a racist?'

'A nasty person,' I said. 'And don't worry about Nazis in Germany – that's like a long time ago. You'll be OK once you get there.'

I carried on looking at her and could tell she was churning it over in her mind. That's when I noticed for the first time how dark her brown eyes were. They had a hard edge, which only comes from seeing things you shouldn't have to see when you're a child.

'So,' I said, 'why did Max Schmidt jump ship and leave you to sort yourselves out?'

'He didn't want to help us anymore.'

'OK, why's that?'

'Because he's a cheat!' she said, showing how angry she was, which made her mum mumble.

I had to stop and think for a minute. She was a bright kid, but was I asking too much of an eight-year-old?

'I tell you what,' I said, 'when was the last time you saw him?'

'This morning.'

'On the ship?'

'Yes.'

'And did he say anything about leaving the ship?'

'Yes.'

'Did he say where he was going?'

She shook her head.

'I think,' said Zammit, 'she is like my little girl, and you will go round and round the roundabout.'

'So,' I said to her, 'he told you he was leaving the ship, but he didn't say where he was going?'

Sonia nodded.

'Did he say he was coming back for you?'

She shook her head.

'You see,' I said, turning to Zammit, happy to prove a point, 'that is why he is a cheat.'

'There are lots of cheaters in this world, my little girl,' announced Zammit, 'but you must not let them win.'

I was going to ask her about the Medusa and then thought better of it. Not in front of Zammit, I decided, who, for the first time since I'd arrived on the island, was showing an interest in what I was up to.

Still, it's not every day you pick up a stray family on a dodgy Russian cargo ship, who were probably running away from some mad crazy war. I would leave things for now and wait until we'd got back to the villa. After all, Tony would have some questions, and I would have some questions for Tony.

Once we'd got through the night-time traffic, we were back in the lanes and close to the villa, when we pulled up sharp and got a dose of whiplash. In front of us was another taxi, which meant we either went back down the lane, or they did. Zammit just sat there with a big fume on his face. I was about to tell him to back off when he flung open the car door and strode up to the other taxi driver, who had been pointing at him to move back. What I thought would just be more pointing, and then some shouting, turned ugly. The other driver got out, but before he had time to do jack, he was on the tarmac taking a serious beating from Zammit.

That was it. I was out of there.

I left Zammit spitting on the guy crawling around on the road.

The Medusa and her kids followed me over a low wall and

18

up the hill to where my villa was sitting pretty. Seeing as things had gone the way they had, I told the family to stay outside and wandered around the back to check that I wouldn't be walking into Max Schmidt, a bunch of Filipino sailors or the international artefact police.

As it was, Tony was asleep on the sofa, with my laptop going up and down on his stomach. I pulled a can of lemonade out of the fridge, keeping the family waiting outside, and sat opposite Tony. The ring pull made him stir, and I gulped down the fizzy pop.

'Christ, mate!' he said, grabbing my laptop before it crashed onto the tiled floor. 'Why do you always do that?'

'Do what?' I said, all innocent and cheeky.

'Creep up on people like some effing ninja.'

'I only do it to you, Tony,' I said, smiling.

'Thanks,' he said, struggling to pull himself upright. 'Who won?'

'Who won what?'

'The match.'

'Haven't a clue. It's not like the footie at home.'

'So, you don't know who won?'

'Nah, fell asleep. As I said, Steven, not my kind of footie. Why, did you have a bet on it?'

'No,' I said, so he knew I was only asking because I was checking up on him.

However, Tony was always going to play dumb if he had been up to no good.

'You got any food in that fridge?' he asked, rubbing his face with his hands.

'Lasagne.'

'Yeah? Don't matter if I eat late, does it. That's what you

do out here, 'cause it's so hot in day.'

'There's a big bowl of it,' I said. 'You'd better heat it all up.'

'You hungry too?' he said, wondering how to get to the kitchen.

I pointed but said nothing.

'How'd you get on then... with the Russian,' shouted Tony, as I heard him opening the fridge door. 'Did he give you that Medusa?'

'Kind of,' I shouted back at him, wondering when the live Medusa would show her face.

'Heh, are you sure you want me to cook all of this?'

I knew Tony would be looking at a big bowl of homemade pasta, beef and cheese, which was cooked by the cleaner who came over once a week.

'Yeah, we've got to feed the Medusa and her kids.'

The silence meant the cogs in Tony's brain were working overtime.

'You what?' he shouted. I heard the beep of the microwave as he turned it on.

'I said... you need to put it all in!'

There was the sound of a bowl being placed on the glass plate and then Tony appeared licking the sauce off his fingers.

'You did say,' he said, looking a bit stressed, 'that you got the Medusa... right?'

'No, Tony,' I said, putting my arms behind my head. 'What I meant was, I have another version of the Medusa, just like the artefact. She's got two kids, but she hasn't lost her head, although I think that's only a matter of time.'

Then I thought about Tony's brain, like a little hamster in

a cage running around on a wheel to nowhere. He looked like he was getting the old cogs oiled and greased, when all the blood suddenly drained from his face, as the Medusa and her kids wandered in through the front door.

So, instead, he said, 'Who the fuck are you?'

I was casual about it.

There was Sonia, still being the big sister, with her arm around Zain, and her mum looking like she was about to fall over.

'You can't come in here,' said Tony, who at the same time realised it wasn't his gaffe to say. 'I mean, Steven...'

And I think that's when he twigged.

'You know what,' said Tony, puffing out his cheeks, 'I can't take that lot home with me.'

That's when I wished I had a proper drink in my hand and not a can of lemonade, not that I was ever much into drinking.

However, I had a plan.

'Right,' I said, standing up. 'You three, come with me.'

I walked to the back of the villa and checked the family were following, pulled down a torch from the shelf and led them to a stone wall outhouse.

I'd had it cleared out when I got hold of the property and had been thinking about putting something in there.

So, now I had something.

'You can stay here tonight,' I said. 'I'll get you some food and something to sleep on.'

Sonia's face was like, you're a mean so and so.

'Listen,' I said to her. 'Your mum's not well, and there's a good reason why the ship's crew don't like you, and it's not just because your mum looks like a walking hand grenade.'

Then the mum flopped down on the ground and the kids

21

rushed down to help her.

'Is it scurvy?' said Tony, looking over my shoulder.

'We still have a deal,' I said to the girl, 'but I ain't going looking for Max Schmidt tonight. Whatever's wrong with your mum, I can't help you with her right now. Let's see how things are in the morning and we can start to sort something out.'

I left the torch on the floor and looked at the two kids hugging their mum.

'Heh, mate,' said Tony, 'you need to have a bit more heart, or else you ain't going to heaven.'

'What makes you think I'd want to go there?'

'If it was offered, I would go,' he said.

'Not likely though, is it.'

I was about to tell Tony to check on the lasagne when an almighty bang, a whoosh and a thud shot through the stonework. It stirred the mum, and the children dived under her long black gown.

'What the eff was that?' said Tony.

I didn't say anything, but it sounded like an explosion, probably in the next valley.

'Heh… where are the kids?' he said, looking around him as if they'd performed some magic trick.

I nodded at the mum, as I went outside to see what I could see.

And I was right, as far as I could tell – there was a billowing smoke cloud appearing just above the hill.

'They looked scared shitless,' said Tony, who had followed me out.

'Yeah, well, I suppose you never get used to the sound of bombs.'

'You think it's a bomb?'

'Don't know…' I said, which was a half-truth.

'Who would do that here? You don't get terrorists on an island in the Med… do you?'

'Well, not at midnight,' I said.

Then the little girl Sonia came out to see her us. She was shivering from head to foot.

It was all fear.

Tony got down on his knee and cuddled her.

'Ah, you poor thing,' he said. 'Nothing to worry about. Uncle Tony's got yer.'

'Christ, Tony,' I said. 'No need to start saying that sort of thing.'

'He's a grumpy so and so, ain't he,' he said to Sonia. 'Needs a family, he does, then he'd understand.'

Tony had a wife and two kids back on the estate and they meant everything to him. Which is why he would want a quick exit from this place, but there was now a big spanner in the works – perhaps one that likes to explode.

Then the mum appeared, helped by Zain, and told Sonia to come over.

'Go back into the villa,' I said to the mum and the kids. 'You'll feel safer in there. Don't worry, me and Tony will check it out. It's just a loud bang, so no need to freak out. If there's one thing you can say about this island, the war ended seventy years ago.'

They trotted off with the mum, looking like she was going to keel over again.

'Heh, mate, she doesn't look too good.'

'Yeah, I've noticed,' I said, as I turned to look back up the hill. 'Come on, let's have a look-see.'

I led Tony for about five hundred yards up to the ridge. As we got closer, we could hear the wind cutting across.

Down in the valley there was a yellow glow and smoke leaning against the sky and the clouds.

'I suppose you're going to tell me that's one of Grandad's villas?' said Tony.

'Yeah.'

'Must be a gas leak,' he said thoughtfully.

'How do you know?'

'Dodgy fitters out here,' he said.

'Yeah, well, something's gone wrong, that's for sure.'

And then we watched in silence, as a blaze took hold and lit up the sky.

It was best to keep our distance, we decided, without saying anything to each other.

No need to get involved just yet.

Earth To Earth

After the scary events of last night, Tony got me to let Medusa and her kids stay in the third bedroom. It was a bit pokey, but they bedded down under their mother's black wings.

After that, I didn't sleep too well because nothing had gone the way I wanted it to go, which usually meant everything was going to keep going wrong until I found out why. And when morning came, it was giving me a headache because it was pulling on my t-shirt and not going away. In the end, I used one eye to look at the two kids.

'Excuse me, sir,' said Sonia, who was being way too polite.

'I'm not making you breakfast,' I said, rolling over to the other side of the bed, so they got the message loud and clear.

'We're not hungry,' said the girl. 'But my mummy won't wake up.'

I took a deep breath.

'That's because she's ill,' I said.

However, I could hear the pitter patter of tiny feet come

around to face me again.

This time, I opened both eyes.

'What!' I said, really pissed.

'Please, sir, can you look?' said Sonia, who had her arm around her brother, who looked super sad.

'She needs a doctor,' I said, as I rolled and then pushed myself up in the bed because I now had to deal with it.

Something was up, like seriously up, because the kids were being way too meek and mild.

As I did my best to get my head together, I wondered if aliens had possessed them and had some big plan to take control of us adults and rule over the world.

'OK, take me to your leader,' I said, scratching my nether regions under the bedsheet.

Now that Sonia had my attention, she told her brother to go and sit on the sofa in the lounge. I hauled myself out of bed and followed her around to the third bedroom. The door was shut and it seemed only right that I should knock. Sonia shook her head, which meant there was no point in me waiting outside. I turned the door handle and let the door swing back on its hinges.

It didn't look good.

Their mum was still draped in her black garb and was lying on the bed looking up at the ceiling, with her arms by her side.

I got up close.

She had that grey pasty look, which meant whatever she had been struggling with had finished her off.

'Is my mummy dead?' asked Sonia.

I didn't know how to say it out loud, so I just nodded.

Her eyes filled up with tears.

She knew really – she just needed a grown-up to tell her.

As I shut the Medusa's eyes, I felt the little girl's arms wrap around my leg.

I let her squeeze.

'You'll be all right, kid,' I said.

She was doing her best, but it was hard for her to stop crying.

And that's when I heard a car on the gravel outside.

I looked through the bedroom window, and it was the kind of visit I was half expecting.

'Look, Sonia,' I said, bending down and holding her arms by her side. 'I know this is tragic, and I know you've seen some things that a young girl shouldn't see. I can tell because when I was a little boy, I saw lots of horrible things as well. So, yeah, you've just lost your mummy, but however bad things are, I think you will do whatever it takes to look after your brother Zain. That means, I need you to focus, because we have some visitors and we need to play a game with them, to make sure they don't get in the way of us looking for Max Schmidt.'

It was a harsh, practical, cold truth, but I could think of no other way of talking to her, given what was going to happen next.

'Now, the police are here, so if you want to stay with me, I need you to pretend that nothing's wrong. You can be sad but don't make anything up because I will do that for you.'

She rubbed her dark brown eyes, wiped away her tears and smeared the snot from her nose on her t-shirt.

'Is that a deal then?' I said, putting out my hand to shake on it.

She took my hand and we sealed the deal.

'Good girl, Sonia, good girl. Now, can you go and piss Uncle Tony off by getting him out of bed?'

She nodded her head like she knew she was on a mission.

'Just tell him the police are here and they are going to arrest him for the murder of his wife and kids.'

Sonia's eyes widened, then she realised I was making a sick joke at the wrong time.

'No, you're right, don't say that. Just tell him he needs to get up because the police are here.'

Sonia wiped her eyes again and trotted off.

I looked out of the window. There were a few of them and they were going to knock on my door any minute. I checked on Zain and he smiled like a confused little hamster. Tony wandered out into the lounge as my doorbell chime was being rung.

'Put some clothes on, Tony,' I said, as he stood half asleep in his pants. 'We've got guests!'

I let the chimes ring for as long as possible then opened the door with a smile and met for the first time Inspector Spiteri, wearing an expensive-looking Italian suit, ventilated for the weather. He was a well-toned athletic type, who didn't look like he had trouble getting on in life because he was so handsome. In fact, I could easily see him strutting his stuff in a mail order catalogue, modelling suits, vests and pants.

He left a constable out front and another one wandered around the back and plonked himself in the middle of the lounge, with me and Tony sitting opposite and the kids in between us on the sofa. He told us he was following up on his inquiries after a major incident last night – an explosion and fire that had occurred in the valley.

However, before he got into some of these details, he just

28

wanted to understand who we were and what the relationships were between us.

He then put his phone on the coffee table and pressed record.

'These are friends and family,' I said.

'Are they your children, Mr Mason?' he asked, as if he knew they weren't.

'No, they're my cousin's kids,' I said. 'It's a cheap holiday for them.'

'But shouldn't they be in school?'

'Yeah, they would normally,' I said, 'but their mother is not well. So I said I'd take them off her for a bit... you know... to get them away from things and help out.'

'That will explain why they look so sad,' he said, looking at the two kids. 'And what are your names?'

I spoke for them.

'This is Zain, the boy – he's the quiet one. And this is Sonia.'

I could tell the only thing Spiteri believed was the names, as he turned his attention to Tony.

'And you are...?'

'Tony,' said Tony.

'And do you live with Mr Mason?'

'What d'yer mean?'

'It's a simple question,' said Spiteri.

'I'm staying here, if that's what you mean.'

'So, you are from the UK?'

'Yeah.'

'On holiday?'

'Yeah.'

'And you are friends of Mr Mason?'

'Yeah.'

'And do you know the children?'

'Yeah.'

'Did you fly in with the children?'

'No.'

'So, when did the children arrive?'

'Yesterday,' I said, to stop Tony from getting us all arrested. 'But they came here by boat.'

'Is that so,' said Spiteri, like he'd discovered a clue to buried treasure.

'So, these children travelled here from the UK by boat?'

'No, they just arrived here by boat.'

'What kind of boat?'

'Look, Inspector Spiteri,' I said, deciding it was time to get him off the scent and sniffing something else. 'I hope you're here to tell me what you are doing about the incident last night.'

'The incident?' he said, pretending he hadn't told us why he was here.

'Yeah, I stood up on the ridge late last night and had to watch what I think was one of my properties burn.'

'My apologies, Mr Mason. It is easy to get distracted in my line of business.'

He then rested his chin on his hands in front of him.

'So, this fire, it must be rather upsetting for you?'

'Yeah.'

'And you stood on top of the hill, watching one of your properties burn, but you did not think to contact the emergency services?'

'No need,' I said. 'We heard them.'

I then got the raised eyebrow treatment.

'So, you watched your own villa being burnt to the ground, but you did not think you should do anything other than watch it burn?'

'No, this is my own villa and the one that I live in,' I said, spreading my arms out. 'And this is still standing, and where we were all safe from whatever was going on out there.'

'But it is your asset, Mr Mason?'

'Yeah, managed by Joseph Borg. I leave it with him to sort out. I am expecting him to phone me today.'

Joseph Borg was my land agent and property portfolio manager, but what didn't appear on his business card was his other important job title: Mr Fixer.

'That, I am afraid, is going to be rather unlikely,' said Spiteri, who eased himself back.

'So, what's happened to him?'

'He is helping us with our inquires,' said Spiteri. 'Unfortunately, the fire tragically took the life of the person who was staying there.'

It was my turn to raise an eyebrow.

'I cannot say what the potential outcome may be for Mr Borg, but you understand that this is a suspected homicide investigation.'

I wanted to say something but I knew it would only sound fake – like "that's very sad news". And if I asked if the guy who had been killed was German and went by the name of Max Schmidt, then I would probably be joining Borg helping Spiteri with his inquires.

But he wasn't finished yet, as he shifted his bum cheeks.

'There are just a few other things I would like to ask you, Mr Mason.'

Here we go…

'You have already indicated that you left the running of this property to Mr Borg, but did you know who was renting the villa at the bottom of the valley?'

'No, I thought it was empty. If I'd known someone was there, I would have tried to do something about it.'

'And what would you have done?'

'Tried to save a life, but by the time we got to the top of the hill, the fire looked full on.'

'Raging,' said Tony, to add corroboration.

'I see,' said Spiteri, who crossed his legs and then uncrossed them. 'And have you noticed a person or persons acting suspiciously, in or around that villa, in the last few weeks?'

'No.'

Which was true.

'OK, Mr Mason, I think that will do for now,' he said, pushing himself forward so he sat on the rim of the chair. 'I must say, you have a very nice home.'

'Thanks,' I said.

'And you have invested a lot in property on this island, in a very short space of time. Do you mind if I ask what attracted you here?'

'To invest.'

'Yes, and to stay?'

'I don't know,' I said casually. 'I suppose I always dreamed of living on an island.'

'To get away from people?'

'Nah… if I wanted that, I'd buy a rocket and look for a black hole.'

That brought a smile to Spiteri.

'OK,' he said again. 'I cannot say what the outcome is for

Mr Borg right now, and I am sure you will have concerns with making insurance claims. If you intend to record the damage with us, I suggest an alternative agent to pursue these matters on your behalf, unless you were to take on these responsibilities yourself. However, a serious criminal investigation is underway and this will always take precedence.'

'I'll look into it,' I said.

Spiteri picked up his phone and stopped the recording.

'So, there is one more final thing, Mr Mason, concerning the persons you have living here with you. I would like to complete the ID checks. No need to show me passports now, but if you could arrange to come to the police HQ with the children's documentation and your friend's, Tony, I would be grateful for your co-operation.'

He then placed his business card on the table.

'Goodbye, little ones,' he said. 'And I hope your mummy gets better soon.'

I followed him to the front door.

'Do you want to see my passport as well?' I asked.

'No need, Mr Mason,' he said smiling. 'We know all about you.'

2

It was a good job Tony knew more about kids than I did, as we set up the laptop in Tony's bedroom so they could watch some children's programmes. Then Tony pulled out of his suitcase some chocolate and their eyes lit up. It had melted but they tucked into like it was Christmas, Easter and Halloween.

'That's all you need to do,' said Tony, as we wrapped up their mum in the bedsheet. 'Put 'em in front of the TV and give 'em sweets.'

'Sounds easy,' I said, as I tied one end of the sheet.

'Yeah, as long as they're happy, you'll be happy, but if they ain't happy, then it ain't so good.'

'Are you sure there isn't more to it?'

'Christ, there's loads, mate, but you need to keep it simple, otherwise you lose the plot.'

'You should write one of them parental guidance leaflets, Tony. Half a sentence and it's sorted.'

'Listen,' he said, 'if you need guidance, then there's something wrong with yer.'

'Well, that's two sentences now.'

'That's a whole book, mate,' he said, laughing as we pulled the knots tight on either end of the bedsheet.

'OK, let's get rid of her,' I said. 'Asap.'

We carried her through the villa and behind the outhouse. After that, we took turns in digging a shallow pit. I then went looking in the kitchen for something flammable and grabbed the lighter fluid from underneath the sink. Back in front of the Medusa's body, I was about to give it a squirt, when Tony piped up.

'We burn this body in the ground, earth to earth, ashes to ashes, dust to dust, health and safety.'

'You what, mate?'

'You need to respect the dead,' he said, with his arms folded in front him, 'or else you don't know what comes back to haunt yer.'

'What has health and safety got to do with it?'

'Dunno, mate, just came out.'

'Look,' I said, ready to light the fire, 'this isn't about respect for the dead, it's about getting rid of something that has died of god knows what and needs to be persona non grata. Plus, I don't think what you said has anything to do with her kind of religion.'

'Heh, I've done my best to respect her. If they then want to cut me head off for trying to be nice, that's their problem.'

The only answer I had was to empty the lighter fuel on the body.

'Matches,' I said to Tony.

'Don't smoke, mate.'

True, neither of us did.

'Your turn,' I said, meaning he had to go back inside and find something to light the fire. 'Or else, we're going to have to rub two sticks together.'

Burning the mum was a kind of sick thing to do but it was still a burial, even if we were a couple of dumb arses about it. However, with the police now sniffing around, and no idea if she had some kind of deadly disease on her, it was the quickest and safest option left open to us. But I knew it was going down on my naughty boy chart, which was making hell look more likely, come the final reckoning and all that.

Then Tony returned with the kids.

'They wanted to say goodbye,' he said.

I looked at Sonia and Zain.

The little girl had her arm around her brother. They stared at the petrol-smelling bedsheet, their faces sending out two kinds of messages: sadness and relief. I didn't think it right they watched their mum burn, but Tony was straight in there with a match. She caught light, fast, the flames spreading from one end to the other. We all watched the sheet burn away and the fire start eating into the body.

It was getting cruel.

'Tony…' I said, wanting him to get the kids back indoors.

But Sonia knew.

She took her brother's hand and they both walked back into the villa.

'It's best they know,' said Tony.

Well, he was the parent.

'Listen,' I said, 'can you get your hat and keep an eye on the kids?'

'Why, where you are going?'

'To check the villa.'

'I'll tell Grandad, then.'

'Sure,' I said, stepping away from the heat, the smoke and the foul stench of burning flesh.

Not good. None of this was good. And now there was something else bugging me: the kids' reaction. I could see they were sad, but there was another thing going on inside their hearts and heads. I couldn't put my finger on it, but it was like they were almost happy to see her gone.

Still, with the trimmed sombrero protecting my head, I strolled up the hill to the ridge and looked down into the valley, where last night's skulduggery had added a large dollop of spice to Max Schmidt and the Medusa. As I walked down through the parched bush, stone and random boulders, I started to pick out odd bits of debris, which must have been launched like a volcano when the place blew up.

The villa was shaded by a well-watered tree line, so I had to make my way through the smouldering bark and branches to get a good look at what was left. Which meant, not a lot, apart from the internal chimney stack, which was charred and broken.

Now, I'm no Poirot, but what was going on at my villa didn't look much like a murder scene investigation. There should have been a load of activity. You know, at a bare minimum, Spiteri's guys in white forensics picking up things with tweezers and putting them in plastic bags, or telling the local press to piss off, or showing the bereaved the remains of a dead man's shoe. But all they'd done was stick a load of police tape around the blast site and left the smouldering mess to bake in the sun.

Of course, I'm not the kind of guy to advocate for more efficient policing, but this had all the hallmarks of a "couldn't give a shit" investigation. I mean, how often is some poor bastard sent to kingdom come on an island the size of a cricket pitch, with the population of a local borough? That's when I noticed, standing at the bottom of the driveway, a lonely Constable Zammit.

'Zammit!' I shouted, all familiar, as I walked down to his little guard duty position outside the gate. 'What are you doing here in your fancy dress?'

I got a stern look and thought I might have to apologise, which is not something I do, when he said, 'No, Mr Mason, I am a constable. My brother is the taxi driver.'

'You're identical.'

'Very... I am Michael, and my brother is Aiden.'

Zammit the constable looked ice cool. I was tempted to ask to see the birth certificates, as I took my hat off and wiped my sweaty forehead. There was not a single blemish or other distinguishing mark that could help me separate one from the other. I suppose there was some logic to taxi driver Zammit keeping his brother out of our very limited conversations, especially when he was driving the notorious local English gangster around. But I was still not completely convinced that he didn't drive a taxi on his day off.

'So,' I said, 'how come you know who I am?'

'Inspector Spiteri said you owned this villa and you lived on the other side of the hill. It is a simple deduction. And of course, my brother tells me everything.'

'Everything?' I said, cringing.

He nodded.

'Your brother trusts you then, seeing as you're on different sides of the fence.'

'It is not illegal to drive a taxi.'

He had a point.

'Do you have a brother, Mr Mason?'

Now, I don't know why he asked that question – it was a bit of a sore point, but worth an answer.

'I had… a half-brother,' I said. 'He's dead.'

'How did that happen, if you do not mind me asking?'

'He wasn't looking where he was going and fell into a hole.'

'So, an accident?'

'That's right, but no love lost.'

'You didn't like your half-brother?'

'It's not that I didn't like him… he didn't like me.'

'Then you are not sad for the loss, which I can understand.'

Good, I thought, not sure why I was having a family therapy session outside my ruined villa.

'Where is everyone then?' I asked, looking back at the

burnt timbers and piles of stone that had been blasted over the front lawn.

'Lunch,' he replied.

'So you're guarding the place?'

'There is nothing to guard. It has all been destroyed.'

'I know that,' I said, 'but this is all evidence. Or have you caught the people who did this and that's why no one can be arsed?'

Zammit the constable shook his head and smiled.

'That's for Inspector Spiteri to solve. My job is to stand guard.'

'Yeah, well, I had a visit from your boss and he's got my portfolio manager. Does that mean he did it? Which, I might add, if he did do it, I will eat my hat – and this is not my hat.'

Zammit shrugged.

I grinned.

Not only were Zammit and Zammit identical, but they also gave nothing away.

However, I could tell he wanted me to pay.

'What's the cost?'

'So, for five hundred euro I can tell you something,' he said. 'And for one thousand euro I can tell you more.'

'Is that cash or do you accept cards?'

'You can pay my brother, Mr Mason. It will all end up in the family.'

'OK, let's see what five hundred euros gets me. Why did they arrest Borg?'

'I do not know why, but I do know Spiteri does not like him. In fact, nobody likes him. However, I believe they will release him later today.'

'And who was killed in the villa?'

'Just one man, a journalist.'

'A journalist? Why, did he expose last year's winner of the best kept garden as a fraud?'

'Journalists can upset people when they tell the truth.'

'So, someone blew him up because he was writing things people didn't like?'

I got the eyebrow treatment.

'You know, you should be a gameshow host: higher… higher… one thousand euros!'

'Is that your bid, Mr Mason?'

'I think you could say it's my final offer.'

'Then you can know that Max Schmidt is the main suspect. They know he arrived on a Russian cargo ship, which has also suddenly left port.'

I suppose it was no surprise to me the Russian had not kept his word and had fled the scene.

'OK, so what was this journalist trying to expose and what has Schmidt got to do with it?'

'Inspector Spiteri thinks Schmidt was hired by powerful people, who did not want the journalist writing stories about them.'

'And has your boss said anything about a statue, a little thing… Greek kind of mythology stuff?'

He shook his head, trying to convince me he knew nothing.

That left me with one question, but I would have to keep it to myself for now: why did Schmidt not deliver the artefact to me and instead take a detour to blow up a journalist, who was being far too honest, and that's if it was Schmidt who pressed the button?

So, I kept it simple. 'Why has Spiteri arrested Borg?'

'With Inspector Spiteri, he usually knows who is responsible for the crime, even before they have done it.'

'That's handy,' I said, struggling to picture Borg making bombs.

'It is good for promotions.'

'And does Spiteri think I had anything to do with this?'

'He is not sure, but he likes you.'

'How's that?'

'Because he came to see you and he did not put you in jail.'

If that was meant to comfort me, it didn't.

'All right,' I said, ready to leave the scene of devastation. 'Can you tell me the name of this journalist?'

'No, I'm not sure of his name, but my brother will know him – he follows his blog.'

'Cheers,' I said, wondering if I should check Facebook for who was leaving RIP messages.

I straightened my Mexican hat to shield me better from the sun, with the aim of walking into town before it reached egg frying time.

'One more thing, Mr Mason,' he said. 'And a bonus prize for you: Max Schmidt has a girlfriend and sometimes uses The Sapori to acquire clients.'

I knew it by reputation.

'Thanks,' I said. 'And send my regards to all the family.'

'I will, Mr Mason… you can be sure of that.'

3

I headed off into town, liking my Mexican hat because the heat was hotter than yesterday, the day before and the day before that. Not that I was complaining because it was a hell of a lot better than the shitty weather back home. And what also made me a little bit happier was finding out Schmidt had a girlfriend – people would know who he was, where he lived and, more importantly, what he looked like. It also meant I didn't need the kids, but I was going to hang on to them, just in case.

As I walked, I got hold of taxi-driving Zammit on my mobile and promised his family – brothers, sisters, cousins, nieces and nephews – the one thousand euros by the end of the day. I then got him to tell me about the journo who had been killed. The guy's name was Tommaso Garibaldi, as in the biscuit. He was based on the mainland but had settled on the island recently, digging up dirt on local politicians and big wigs.

Now, that's not much of a revelation to me – people who appear legit are as about legit as a ferret in a rabbit hole. But I suppose it meant a lot to two hundred and fifty thousand people on the island who were getting ripped off by a load of bosses who controlled everything and put a bomb up your arse for telling everyone what everyone already knew.

Zammit was angry, he said, because this time the racists had gone too far, stepped over the line, and there was going to be a load of trouble unless they caught the people who had killed Garibaldi… real quick. That's when I asked if it was out there, that this Max Schmidt was in the frame. He'd heard rumours, he said, but the constabulary were keeping their cards close to their chest. Well, his brother wasn't, but I told Zammit to let me know if people get so pissed they want to raise a posse and get hold of Schmidt, because I need to get hold of Schmidt before he gets strung up.

Whether I liked it or not, I had to deliver for Grandad, and he would not be a happy bunny losing a villa and the Medusa all in one go. Not that any of this was my fault, but I would have to be the solution to sorting out these kinds of problems – why else was he paying me? And as I told you before, it's all transaction.

When I got into town, I had some lunch in a café opposite Borg's offices. The metal shutters had been pulled down and a handwritten note stuck up outside to say they were temporarily closed. Also, his phone was dead, which meant he was dead, or he was still a guest of Spiteri, or he was trying to swim across the Med to get to the mainland, which, if anyone wants to know, is also a death sentence. Even if the constabulary did let Borg go, he can run, but he can't hide. He had a few clients like Grandad, who would then get people like me to find him, dead or alive, or alive and then exterminated.

Once I'd scoffed my tuna mayo, I went to the bank, got some money out and then did some shopping for the kids. I was picking out toys that I would have liked when I was kid, and I couldn't help feeling how good it was to say yes to this and yes to that, like I'd won the lottery or was doing some toyshop *Supermarket Sweep*. But then, I got stuck on the doll stuff for Sonia, so I put some of it back and added in a PlayStation. Whatever… they could choose to play with what they wanted. It was just a surprise Santa, to make up for the hell they'd been through.

However, I should have known better. Just because you plonk a load of toys down on the floor, doesn't mean they're going to be appreciated. The kids didn't know what to do or how to deal with it; they just looked at them. After all, why was this strange man, who had lied to the police and burnt their dead mum, giving them toys to play with? That's when Tony said it's like being in a desert and gulping down water because you're dying of thirst – too much too soon and it only makes you sick. It was not that they didn't want them, they just didn't know what to do with them.

Tony was a proper dad. He understood. He told me that these kids were traumatised. They're not going to be like normal kids, and they had to grieve because they'd just lost their mum. They would play with them, he said, when they felt more comfortable about things, which would be a sign they were starting to trust us.

He carried on being the good parent and did some cooking. We sat down in the dining room like we were a family. Tony and me were at each end of the table and the kids next to each other. Sonia kept telling Zain he needed to eat, but all he could do was drink some water. I didn't know if the kid was too sad to eat or he was ill and had caught something off his mum. The thing is, we didn't know what had killed her, and I reckon it wasn't just her shit personality that had the sailors on the cargo ship keen to throw her overboard. Still, it could just have been worries about transporting the scary Medusa, who was more than likely on Interpol's most wanted, but sailors are a superstitious lot and anything bad didn't get tolerated.

I let the kids go back to the bedroom, which Tony said

was where they probably felt safe. He said he'd put some toys in there later, as he washed up and I dried the dishes.

Tony then told me what Grandad wanted, which was kind of ABC stuff: find Schmidt, get the Medusa, and minimum, break his legs, but far better if we drowned him. However, the villa thing got Grandad raging, and I had to be on the case with the insurers. I wasn't to take any BS off the local coppers about murder holding up getting the money we were owed.

I asked if he had said anything to Grandad about the kids, the mum and everything. Tony said he was not an idiot and he wasn't going to start telling Grandad about things that would only get his blood going from raging to boiling. But that's when Tony brought up the whole thing with the kids and how I couldn't go using a little girl like Sonia. I told him it wouldn't come to that because I was following up on some leads. Then Tony said we should stop it all here and now and hand them over to the police or the social services. I could easily find Schmidt if he was on the island and didn't need the little girl to ID the two-faced bastard.

He was right, but I wasn't going to do that. None of which made sense to Tony, and I'm not sure it made much sense to me, but I was going to hang on to them.

As he handed me the last dinner plate for drying, he said, 'Make sure that death don't follow you.'

'Yeah,' I said, wondering what had got into him. 'I will make sure that death don't follow me.'

And then he wandered off in a huff.

I put it down to Tony taking all that Greek mythology stuff too seriously, or he was having a moment because he was missing his own wife and kids.

To keep Tony happy, I set him up on the laptop again. I

then sat outside on the swing seat with a beer.

That's when Sonia poked her head out.

I could tell she wanted to talk.

'Did you like your dinner?' I said, swigging the ice-cold beer as she stood in front of me with her head down.

She nodded.

'Do you like Tony?' I asked.

She nodded again.

'He's got kids, you know,' I said. 'Back in London. Do you miss that, London?'

This time I got a shrug, like she wasn't sure.

'Yeah, well, I'm the same,' I said. 'Funny old place, London. Can't stand it when you live there and as soon as you're away, you start to miss it.'

'I miss my friends,' she said.

'Yeah, so how long you been away?'

'We left when I was six.'

'How old are you now?'

'I'm not sure. I think I might be eight.'

'You mean you can't remember your birthday?'

She shook her head.

'Well, that's not a bad thing,' I said, sitting forward. 'It means you can choose when to have your birthday. Which means you don't have to wait!'

It didn't cheer her up. All the mouth, all the cheek and fight had been sucked out of her.

'Do you want to sit down?' I said, nodding at the space next to me.

No, she didn't want that either. Life ain't fair, having to put up with doing whatever it is your parents want to do and then ending up way worse off. Still, I was keen to know what her parents had been up to.

'Was she religious then, your mum?' I said, easing back on the seat.

I got the nod again.

'But you and your brother, I haven't seen you doing any praying?'

'She told us not to do it when we left. She said we had to pretend we weren't like that.'

'But anyone could see your mum was... you know... dressed all in black?'

'She said she was going to change and pretend like us, once we got back to... Europe... I think...'

'And do you want to do it... the praying stuff?'

Sonia shrugged.

'Well, maybe your mum was right, just for now, until you can feel safe. No need to draw attention to yourselves. So, why do you want to go to Germany?'

'Because that's where Mummy said we should go.'

'Don't you want to go back to London?'

'I do, but Mummy said they won't let us go home because of what Daddy did.'

'Yeah, and what did your daddy do?'

'He was fighting, in the desert.'

'Yeah, and where's your daddy now?'

'He's like Mummy.'

'You mean he's dead?'

'Yes, he was fighting, and Mummy said he got killed by a bomb.'

I took another swig of my beer. It was the picture I had in my head about the family, so no surprises.

'Are you going to tell the policeman about me and my

brother?'

'Well, they already know about you.'

'Are you going to tell them where we came from, and about my mummy and my daddy?'

'I don't know…'

'But you said we had a deal. We were shaking our hands.'

'I know I did, but you and your brother are children – you need to get back to something that's a bit normal.'

I must have said the wrong thing because I could see she was starting to cry.

'What's wrong?'

'I don't want to go to jail.'

'Listen, you won't go to jail. They'd more than likely send you back home. You must have relatives, family back in London… cousins…'

She wouldn't answer.

'Or are they in Germany? Is that why you want to go there?'

'It's where Mummy wanted to go,' she said. 'Mummy said it would be safer there.'

Perhaps she was right. I didn't know. I was going back on my word, and I had promised. And who knows, perhaps she could help with tracking down Schmidt, whatever Tony said.

'OK, let's stick to the deal. Do you still have your passports?'

'Mummy had the passports. They got burned when you put her on fire.'

'Shit!'

'We need our passports to go to Germany,' she said, looking at me like it was my fault.

'Right, don't worry. I will sort it. Now, go inside and see

Tony. Ask him if you can watch some TV.'

'But he's watching football.'

'Don't worry, he'll let you watch what you want. He'd like that.'

4

It was about one in the morning by the time Zammit had dropped me off in the main bar district. If it were peak season the place would have been heaving with tourists, but it was late summer and the place was returning to the locals and expats, which meant the bars were going to be empty.

There were about a dozen outlets that plied their trade, starting at the top of a hill and running all the way down some steps to the bottom car park, which then took you out of the tourist area and along the coastline. The Sapori was tucked down a narrow alleyway and it was easy to miss unless you noticed the chalkboard that pointed the way to something more savoury.

It was a Tuesday, so a quiet night for bars anyway, and The Sapori was no different. You could get a drag night on Fridays and Sundays, but during the week it tailed off to pick-ups, escorts and the odd alcoholic. The place had as much lighting as a coal mine and stank of booze-soaked walls, floors and ceiling. There were battered spring-loaded sofas, with a small stage for drag acts. Just above that, hanging down from a vaulted roof, was a cracked glitter ball shooting laser lights at punters.

I got myself a Coke and looked around for anything that

49

would pass for pond life attached to a slimy slug. There was a straight couple kissing on a sunken sofa, a lost drag act sitting at the bar and two loner guys trying to be cheerful about tomorrow. I didn't expect to spot a woman with a flashing light on her head that said "my name is Greta and I am that bastard Schmidt's girlfriend", because I was here to talk to Pissing Willy.

I downed my Coke and then went to the gents.

His eyes lit up when I walked in, and he didn't waste time letting me know what he could do for me.

'Do you want your cock sucked?' he said, desperate for some action, laying on his backside in the trough of the urinal.

Pissing Willy was an expat who had got himself stranded on the island. He was pockmarked and red-faced, with odd rubbery lips that were always wet with spit or someone else's dribble. I'd heard he'd been educated at Eton but had fallen out with the system, his family, his destiny, and anything else that he was given and didn't appreciate. He liked it here, doing casual labour during the day and then hanging out in The Sapori all night in his buttoned-up raincoat, pleasuring anyone who was willing – and liked the smell of bleach when they came. It was an odd mix to get off on but everyone needs to earn a living I suppose.

'No thanks, Willy,' I said, as I unzipped and relieved myself.

As I let my stream empty and flow down towards Willy, he didn't seem too bothered with what was coming his way.

I did the polite thing and washed my hands. I then gave Willy fifty euros because I had a few questions.

'Do you know who owns and runs this place?'

'You'll never guess who owns this place,' he said, pleased with himself that he had intel of value for once.

'Yes, you're right, I will never guess, because I am not guessing, I am asking you.'

'So, why do want to know?'

'Well, if I told you that, I would have to cut off your penis and stuff it in your mouth.'

Pissing Willy was afraid and excited by the opportunity.

'Just tell me,' I said, like a frustrated parent, wondering why I sounded like a parent.

'It's owned by a monkey,' he said, full of himself.

'A monkey?'

'Yes, old monkey face.'

I got it. He meant Grech.

'OK, and the next question is a bit more difficult, but maybe your university education will help. Have you seen a German guy in here with a woman over the summer?'

Willy shook his head.

It was way too vague. There were thousands of Germans over here on holiday in the summer and a lot of them would spend time in a place like The Sapori.

'The guy's name is Max Schmidt,' I said, 'and I was told his girlfriend hangs out here?'

That's when Willy smiled.

He nodded.

'So, you know them?'

'Yes, I did some hand-jobs for him.'

'You mean Schmidt has clients?'

'Yes, but I'll only suck their cocks in here.'

Fair enough, I thought to myself.

'Do you know where he is then, where his girlfriend is or

51

where they live?'

'No, sorry.'

'What about his girlfriend, I heard she comes in here?'

'I think you mean him/her.'

'She does drag stuff?'

'Just because somebody is in transition does not automatically mean they are a stage act.'

'OK, does Schmidt manage her... him... then?'

'It is him to her,' corrected Willy. 'And everyone is managed by Max Schmidt. He does not do relationships. Although, having said that, I think there may be something more in his dealings with Mila.'

'Yeah, do you know where I can find her?'

'You know,' said Willy, who looked a bit put out, 'I am an expert at cock sucking. I don't believe Mila has the same level of expertise.'

'Well, perhaps they will when they complete their transition.'

'That's if Schmidt lets her. He likes ambiguity.'

I pulled out another fifty euros.

'So?'

'She could be anywhere,' said Willy. 'Max Schmidt has gone off on one of his little trips and left his children to play.'

'And you really don't know where this Mila lives, or Schmidt?'

'You had better cruise the bars if you want to find Mila. But just remember, you will not get a better service than from *moi*!'

'OK,' I said. 'I'll be back if I'm desperate.'

'No need to be desperate – everyone should try things out at least once before they die!'

'Heh,' I said, smiling. 'You're on my bucket list. Thanks.'

I left Pissing Willy stuffing the fifty euros into his raincoat pocket and scanned The Sapori. Nothing had changed so I headed outside, back up the alley and into the bright lights of the bar district.

In front of every bar were sad empty chairs and tables, struggling to have any meaning. I had to tell a few chuggers to go eff themselves as I slipped in and out of one bar after another. I was relying on my gut instinct to find this Mila, hoping they knew more about me than I did about them so they would look scared or startled. But by the end of it all, I had an overpriced drinks bill, a couple of offers to have sex – that's where the car park was useful – and a timeshare application form that I needed to fill in without delay.

I was wasting my time and headed up to the taxi rank where I knew Zammit would be waiting for fares. As soon as he saw me, he pulled out of the taxi queue and I jumped in.

'I'm shattered,' I said, as I closed my eyes and rested my head on the back seat.

'Come, you need to wake,' said Zammit, who was being far too alert for the early morning hours.

'Why?'

'I have good news for you. My brother has told me something which you will like. He thinks the one thousand euros was very nice and you deserve full value for what you pay.'

'That's a first for this place.'

'Yes, I think you have come first,' said Zammit, whose pupils had disappeared because of all the amphetamine he was on.

'Well, I've heard points make prizes, so what does my

money get me?'

'I have seen her,' he said, grinning all over his sweaty, spaced-out face.

'Whose her?'

'The girlfriend.'

'You mean Schmidt's manfriend... girlfriend?'

'Yes, the girlfriend, the man who wants to be a woman.'

'You know about Mila?'

'Yes!' he said, all excited.

'For eff sake, are the police following me?'

'A little,' he said, 'but not as much. My brother says that he knows some but not all, but he knows Schmidt's girlfriend likes to visit.'

'Visit what?'

Zammit started giggling like a child.

'Wait,' he said, dipping his head down like we were on surveillance.

I looked around at the line of people catching taxis.

'See,' he said, keeping his head low.

All I could see were drunks falling over each other and falling into taxis.

'The red,' he said, as he popped his head up and pointed.

And that's when I saw her, Mila, with her back towards me, long, sleek and in a strong fiery-red dress.

'She looks hot,' said Zammit.

'Are you sure that's her?'

'We can ask her if you want?'

'Not funny...'

Then it was Mila's turn to jump into a taxi. Zammit was on it like a trained sniffer dog. I don't know why but I kept down low in my seat, like a useless Private Dick.

He followed Mila's taxi back along the rows of hotels that hugged the coastline. I was surprised that she didn't jump out and go into one of the hotels for a trick. Instead, we carried on through the old town and up windy streets to the top of a hill. This was where all the administration buildings had been sited: old and historic, smooth brown stone outsides, with tall windows, well spruced, with proper paving and clean streets.

Mila's taxi drove into a cobbled circle and stopped outside an old, grand gated building. Zammit pulled up about a hundred yards down a narrow lane and we both stretched our necks to see where she was going. She pressed the intercom on one of the column gates. That's when she turned and waved away the taxi so I could get a good look at her. Yeah, Zammit was right – that changing into a woman thing was not going to be difficult. She had high cheek bones, heavy red lipstick lips and bleached white eyes, which seemed to glow in the dim streetlight. She bent down to speak into the intercom and her long black hair curled around her shoulders. Then Zammit burst out laughing and started thumping his hand on the steering wheel.

'Christ, what's wrong with you?' I said, wanting to slap him for making me jump. 'You need to take a horse pill.'

Zammit carried on laughing, shaking his head as the gate to the grounds of the building opened automatically and closed.

'She must be going to see a client,' I said, hoping this would calm Zammit down.

'Yes, yes, yes!' he said. 'And do you know who lives there?'

'No, but I reckon you're going to tell me.'

'Yes, I am,' he said.

55

I waited.

'The president. It is the Presidential Palace!'

5

I made sure I wasn't going to be woken up too early in the morning by locking my bedroom door. When I did come out and look for breakfast, I was happy to see the two kids playing with some of the toys I'd given them. Once I'd drunk a tonne of orange juice, I let Tony know about last night. I then had Zammit do two trips for me. One was to take the kids and Tony round to see Zammit's kids, which meant we could also get the photos for the passports they needed. And two, I'd had a call from Mr Vella, from the Department of Environment, who was keen on meeting me this morning and had gone out of his way to book a table at Grandad's restaurant for lunch.

Now, me meeting Public Official Vella was never going to happen if Borg was still around – I would have left it to him to handle and that would have been that. I didn't feel the need to go running around looking for Schmidt because one way or another, I felt sure these things were going to come my way by just meeting people who were suddenly keen on talking to me. Also, Vella would be linked to everything else going on: Spiteri and the no-show police investigation of an explosive homicide in one of Grandad's villas, and the early morning visit of Schmidt's girlfriend Mila to the Presidential Palace, which was either to service a randy butler or someone a lot higher up the food chain. It didn't need a genius to work

56

out there was a potent brew that was stinking out the whole island.

Zammit dropped me off at the restaurant, which was called The Seashell, and was meant to be one of the best places on the island to eat fish with a sea view. Grandad was keen on buying it as soon as Borg had told him it had come on the market. I did my usual thing of being the formal buyer and, at least legally, was the owner of a seafood restaurant. In fact, I thought about changing the name to Seaview but heard the locals would get upset about it. And just to make things a bit weirder, I didn't like fish that much, so I've only been there once to buy the place with Borg and another time to throw the manager out because his fingers were seriously light-fingered.

But, The Seashell had one big thing going for it, more than its cooked fish and fish soup, and that was its prime location. If you were to follow the walk along the coastline, starting with the old port and the old town, you'd run into the hotels. They all looked out onto the deep blue, shiny sea, with their reception fronts, balconies and potted palm trees. It was what people wanted and paid for, except the smell of rotten eggs caused by the exhausts from too much traffic. Once you'd removed your gas mask, you'd then be into the bar district and down into the car park. Avoid the rutting back seats and take a curving stroll all the way down and then up to the headland that sticks out into the sea, and there you will find The Seashell.

There was not much room inside the small stone house that boiled lobsters and fried squid. The locals took over out of season and a few were spread out on the decking for lunch. The new manager had already seated Vella, with a shaded sea view and well away from the rest of the punters. He was upright and standing as I shook his hand, and told me he had already ordered, as I asked for some water.

'Mr Mason,' he said, waiting for me to sit down, 'this is a beautiful view, and I am so grateful for you agreeing to see me today at such short notice.'

I nodded, pushing my Mexican hat down lower.

Straight away, it was easy to dislike Vella. He had a thin patchy moustache above his lip, thick black eyebrows and a slimy grin that only slimy public officials like him knew how to use.

'A shame, I think, that Mr Borg could not be with us as your representative. I appreciate this may be inconvenient for you because I know and I understand the circumstances regarding your villa. But, as we both know, a tragedy, a horrific crime has occurred. So, some suspicions are about and therefore it is perhaps best we meet now, as we cannot tell what the outcomes will be.'

'That's OK,' I said, as my iced water arrived in a jug.

'Yes, it is lovely here, I think,' carried on Vella, looking out over the cliff wall and pretending to absorb the view of the blue sea like a tourist.

'Yeah, I like it.'

'But do you, Mr Mason?'

'Yeah, that's why I bought it.'

'Forgive me, if you don't mind, but it is my understanding that you rarely come here to eat. If you like it so much, why do you not eat here regularly?'

'Because I don't like fish.'

This threw Vella off for a few seconds and then he got back on track.

'Well, anyway, you have made an interesting purchase,' he said, looking over at the kitchen to see if his food was coming. 'But the main point of me asking you to meet is to explain and articulate the government's point of view regarding the legal issues which surround the ownership of this property, and the land it occupies.'

I took a sip of water and waited for the land-grabbing bomb shell, which I suspected was going to be lobbed my way.

'The government is continuing to launch many schemes to facilitate the island's transition to a more sustainable, resilient, greener and more carbon neutral economy. That is why my department, the Department of Environment, oversees all the developments on the island, to ensure they do not just bring economic benefits but also added value to support our local communities.'

'You have my support,' I said, in a tone that meant I didn't give a shit about his bullshit.

Vella ignored me and was about to launch into more twaddle and gibberish when his soup arrived.

'You will not be eating then, Mr Mason?' said Vella, as he tucked a napkin into his shirt and tie.

'Is it fish?'

Vella laughed.

'Well, I am afraid it is fish soup. I can order something else if it makes you feel queasy?'

I was tempted to say it wasn't the soup that made me feel sick.

'I'm not hungry,' I said.

Vella broke a bread roll and dropped it into his soup. He then started slurping, like his mum hadn't taught him how to eat.

'So,' he said, as he carried on draining the bowl like he'd been out in the desert for six months, 'there is this important matter of some legal status of things, which perhaps, if you are not overly familiar with our legal processes and ownership rights, would have been far more judicious if Mr Borg had been... available.'

'It's not a problem. I am the owner and have experience of the law.'

'Not our law,' he said sharply, as bread fell off his spoon and into the bowl, so soup splashed down his trouser leg.

'Apologies if I am being offensive,' he said, getting his emotions back under control. 'However, land and property rights, especially on the island, is a very detailed legal process. Also, law is not fixed in stone and needs to be responsive to the significant challenges in the global world we live in.'

'I own a seafood restaurant, not an oil company.'

'From the micro to macro, it is all now integrated.'

'Well, anything less and I would be disappointed.'

Vella stopped slurping and gave me a sly, slimy look.

'You have what I think is called a dry sense of humour. Which I like, I just need to get used to it, because then I can be sure I am not being insulted.'

'No probs, I'll let you know when I insult you.'

Again, this threw Vella off for a second, before he got back on his legal BS hobby horse.

'The point is, Mr Mason,' he said, giving me his harsh look, 'and I am sorry to be the one to have to tell you this, but you need to return this land to us.'

'Really,' I said, full of a lack of interest. 'Does that mean

I get to keep the restaurant?'

'No, they are one and the same thing, in our law, in this instance.'

'Really...' I said again, convinced he didn't have a legit legal leg to stand on.

'This property,' he said, spreading out his arms like he already had it in the bag, 'had been identified for future development. There would have been a seamless transition of land deeds and ownership to my department but for the unfortunate mistake of not preventing Mr Borg purchasing on your behalf. Call it the fog of a competitive market, but the previous owner, through some sleight of hand I suspect, took your offer while he was contractually obliged to complete the sale with our government. We can call it an administrative error, or perhaps just a lapse in concentration from all parties involved. But, with so much development going on, we dropped a ball, a clanger, I believe you might say. So, whilst you legally own this land and property, it can only be temporary, as the moral, democratic and, finally, legal process is enacted and the true owner is formally established. In other words, it does and will belong to the government's Futures Land and Property Fund, who have earmarked it for community and commercial development.'

No wonder he wanted to talk to Borg. It would have been easier to pass the brown envelope under the table and have Borg spin me a story.

'As you know, one of my villas was blown up the other night,' I said, leaning forward. 'Is that also earmarked for community and commercial development by the Futures Land and Property Fund?'

Vella looked intense.

61

'Trust me, Mr Mason, the government takes very seriously the killing of a journalist. He was only doing his job in exposing some of the corrupt practices that have on occasions caused some reputational damage to the island. I am sure the investigation will rapidly conclude and identify who was behind such an appalling murder and help compensate you for your losses. But the two matters are not related in any way at all.'

It was possible, but I didn't believe him. I just needed more time to draw the dots.

'So,' I said, easing myself back in the chair, 'you want me to sell you the restaurant, to avoid a long and drawn-out courtroom battle to establish who rightfully owns The Seashell and the land?'

'It is a case of what is convenient for both parties, because ultimately the government will win, or obtain what is rightfully theirs – something which will happen sooner than you think.'

'You mean, sign the papers now or get shafted a few days later?'

'This is not personal, Mr Mason. Nothing will transfer to me, you understand, but to the Fund. And as an indication of our own good will in this matter, we are prepared to offer an additional five per cent on top of the price you paid. Also, as we both know, Mr Borg is in some difficulties, which may preclude his ability to practice in the immediate future. I would be willing to identify suitable alternatives to act as an agent on your behalf.'

It was my turn to look out to sea and pretend I had some interest in the Mediterranean blue.

'OK, let me think about it.'

'And how long do you think you will need to think?'

'Not long,' I said, picking my nose and flicking what I had found over the side of the wall.

This seemed to cheer Vella up, and I don't mean the skill in picking my nose.

'Excellent,' he said, as he drained his bowl of soup by using more bread to it mop up.

I decided to remember my manners and poured him a glass of water, which seemed to make him think he had somehow sealed the deal.

'Now,' he said, using his napkin to clean his moustache, 'I have a special kind of invitation for you.'

He unzipped his leather wallet briefcase and pulled out a fancy-looking invite. He then announced: 'The prestigious Evening Gala at the Presidential Palace.'

'I've heard of it,' I said, smiling. 'I mean, I know where it is.'

'We have obviously noticed your investments on the island and this would be an opportunity for you to meet with some of our more substantial corporate property investors.'

'You mean bring me in from the cold.'

'It is never cold out here, Mr Mason, only warm, hot or very hot.'

'I've noticed,' I said, folding the thing up so I could stuff it in my pocket.

'Such an invitation is quite a high honour. And of course, you can bring someone with you, a plus one. Do you have someone in mind?'

'Yeah,' I said. 'I just need to find them.'

Again, Vella didn't know if I was being funny or not, as he signalled to the waiter he was going to go.

'Hopefully, I will see you there,' he said, putting cash on the table.

'If pumpkins can turn into a carriage, I can't see why not.'

6

I'd had a text message before I met Vella and had in mind who Cinders could be for the night. I didn't know who the text was from but it said "Mila", with an address in the old town. It might have come from Pissing Willy, but he would have wanted more money, so I was hoping it was from Zammit's constable brother. If it was, then it was less likely I was being set up for a nasty surprise. But it also meant I was being led by other people, and not being in control is not the way I like to do things.

I left Vella's cash to flutter in the sea breeze on the table as I had a chat with the new manager of The Seashell. I asked if he knew anything about Borg, what he'd been up to with this place, or if he knew how Borg could ever be released from the island's criminal justice system. He didn't and he was getting all anxious and worried about what might happen, because if you get a visit from the Department of Environment, it meant they were going to close the business and sell it to the developers. This is what worried him more than anything else, he said, because the people get nothing back in return, except poorly paid jobs with no skills required.

I told him not to worry, I wasn't selling the restaurant, not that it was my decision to sell. This got the manager all excited and he said the people would rally to protect The Seashell from the developers. I was about to go all Churchill on him and start talking about fighting them on the beaches, when I decided it would sound like I was reminding him of what the Brits did for them during the war. So I backed off from taking the piss because they took this whole development thing seriously. I said I'd be back in a few days and told him to buy some meat.

I took a slow stroll back into town, along the road that kept to the coastline. There were a few yachts and boats lying flat and peaceful in the bay area. On the surface, the world was perfect: Mediterranean sun, blue sky, blue sea, sand-coloured rocks and busy insects chirping away like they were always on heat. But go under water, beneath the surface, and it was just like life back in the shithole on my estate. But being as the island was only about fifteen miles across, things felt a lot more intense. As far as I could tell, a load of rot had got in and was killing off anything that was good and wholesome. Still, it was none of my business – it was not like I was going to be standing in an election to take on old monkey face. All I wanted was the artefact, then pack Tony up and send him back to Grandad, get the kids on their way and buy a few more villas.

Anyway, the address I had for Mila had me going up and down small alleyways off the main streets, which had a serious number of steps and cobbles. It's always a bit hit and miss to find any address in the old town, and even then, you couldn't guarantee you had found the right place. You really had to know where someone lived or have a five-hundred-year-old memory of what had been built, then built on and adapted. Something I was working on, but I was still a few hundred years away from cracking it.

When I found what I reckoned was Mila's address, it was nicely tucked away. There was a narrow alley and a wall, which I followed around until I could look over into a tiny courtyard. There was a table with an umbrella, a white metal chair and a few potted cactuses. The back door was open and a string of plastic beads covered the doorway, moving in the breeze that was channelling into the little cubbyhole.

Now, I have been over plenty of walls in my time, so it was easy for me to hop over and land as quiet as poss. I stood there like a statue for a good ten seconds, waiting to see what came out of the doorway. With nothing happening, I put one foot forward, and then another.

Then I stopped.

Something that looked a bit like the barrel of an elephant gun pushed through the plastic screen.

'I come in peace,' I said, putting my hands up.

'Don't you move, you dirty little scumbag, or else I will blow your fucking balls off, cut your stinky little heart out and feed it to those noisy filthy seabirds.'

They sounded Spanish.

'I'm looking for Mila,' I said, keeping my hands up.

'You are not looking for Mila, gangster man. You are looking to have your tiny little prick blown off and splattered all over this place. So, you had better go, before cock sucking is something you envy because your silly little penis is a plastic fork.'

'That's not what I want,' I said, trying to see through the beaded screen. 'I'm not looking for services, I'm looking for someone.'

'You said you were looking for Mila. Now you say you

are not looking for Mila. You think you can put your sandals in my courtyard and pretend to say hello. You need to go to the police. They can help you find someone. They can help you find anyone, if you pay them the money.'

'Well, the thing is, the police came to see me and I don't think they can help. But you might, if you can tell me where Max Schmidt is?'

It had to be Mila because there was a long pause before she said anything.

'What's your name, gangster man?'

'Steven... Steven Mason.'

'And why do you want to find Max Schmidt?'

'He's got a parcel for me. I was expecting him to deliver it a couple of days ago and I'm worried that something might have happened to him.'

'Then you need to look for Schmidt. You do not need to look for Mila because Mila is not Max Schmidt.'

'Look,' I said, slowly lowering my hands, 'let's just cut the BS and talk.'

'No way, Steven Mason. You get out of here or else I will shoot your head off!'

Oh well, I suppose that was better than losing my balls and my cock.

'Do you have a photograph of him?'

There was laughter.

'Do you think a man like Max Schmidt has photographs of himself. Anyway, you can have a thousand photos of that man but you will never find him if he does not want you to find him.'

'To be honest with you,' I said, trying to creep forwards, 'I'd not heard of him until a few days ago.'

'So you have one piece of luck. Not to see Max Schmidt is a good thing for anyone. Also, even if you find him, he will never give anything back to you. He will say it is finders keepers. You need to forget and move on.'

'Have you seen him then?'

'No, like you, I have only seen the police.'

'You mean Spiteri?'

'Yes, a handsome man, a lovely suit – not like you, Mr Tatty Man.'

'Come on…' I said, trying to ease myself down onto a chair. 'Why don't you put the gun down.'

'The gun stays like this until you leave.'

'OK, I'm leaving, but when was the last time that thing was fired?'

'When I shot my papa.'

'Was that a long time ago?'

'When I was a child.'

'Did you want to kill him?'

'I tried, but he lived.'

Interesting story, and one I was going to treat with respect.

'Well, my point is, that thing is more likely to blow your arms off than do any kind of damage to me.'

'You know a lot of things about guns do you, Steven Mason?'

'A little.'

'That doesn't surprise me. You know, I'm not some stupid pimped out drag queen. You need to show me respect if you want to talk to me, and not think you can fly over walls and do what you like.'

'My apologies,' I said, opening the palms of my hands. 'But I've found when I knock on people's front doors they jump to the wrong conclusion and then it's too late. This way, you've had a chance to think about it before you shoot me.'

'Willy told me about you.'

'Did he…'

'He said you didn't want your cock sucked but that you'd think about it.'

'Well, he'll get piles sitting all day in that urinal waiting for me.'

I heard a little laughter.

'OK, Steven Mason, I don't know why but you can have one more second, then you can fly back over that wall.'

'Thanks. I know you work for Schmidt and he has something of mine, which he has stolen. I will find Schmidt and I will get back what is mine.'

I then got up to leave.

'But there is one other thing,' I said, still looking down the barrel of the gun.

'Go on…'

'I would like to invite you out. I have an invitation to the Evening Gala at the Presidential Palace tonight and I would like you to be my guest.'

As soon as I said that the string beads parted and out came Mila.

'Well, why didn't you say!'

And so began a different kind of relationship.

7

When I got back to the villa the place had been turned into a bunch of happy campers. Knowing nothing about kids, I didn't know they talk about a thousand words a minute, want a thousand things doing in a second, and jump up and down like Duracell bunnies like they've been plugged into the National Grid. I was like, what the eff is this?

But Tony was in his element. He knew how to be with kids and the kids were all over him. They'd had a great time, so Tony said, with Zammit's kids, and Sonia and Zain wanted to know when they could see them again. In my head I was thinking, when we pick up the passports and drop in on Inspector Spiteri. Then Sonia said they could come round tomorrow and they had it all sorted because Zara wanted to see all the new toys she had got, and Zara was Zammit's daughter, who I think was the same age, and she was going to be Sonia's best friend...

I mumbled something and hid in my bedroom. When Tony tapped on the door and poked his head round, I felt like the dad who had come home from work grumpy and needed some time alone. Then, like the pissed off dad who hated his job, I told him what I had been up to and how I had the lead on Schmidt through Mila, and how the bosses on the island wanted to get hold of the Seashell – but that was never going to happen – and how it was probably all connected, but I didn't know how... yet.

I thought that would be it but he stood there wanting to say something.

'What?'

'The kids...' he said, like he was the mum who had to spend all day with them and I needed to understand.

'What about them?'

'We should let the kids go back to normal.'

'What's normal, Tony?'

'You know, like they're doing now, toys and friends, going to school, even if they teach you a load of crap.'

'Tony, they ain't going to get that if we hand them over. They'd spend ages in some fucked-up system and then get shunted from one useless care home to another. No one wants to adopt these kinds of kids – they're too old. It would be foster this, foster that, and then they'd be more fucked up than if they'd stayed out in the effing desert.'

'They've got relatives. They'd take them back, I reckon.'

'Did they tell you that?'

'Yeah, they said that they had lots of family back home.'

'And did the girl say that's what she wanted?'

'Well, no, she just said she had relatives.'

'That's not saying she wants to go back home, is it, Tony? And let's face it, they've been with a mum and dad that ain't exactly been honouring Queen and Country.'

Tony looked at me like I was supposed to know what was right.

'What?' I said again.

'Don't you think these kids could get hurt?'

'Tony, they've been living in an effing war zone with laser-guided bomb shit coming down on them and you're telling me that having them here is deadly?'

'Well, if you told me to bring my own kids over here now, I wouldn't.'

'That's different, Tony. That girl and boy are as safe as they're ever going to be.'

Tony shrugged.

'Look,' I said, 'all we're doing is looking after them for a bit.'

'For how long?'

'For as long as it takes to find Schmidt.'

Tony bit his lip and then he said something he shouldn't have said. 'You're using that little girl.'

I stood up.

I was angry.

'We all get effing used, Tony! Don't make out you're like Santa Claus, the pope and Mother effing Teresa all rolled into one.'

'All right,' he said, putting his arms up in case I swung at him.

'I need her,' I said. 'Schmidt is like this bloody Scarlet Pimpernel – everyone knows him but nobody wants to say jack shit. They're all scared of him. So this idea that he's just some messenger boy is fake news. And he could be standing right next to me or you and we wouldn't have an effing clue it was him. But Sonia, she would know, and we could trust her on that.'

He thought I was wrong, but he knew he had to back down.

'I'm going to make some dinner,' he said, as he turned to walk out in a huff.

'Not for me,' I said, laying back on the bed. 'Forty winks and then I've got to go.'

Then I'm sure he said I could piss off.

Anyway, early evening, I got suited and booted and left without saying a word, just in case Tony thought of something else to beat me with. Zammit drove the taxi carriage into town, picked up Mila and then dropped us off outside the Presidential Palace.

Mila forgave me for not arriving in a limo. She'd also

done herself proud and gone out and bought herself a nice new dress, tight as a baboon's arse and with enough sparkles on it she could be seen from outer space. As we walked up to the front gates, with all the posh end of the island waltzing in past us, there was a tarted-up soldier in full dress. He recognised Mila because he put his arm out, but there was no way she wasn't coming in.

'Trust me, the invitation's genuine,' I said, as I pulled out of my pocket the crumpled card. 'I'm Steven Mason and this is Ms Mila Morales.'

He got the sideways look from Mila.

'Thanks,' I said, as we entered the Presidential Place, guided by lanterns that lighted our way along a paving stone path.

'You should know your way around here,' I said to her, as we brushed past the foliage on either side of us.

'If you are going to be horrible to me, Steven,' she said, winding her way elegantly along, 'then you can do this on your own.'

I didn't think I was being horrible, just cheeky. But I needed Mila with me because I wanted to put the shits up the big chiefs. And having Mila around would get them all nervy and anxious – put them off their balance.

Then we entered the gardens.

She got me to hold her arm as she paraded like a peacock, with her highlighted cheek bones, long eyelashes and ruby red lips flashing and bleeping like a traffic light.

'Now that's what I call an entrance, Steven Mason,' she said, as all eyes from the flowered presidential garden were looking our way.

Nobody needed to tell us we were different, but who

would want to look like them! The women must have been made in the same factory: same hairdos, same eyelashes, same make-up, all with false boobs and long legs. And all the men looked like they'd been painted using the same pot of orange, with their white teeth and Botox plastic shiny eyes, to hide the fact they were lizards from another planet. And they were all talking at the same time to each other but it didn't look like any of them were listening. And they all laughed together but it didn't look like any of them knew what they were talking about.

They were spread out on the grass, which was green and had been watered, just like the blooming flowers growing out of baskets hanging down from the seafront colonnade. There were also palm trees and cactuses packed into tubs and sandy troughs. And then rising above the garden were the sandstone bricks, columns and carvings of the grand palace, where the president lived, which was guarded by ceremonial police and off limits to the guests.

We headed straight for the marquee, which had round tables littered with big bunches of flowers. Even I needed a drink as we grabbed a glass of champagne from a passing tray.

'Well, it's not what I am usually asked to drink,' said Mila, as she downed it in one.

'Yeah, so who did you visit here last night?'

'That is client privilege,' she said, placing her empty glass down on the table, 'but what I will tell you... you will not find Max here.'

'I'm glad to hear it,' I said, 'otherwise there'd be a lot of explaining to do.'

'Is that a threat, Steven?'

'Yes,' I said, scanning the monkey cage. 'I don't know how you can do it, servicing all these dodgy-looking politicians and businessmen.'

'But Steven, you are much like these men. The only difference is you do not look legal. In fact, I would say, in your tuxedo, you look more and more like the Italian mafia.'

Little did she know…

'Ah… Mr Mason…'

It was Vella.

'How wonderful to see you and…'

He took a few seconds to take in the fluttering eyes of Mila.

'Ms Morales,' I said.

'Your plus one,' he said nervously.

'Do you know each other?' I said, grinning like a Stan Laurel.

Vella broke out in a mini sweat. He wanted Mila to say they had never met before but she wasn't going to confirm or deny.

'Anyway, Mr Mason,' he said, which I think meant he did know her, 'as I said at our little meeting earlier today, this is a perfect opportunity for you to meet some of the investors and developers who have been driving forward the very important land and property transformations on our island. I have already said to a few of them I believed you would be coming tonight, and it would be a personal pleasure of mine to introduce you.'

I looked at Mila.

'I am sure Ms Morales can amuse herself with some of the other guests for a short while,' said Vella, like he knew she would be making a nuisance of herself.

'No problem,' she said, her eyes drifting around the light and shaded garden. 'I know most men would have left me before we got to the gate.'

'There you go, Mr Mason, you are actually a perfect gentleman.'

'Not really,' I said, 'it's just the suit.'

I could see Vella trying to remind himself about my sense of humour.

'Oh, I can see some more champagne,' said Mila, as she made a beeline for a wandering waiter.

Vella looked relieved.

'Eh, how long have you known Ms Morales?' asked Vella.

'Let me think,' I said, scratching my chin. 'I would say… about five or six hours.'

'Well, I have heard,' he said, 'he or she charges by the hour.'

'Not me,' I said. 'We're just good friends.'

'Of course,' said Vella, the slimy creep.

He then waved at two guys about twenty yards away. They looked like well-groomed bouncers, fit and suited, which meant they had to be Fund managers.

'Please,' said Vella, 'you will meet two important people, I think, both of whom have substantial interests in the topic we discussed at The Seashell today.'

'You mean they want to buy my restaurant?'

'No, Mr Mason, it is not exactly like that. As I explained to you earlier today, your purchase was in error and needs to be resolved to the satisfaction of all parties involved.'

'Vella!' was all I heard from a guy wearing sunglasses.

He was American, which wasn't a good start.

'This is Mr Cyrus Miller,' said Vella, who now looked small up against the two six-footers. 'And Mr Simon Colindale.'

'From Global Venture Capital Group,' said the Brit. 'We were just admiring your lady friend while Mr Vella was talking to you. Some unique features… and a very attractive person.'

'Yeah, well, she can suck cock,' I said, 'if you're interested.'

Colindale smiled, like nothing phased him, but I reckoned he could talk shit all day and still sound like he knew what he was talking about.

'So, gentlemen,' said Vella, 'it is a good opportunity to meet tonight. Mr Miller and Mr Colindale are fully aware of some of the…'

But before Vella could finish, Miller butted in.

'I tell you what, Mason, you look like a nasty piece of work to me, and I've heard that all you're doing over here is laundering dirty money for your boss in the UK. Now, we don't have to get into the ins and outs of what's right and wrong, but when push comes to shove, we are legitimate investors, generating wealth, creating jobs, thinking about the earth, making sure things are clean and sustainable. You, on the other hand, have dirty lumps of cash that need putting in the laundromats. Now, as far as we're concerned, you can carry on doing that if you keep it away from the projects – projects that are going to raise this pissy little backwater into a viable economy, and one that will give it a future. And, just so you know, we're the good guys here. All you need to do is handover what's ours and then disappear up that little hill of yours and rest easy while you accumulate – out of sight and out of mind.'

'Sorry,' I said calmly, 'but I don't know what the fuck you're talking about.'

'Mr Mason,' said Colindale, 'what I, Mr Miller, and all the other investors want is for the mistake made by Mr Vella and his department to be corrected. It requires cooperation on your part, an acceptance that the restaurant you think you purchased is effectively in the wrong hands.'

'That's not what the locals want,' I said.

'Heh, Che, don't get motherfucking revolutionary on us!'

I looked at Miller, ready to slap him.

'Gentlemen,' said Vella, keen to calm things down as people started looking our way. 'Please, I had assured Mr Mason that he would be meeting investors, reasonable people, and the department is working to resolve this matter without delay.'

'The thing is, Steven,' said Colindale, 'we know that you will not have a leg to stand on if your dealings on this island were to be investigated by the constabulary. Your boss will not be happy to see his hard-earned riches scrutinised for its legitimacy. This would also, I believe, cause some level of instability for you, drawing unwanted attention, putting at risk the quiet process of money entering through the back door and into the system. There is a good offer of a five per cent profit on your investment, which I think is a generous return in the short period of time you have... how shall I describe it... held the deeds to The Seashell.'

'You mean owned,' I said.

'Let's not get into that shall we, but we are open to negotiation.'

'Yeah, well, I'll think about it, if you give me double what

I paid.'

'Mr Mason,' said Vella, almost coughing up his corrupt vomit, 'the offer is a reasonable one, and it would be unrealistic for the Department of Environment to find unbudgeted capital to merely correct an administrative error.'

'Perhaps these guys can help make up the difference then,' I said, still thinking about decking the sun glassed Miller.

That's when Miller got up close and personal with me.

'I've dealt with punks like you before,' he said, breathing in my face. 'And everyone I've taken down and put on the floor.'

'Yeah, I suppose golf can be a bit mean and nasty.'

Miller stayed where he was, in his big-boy pants.

'Steven!' screamed Mila out of nowhere, pushing her way into the middle. 'You are a naughty man! You need to keep me in the loop, you know. All you tall men look like you're about to burst. Must be something serious, and Mila likes to know everything.'

'Let's go,' said Miller, like he was going to wait for me after school finished.

Colindale tried to shake my hand but he was wasting his time.

'Did I say something wrong?' said Mila, spinning around on her high heels with her champagne.

Vella was all shaky for about two seconds and then ran off after the dickheads from Global Venture Capital Group, trying to work out how much his next brown envelope was going to shrink.

'What an odious man,' said Mila, fluttering her eyelashes.

'Yeah, you're the star of the show,' I said. 'But give it five minutes and then go over to the American guy in the sunglasses and slap him hard for me.'

'I can't do that!'

'Yes you can. I'm paying you by the hour, so go and slap him! If they throw you out, I'll pay you double.'

Mila hated me for saying that.

'You know, Steven, I'm not a cheap whore. I'm a human being and should be spoken to with respect.'

'I'll make it up to you,' I said.

She hated me for another second, then kissed me on the cheek.

8

Mila had real balls. She whacked Miller so hard he was almost on the floor, and then she followed it up with some raging Spanish, hopefully accusing him of shagging animals and dead people. With all eyes on the shock and awe of Mila going at it, I slipped under the canvas of a marquee and jumped up onto a low wall, which ran down the side of the old palace.

I looked straight down.

The lights from the palace and the garden lit up the cliff edge, all the way down to the hard-edged lines of rock, a good three hundred feet, all the way down the steep and jagged lines that dropped into the sea, bashing against the bottom of volcanic rock. Heights was never a problem for me, but I spent a good two or three minutes looking down at the sea. I wasn't thinking of jumping, but I felt this strange pull, like a magnet, attracted to falling all the way down to the busy waves. I was stuck in that moment, suddenly caught out by how shaky life is. It didn't make sense because I'd never felt like that before, even when my life was threatened. I could feel being outside of my body, hovering above the cliff edge, the rocks and the sea, wondering whether it was worth it, whether I should carry on or just let myself go. It wasn't suicide I was thinking about, it was just death.

Then I told myself to get a grip.

What was I thinking?

I pulled myself up and pressed my hands against the palace so I had leverage to shuffle along. I didn't get too far because the wall was all gritty and sandy and my leather soles made things slippery. So I got down on my hands and knees and started to crawl.

The idea was to get inside and nose around before I was escorted off the premises. And I was banking on all the windows being open to let the cool breeze in so I could introduce myself formally, but it was all shuttered up. I kept on crawling as I heard my mum in my head telling me off for ruining my nice trousers. It was only when I got to the end of the wall that I got lucky – the shutters were pressed back and a window was wide open.

I looked in.

It was a fancy bedroom with the biggest bed I'd ever seen. In the middle of the bed was an old man, surrounded by medical equipment. There was a crest above his bed, something royal and grand – swirly things and crossed swords. He was sleeping, as far as I could tell. I put my foot on the windowsill, pulled myself over and jumped in.

I made a thud.

His eyes opened and he looked at me. I stood there, pretending to be a statue.

It was too late. He could see me.

I was waiting for some panic alarm to go off but he held up his hand and waved me over.

I could have told him it was just a dream and walked out. Perhaps I should have, but he seemed keen on me going over to see him. So I sat on the bed.

His mouth was all dry and crusty. He held my hand real tight, then started squeezing like he was seriously constipated. Then he started moving his mouth, trying to say something, but he couldn't get his words out. I tried to pull my hand away, thinking the old man was totally gaga, but he pulled down harder. It surprised me, how strong he was, and his breath stank. But he was trying to say something. It was foreign, sounded Spanish. I blamed Mila for making everything sound Spanish.

'Speak up, mate,' I said. 'I can't hear yer.'

That's when his eyes bulged like they were going to pop.

'Diablo...' he said, as if it was the end of the world.

'You what?'

He licked his lips. He was going to have another go.

'Diablo,' he said again.

'Yeah, I get it. Diablo. What's that then?'

That's when he began to fade a bit, sinking his head back into the pillow. It had taken it out of him.

I poured out some water and got him to take a sip. The old guy must be at the end. Who knows what goes on in your head when it comes to the final reckoning.

However, he wasn't the kind of thing I was looking for, not that I knew what I was looking for, except maybe a

German guy in leather lederhosen carrying a tray of Bavarian lagers.

I decided to do the decent thing and tucked his bedsheet in so he felt nice and comfy. I then had a quick nosey in the drawers, but there wasn't the odd Medusa just lying around. Anyway, I do like a good butcher's in people's houses, or a grand old palace will do, but an old man talking gibberish was not the kind of return I was looking for. The golden goose had to be Schmidt tucked away in some cupboard, but that was about as likely as Grandad becoming a saint.

I opened the door into the corridor and poked my head out. There was no one about. I noticed a light switch on the wall, so said goodnight and turned the lights off.

The corridor was all mirrors, gold-framed paintings and vases. I tried to look casual and get back to the garden party.

As I headed for some big open doors, with a couple of ceremonial guards standing outside, I heard a shout:

'Excuse me!'

The voice came from inside a room that had its own big double doors wide open. I could have carried on but then I had a feeling they wanted to do more than just tell me off.

'Can we help you?'

There was two of them in the room.

I recognised Grech, sitting behind a finely carved desk, and by his side was this woman in a seriously decorated uniform.

'What are you doing?' she said.

'Oh, yeah, do you know where the toilet is?'

I got a stony look.

Then she said, eyeing me up and down, 'You look as if you have fallen over.'

'Yeah, a bit of a scuffle outside. Some American guy was going around groping all the ladies. Got a bit ugly, so I needed to clean myself up.'

'The knight in a shiny tuxedo.'

'Well, you know, I do have me standards.'

'I am sure you do, Mr Mason,' she said. 'Please, come in for a minute. My name is Police Commissioner Attard and this is Prime Minster Grech.'

Christ, I thought, I'm getting popular. Maybe I should stand for election.

Grech looked just like his poster plastered all over the island with Zammit's spit dripping down his face – Zammit had hit the target on the way down here.

Attard was a thin rake, black trousers and badges all over her constabulary jacket. She had her cap under her arm and had the look of a sleepy dog, with bags under her eyes and a long face.

I dusted down my trousers and then noticed on one side of the wall a bank of security cameras, which also showed the old man's room.

'We see you also popped in to talk to the president,' said Attard.

'Yeah, I wanted to get his autograph.'

'Don't worry, Mr Mason,' piped up Grech, 'we understand that a man like you may need to resort to unorthodox methods when nature calls.'

That was nice, I thought. They must get on with villains like me.

'He's not a well man,' said Grech. 'Age rather than disease, you understand.'

'Well, I suppose it's good of you to keep his seat warm.'

Grech smiled.

'A president on this island is merely constitutional, much like your queen back on your own island. And if there is a need to keep a seat warm, it is only a soft cushion to ease the pain of long hours reading and signing papers.'

'They say it's tough at the top.'

That's when Attard had something else to say. 'Mr Vella said you had a strange sense of humour... very British. Fortunately, we are no longer morally in debt to your country and our independence means a zero tolerance of sarcasm.'

'Fair enough,' I said. 'But does that mean you don't mind the odd murder now and then?'

I got the look that said they'd only tolerate so much before I faced the firing squad.

'The Garibaldi case has shocked everyone on the island,' said Grech. 'It is extremely troubling that there are people who seek to undermine our democracy by egregious methods. Mr Garibaldi was a brave and fearless journalist, even if much of what he wrote was often critical of myself and my administration.'

'Well, I know I didn't do it,' I said. 'You don't happen to know who did?'

Attard was going to say something back but Grech held up his hand so he could carry on.

'We can be realistic with each other, Mr Mason. There is no one else listening and we both know who and what you are. But you may not be too familiar with the world of politics and politicians. It may be your job to protect the interests of your investments here, but it is my job and in my interest to protect the things that sustain our democracy. And there are two things that are trying to undermine our democracy at this moment in time: corruption and the truth about corruption.'

'Isn't that the same thing?'

'Yes and no. Let me tell you a story about how things used to be on our little island. There was once a young man who knew he was going to marry one of two sisters in the next village, but he also knew that one was ugly and the other one was very beautiful. The families shook hands on the basis that the young man was promised the beautiful one, on condition that the veil was not removed until after they had been officially married. Then, come the day of the marriage, the veil is removed and he discovers he has been tied to the ugly one.

'As you can imagine, the young man and his village are outraged, they want revenge, because the family and the village have been tricked and made to look like fools. Feeling duped, they rampage and riot, lashing out at those they hold responsible. But, in the end, once the people have calmed down, all that has happened is a village has been ruined and is in need of repair. And after all, the fields were ready for harvesting and no one wanted to go hungry with winter only around the corner.

'The young man didn't get everything he wanted, but at least he was married and could still have children. Whilst everyone knew the truth, no one wanted it to be known forever and people got back to being married again. So, you see, the point is to maintain balance because it is in everyone's interests to preserve the status quo, which in the long run is not as bad as it may seem, even if a few principles get broken.'

I was trying to think of something to say back after that fairy story but Attard was keen to refocus.

'Now, Mr Mason,' she said, 'we will forgive your little indiscretion regarding your entry point into the building and subsequent trespassing. However, I have a question for you: do you know where Joseph Borg is hiding?'

'I thought he was staying with you...'

'Borg, regrettably, was released before we had time to act on information pertinent to the Garibaldi case.'

'Was that Inspector Spiteri? He's a nice bloke but a bit slack.'

'Well,' said Attard, 'you'll be able to tell him yourself when you present the passports of the guests residing in your villa at constabulary HQ. We look forward to seeing you tomorrow.'

'OK, but I have to warn you, I'm not a morning person, better make it the afternoon.'

'And how are the children?'

'Oh, you know what kids are like,' I said, turning away to leave, 'always up to all sorts of things.'

'Just remember, Mr Mason,' said Grech, 'the longer you stay here, the more likely it is you will earn the right to vote for me one day. And of course, that will always make your investments more secure, if you are in the club.'

I got to the door and looked back at them.

'Oh, by the way,' I said. 'I just thought you'd like to know people keep spitting at your poster. Rude, isn't it, but that's people for yer, they never appreciate what you do for them.'

And then I was back down the corridor, starting to feel the pressure for the first time.

I was ready to get Zammit to pick me up when a few of the ladies made a beeline for me. They were keen to give me the lowdown on Mila's big scene and then wanted to know what it was like to have Mila as a girlfriend. They said she looked stunning as a woman, even though they knew she was a man.

I couldn't help myself and gave them a picture of our life together, how Mila had been working extra hard to raise the money for her transition and how we were planning on a family. Of course, there was her pimp Schmidt, who might be a bit of a problem, but seeing as he was a suspect in the murder of the journalist Garibaldi, we could get lucky and spend the rest of our lives together. Oh, and one final thing: Mila said she'd fucked all the men here anyway, so she had a load of intel on what their husbands liked, but that kind of information didn't come cheap.

That pissed them off and so they left me alone to drink a few glasses of champagne.

I decided to wait for the fireworks and sat on the gritty stone wall I had crawled along. I looked down the cliffside into the wavy sea. I wondered if you would die if you felt like jumping. Yeah, I thought to myself, there's no way you'd survive if you dived off the cliff.

I looked along the colonnade, which stretched into thick bunches of palm trees. Then through the foliage came the swinging hips of Mila.

She looked pleased with herself.

'I thought they'd thrown you out,' I said, easing myself back so I could hear more of the waves below and not the noise and music in the garden.

'You are joking, Steven. I've had two hand-jobs tonight, and one of them was the American.'

'You mean he wanted you to slap him again?'

Mila burst out laughing.

'I bet they caught you,' she said.

'Sort of. I also bumped into an old guy.'

'Oh, you mean the president. He's waiting to die.'

'Yeah, he didn't look too good. But he seemed desperate to tell me something.'

'Why you?' said Mila, who was using her beady eyes to scan for more targets.

'Who knows, perhaps he'd rather talk to me than Grech.'

'And...'

'And what?'

'What did the president say to you?'

'He said, or I think this is what he said, Diablo. It sounds Spanish, so do you know what that means?'

'It is Spanish, Steven. It means "the devil". Maybe he thought you were Diablo, come to take away his soul and send him off to hell.'

'I don't know,' I said. 'He kind of said Diablo... like they existed... the devil... like Diablo was a person.'

'You know, Diablo is everywhere. It is not one person. It is the spirit of evil. It runs like a dirty stain on this island, and all these people here worship Diablo.'

'Well, I'm no fan, but I don't buy into this lot being a bunch of devil worshippers.'

'No, Steven, it is not that they go to a satanic church and kiss the feet of the devil. No, but they have the strength and the power of Diablo. Diablo is in the hearts of many. There are diablos on this island who seek and steal. Diablo is their business; it is the fear they trade on.'

I wondered if she was talking about Schmidt, rather than anyone in the presidential garden, but I didn't have time to say anything as the first fireworks suddenly came whooshing out of nowhere and cracked up in the sky.

This changed Mila's mood, and everyone else around us, as the fireworks got people to look up at the sparkles and fizzles. It made Mila's night as she jumped up and down, clapping her hands. For a moment, she looked like all the things that were weighing on her were being lifted off her shoulders – turned into two-second explosions of glitter and fairy tales.

Like everyone else, I watched, but after five minutes, I just turned my head and looked back down the cliff.

I wasn't looking at anything until the fireworks lit up the dark and that's when I was sure there was someone standing there, about a third of the way down, looking back up from steps cut into the cliff. It was only for a second or two, and then the light went.

Another load of fireworks shot up but whoever it was had gone.

Then two words popped into my head: Schmidt and Diablo.

9

By the time I got back to the villa, all I wanted to do was crash. The sun was coming up, so I got a pen and paper and scribbled on it:

GO AWAY

I then stuck it on my bedroom door, pulled the curtains

across and slept like a baby. But when I woke up, I had mother hen bugging me again.

'Tony, my brain hurts, and you're the reason why my brain hurts.'

He was standing there, just like he did yesterday, trying to tell me something about the kids.

'Look, Tony, I don't give a flying fuck right now! My head is throbbing and your negative vibes means it's going to explode.'

'I'm just saying, the little boy, he got ill last night, and he's got a temperature. You know, we didn't know what was wrong with their mum, and I don't want to be burning some kids body around the back because we couldn't be arsed to do something about it.'

'Then get a doctor, phone for a GP, or whatever it is you do when kids are ill.'

'Listen, mate, this is your gaffe. I don't know what you do around here to get a doctor.'

I held my head in my hand.

I had drunk way too much.

'OK,' I said, 'I'll be up in a minute.'

I needed to drink a gallon of water and a litre of orange juice so I plodded out into the kitchen. Sonia was there looking sorry for herself as I poured out the juice and drank.

'How's your brother?' I said, wiping my mouth.

She shook her head, like she couldn't speak.

'No worries,' I said, 'I'll get a doctor to take a look.'

She didn't look happy with that idea.

'What's wrong?' I said, downing a load more juice.

'He's going to die, just like Mummy,' she said.

I didn't answer that.

91

Then Tony came in and looked at me like I should go see the poor kid. I took one more swig and then followed Tony into the bedroom.

'He's burning up,' said Tony, as I pushed past him.

The kid looked in a bad way.

He was in his undies and was lying on his back, shivering and moaning.

'I've got a thermometer in the bathroom,' I said to Tony. 'Have a look in the cabinet above the sink.'

I sat beside him on the bed and put my hand on his forehead. He whimpered as I felt how hot he was.

There was a serious fever going on.

'Heh, Zain,' I said. 'Does it hurt anywhere? Are you in pain?'

He wanted to say something, but he was in the grip of being ill.

Tony came back and stuck the thermometer under his armpit.

He took it out.

'Christ!'

'What?'

'I'll do it again,' he said.

He kept it there a bit longer.

He looked again and just nodded for me to follow him.

We stood outside the bedroom.

'Well?'

'His temperature's not good,' said Tony.

'Yeah, I can see that.'

'It's forty degrees.'

'And?'

'That's dangerous,' said Tony, biting his lip.

'How dangerous?'

'Deadly,' said Tony. 'You need to phone for that doctor.'

That's when I went quiet.

I needed to think.

'What are you doing, Steven?'

I carried on thinking.

'Steven, there ain't no other solution. The kid's going to die if his temperature stays like that.'

Then Tony looked behind me.

'All right, Sonia,' he said. 'Don't you worry, we're going to get a doctor, ain't that right, Steven?'

I didn't say anything.

I went into the bedroom.

I picked the kid up in my arms.

He was as light as a feather.

I pushed past Tony and Sonia and went out back. I could hear them shouting after me. I started running and as I ran, I was talking to him.

'Come on, kid, you aren't going to effing die, do you hear, you ain't going to die! You're going to live! You're going to be a hero! You're going to be the greatest! Yeah, I know that for a fact. Yeah, there's no way you're going to die. You're the best, the best kid on the block. And fuck me, we're going to have some fun. We're going to party. Yeah, a big party with chocolate and ice cream. Would you like that, kid? Yeah, I used to love parties. Not that I had too many of them but you know, when there was one, I was like right into all that chocolate and ice cream and cake. Yeah, I loved a nice piece of birthday cake. You know, with lots of icing and jam in the middle. And I'd take all the icing off first and eat all the jammy cake, and then I'd tuck right on in because I'd left the best bit till last, which was the icing on the cake. I tell yer, you can't get anything better than that. Yeah, love that birthday cake. And, you know, I don't know when your birthday is, but that's something you can tell me about, you know, when you're ready to speak. And not speaking is not a problem. I can understand that. Who needs to speak? You know with us grown-ups, kid, that's all we do all day – prattle on and talk a load of shit. But it would be great to hear you talk, you know, when you're feeling better. And that's all we need to do right now, is get you to the hospital, get you in front of them doctors.

'I knew a doctor once, a crazy guy really. Well, what I mean is, he was a doctor for crazy people. And he was a nice guy. Talked too much. Used lots of big words so you had to have like a dictionary in front of you just so you knew what the eff he was talking about. But a good guy, like I said. And he was all into helping people. If he was here now, I know he would be into helping you and your sister, trying to find a safe place for you to live. Which I know ain't much to ask, just to have a safe place and a bit of sanctuary. And trust me, Zain, I've promised your sister that we're going to get you both to Germany. So, what I'm trying to say is, I don't need you dying on me because I've been putting some hard graft into this – I've been sorting things out, talking to people, greasing a few hands, making sure them cogs get moving so we can get some new documents. I know, it's crazy isn't it, that you need bits of paper just to prove that you're a human being and not a monkey. But that's the way the world is. And that's not your fault. You know, when you're a kid, you just get born into it, and you must sort out all the crap that's thrown at you. And none of it's fair, being treated like some old boot that gets kicked down the road. Because as a kid, I know, all you can do is follow. You might know things ain't right, you might know that something is wrong, but that ain't going to give you a voice. And I know, as a kid, all you want is a nice mummy and daddy. And I get that, you know, that's something I would have liked when I was a kid. But we get spewed out into this fucked-up world and told to just get on with it. There ain't no helping hands, there ain't no nice people out there too often. You just have to get your head down and push on through.

'And I can see that, I can see that in your eyes – I can see that you ain't trusting nobody. And that's a good way to be. There's nothing wrong learning early on that people can be really mean and nasty. And it doesn't matter how old or young you are, they're going to do what they want to you because that's how they're wired. It's like they plug themselves into the nasty bastard plug socket before they get up in the morning, just so they're recharged and ready to go. I had a lot of that sort of shit when I was a kid and the way I used to survive was to go somewhere and hide. Maybe that's what you're doing in your head. I get that. It must be nice in there, a safe place where you get some control. Yeah, I can see how that's all you really need, to live in your head and just let all the other rubbish go on around you. But the thing is, Zain, go too deep and it can be hard to come back. It's early days for you, but you don't want to go too deep. Some things ain't that bad after all. I mean, there's your sister, and I know she's done a good job of looking after you, but I think in your own little way, you look after her. That means your sister needs you. She needs you to be around so she's got more than just the memory of your mum and dad. I know that

95

sounds a bit weird but you're the most important thing to her and she's banking on you still being here. That means you can't just wander off and hide and not want to be here anymore. You've got to live because your sister needs you. And you know what? Tony needs you. And you wouldn't want to let old Tony down now, would you?

'OK, so let's keep on running a bit here. I don't think we've got too far to go and then we can get those doctors and they can have a good look at you. Once you see them doctors, they will know what to do. I don't remember if I saw too many doctors when I was your age, but I suppose there wasn't too much wrong with me. Probably a bit lucky with that. But we all get ill at some point in time. That's all normal. So just remember, kid, this is all normal. It might not feel like it right now, but it's all going to be all right. I can tell. You just hold on tight. That's it. You hold on tight because I reckon we are not too far away – if I get it right. Yeah, just around the corner here, where this is… the hospital. And then we can see how things are. Everything's going to be all right. Trust me, Zain, trust me…'

10

I was sitting in the waiting room on my own when I saw Tony and Sonia come into the hospital.

'How is he?' was the first thing Tony said.

'I don't know,' I said. 'He's in there with the doctor.'

I nodded at the doors where Zain had disappeared.

'You could have told us what you were doing,' said Tony.

'You had us freaked out.'

'What do you mean?'

'Well, you know…' said Tony, with Sonia by his side.

'No, I don't know,' I said.

'Well, it's just… like…'

But before Tony had time to finish what he was saying, I felt a punch into my stomach and then a load of small fists flying.

It was Sonia and she was going into one.

'I hate you! I hate you! I hate you! You're evil! You're the devil! You should die. You killed my mummy. You killed my mummy!'

I stood there, taking the beating.

Tony tried his best. 'Come on, Sonia, ease off. No one killed your mummy. You know that. Zain's going to be fine.'

But I let her carry on beating me, crying, letting it all come out, all the hell and all the other shit she must have been through.

Then Tony thought enough was enough.

'Sonia!' said Tony, grabbing hold of her arms to stop her hitting.

She then looked at me like I was all the things that had turned her world upside down and caused all the pain, fear and death. And I knew the look. I had always aimed it at other people who had caused me pain.

'She's just upset,' said Tony. 'You know, running off with her brother like that.'

'Why, what do you think I was going to do, break his neck and burn him?'

Tony looked at me like I had said the wrong thing. And I had.

Sonia burst out crying, full on, and buried her head in Tony's big fat belly, holding him, needing him.

I'd had enough.

I was off.

I had done my bit.

'Heh, where're you going?' shouted Tony.

I didn't answer as I walked back along the corridor and out of the hospital.

The next thing I did, which isn't normal for me, was head straight to the bars. I started on pints, a few lagers, and then got into some snakebites. I went to every bar I could find along the strip. I was rat-arsed in good time. I puked up just as the sun was going down and then wandered out onto the flat volcanic rock, which was on the other side of the old town and looked out at the darkness covering the blue bay.

For the first time in a long time, I felt like things were falling apart. And I don't mean around me, the things outside of me, the doing stuff. I mean inside me, inside myself. I didn't just feel sick because I had a serious hangover, I felt sick to my stomach because the whole world inside my head was going off beam and spinning out of control. I always banked on things being certain, no ifs, no buts, no other way of thinking about things, but the kids were giving me the heebie-jeebies and I didn't like it – or I didn't know how to handle it.

In a way, I wished somehow I could make it better for them, especially for Sonia, but I had no real power to do anything. Perhaps Tony was right and they deserved to be back with people whose job it was to look after lost and damaged kids. That's what a logical, sensible brain would be thinking. They didn't need me. They didn't need some hard-arsed villain pretending to look after their interests. Someone like me was only going to bring them more trouble, more pain, more shit that they shouldn't have to deal with.

Perhaps it was the booze – too much booze had blown a few plug sockets. I was feeling dead sorry for myself, feeling like I should be the one who was being looked after. I was the one that needed a hug and cuddle. Even a nasty piece of work like me needs someone, something, anything in my life to hold on to. But Britney had gone – someone who was close to love. And having finished off my useless shithead of a half-brother, I was stuck out here on this effing island and it felt like my past was coming back to haunt me, I was sure of it, because my threat radar was screaming in my ears.

Or was I just evil? Had I done so much bad shit I was like the devil? Maybe I am Diablo. Maybe there is no other Diablo but me. Perhaps I am like this Schmidt.

After all, how long did I think I could carry on living this way of life before it all caught up with me? It's always just a matter of time in my line of business that you come against things, people who are better at it than you, who have more power than you. Perhaps this is what is going on. Do I really have a chance of tracking down Schmidt unless he wants to find me? And if he does want to find me, why is he in control and what is he trying to offer?

But one thing I was sure of, which was staring me in the face: there were people here on this island who knew a lot more than me. And I am being singled out, targeted. There's an effing puppet master pulling my strings, and it wasn't Grandad. I could feel it, I could feel there was something coming for me. I didn't know what it was and where it was coming from but I just knew it was going to cut to the core like a knife into the heart.

And then I puked up again.

So I moved away from all the sick.

I looked at the red sun, the old fortress, the old defences of the old port, and then headed back to get doubly rat-arsed. I was on the absinthe by the time I got to The Sapori. As far as I could tell the place only had a few people in it. I needed a piss and had to put up with Pissing Willy lying in the urinals again. He didn't recognise me at first, maybe because he only went on cocks.

He then offered his usual services at a discounted rate.

'Eff off, Willy!' I said, fumbling around because I was well fucked. 'Why don't you go butter your arse...'

'Oooo... I heard Mila had already done that for you.'

I said something like, 'Ha ha,' as I bumped off a couple of walls and back into the bar. I kicked a few tables and chairs, got a drink and sat in front of the small stage waiting for some dumb act to come on.

I was nodding off when suddenly the music came flying out of the PA system. It was some musical shit, something to do with cabarets, and an ugly-looking drag act who strutted her stuff. I was struggling to keep my head together. The absinthe had lit the trippy stage and a load of rainbow colours started shooting out of the glitter ball, hitting the back of my eyeballs. It was turning my brain into a laser gun. Then my head started falling off my neck, so I put my hands out to catch it and my arms started extending like a telescopic ladder. I watched my head fall off and held it in my hands.

'You crazy motherfucker!'

That made me laugh... whoever said that... yeah... whoever said that... needs to say that to my face... because you know...

But I didn't know. Not anymore. My eyeballs were trying to jump out of my brain. I put my hands up to my face and started rubbing my cheeks and my lips, my eyebrows and my hair.

I'd had enough.

I wanted to puke.

I stood up.

I had to go.

But something was missing. Oh yeah, my legs. Where were my legs? Someone had them. I had them. These are my legs. They were sticking out and they were drilling into the floor, so now I couldn't move.

Fuck!

I needed to be put out of my misery.

I needed someone to pick me up, just like I'd done to Zain, and carry me back in their arms and lay me down on a soft bed and tell me everything will be all right in the morning.

Whoa...

Christ!

A red painted face. Their eyebrows were like thick tree branches and they were zinging off to each side and spinning around in front of me. Then I was lifted. I was smiling, or I was laughing, and I could feel myself dancing. A drag act was carrying me around the bar. I was draped over them like a useless puppet, going with the flow, floating down the river, gently rocking myself to peace and quiet.

And then I had no idea where I was. I thought I had opened my eyes but there was just darkness. I stretched out my hands like a blind man. I walked forwards and felt myself falling. I didn't hit the ground. I felt some arms touch me, hold me, stand me up.

'*The rivers of hell fire are going to burn...*'

I couldn't move. I was being held in a tight grip.

'Hell fire!' screamed everywhere, echoing, thumping off the walls, ringing in my ears.

This was music – some sixties-sounding, pounding devil music.

And I could feel the grip, like they were not going to let go. And then my face filled up with a blinding sequined red, a spiteful menacing streak of a pulsing blood boil.

And eyes, eyes like Diablo.

I don't know why, but I am sure I said, 'Schmidt...'

I was swung around like a piece of meat. I was in the hands of the beast, the devil's breath, the evil mask, the goat's head.

The music was screaming in my ears. My head was exploding. I was going to die.

My time had come.

I felt the cold cheek of Diablo, the saliva dribble, as it whispered again in my ear:

> '*They seek him here*
> *They seek him there*
> *They seek him in*
> *Medusa's hair,*
> *But what they'll find*
> *I have no doubt*
> *Is something they are*
> *Scared about!*'

'Schmidt!' I shouted, as I hit the floor.

11

I don't know why but I woke up the next morning lying in a
load of fertiliser at the back of my villa. That was weird, but
so was tripping off my head in The Sapori. I got on my hands
and knees and like a brain-damaged insect, crawled into the
hot sun. I knew I couldn't stand up, shaking from the alcohol
poison, desperate for water, juice, pills, more water and a
shower. That's when I noticed, through my half-closed eyes,
a flower bed where the kid's mum had been dispatched to a
better life.

And that's when the old recall kicked in.

Having dragged myself out of The Sapori looking for
Schmidt, and not finding him anywhere except maybe in my
imagination, I had got it into my head to do something for the
kids. I'd made my way along the cliffs and crept up into the
Presidential Palace. I then nicked from the garden a load of
hanging baskets and swung them over my back. I hauled the
lot over to my villa and planted the flowers where their mum
had been burned and buried. And they looked very nice, even
if the smell made me feel like puking on them. I also said
something like, 'Earth to earth,' before I passed out.

Anyway, I crawled into the villa and headed straight for
the kitchen. There was a large bowl on the floor with water
in it. That's when I heard Tony say, 'I thought you'd be
thirsty.'

I suppose his point was, that's what dogs do.

Whatever, I said to myself, and yanked open the fridge

door and started pouring orange juice down my throat.

'I see you done some gardening last night,' he continued.

I wasn't going to talk; I was just going to listen.

'If you're interested,' he said, 'I've left Sonia with Zammit and his family. I also got the passports off him for the kids.'

I took another large gulp of juice.

'And Zain is going to be OK. The doctors think it's just a virus, but they're going to keep an eye on him, just in case.'

That was a relief.

'And Grandad's got the 'ump,' said Tony.

That was no surprise.

'He said because you're having so much trouble finding Schmidt, you should concentrate on tracking down that guy Borg. He says he was more likely to still be on the island and he knows enough to help.'

I didn't say anything but couldn't help thinking that I should have known this before I started running around like a blue-arsed fly.

I thought about crawling away but I knew Tony had one more thing he wanted to say.

'Get a grip, Steven,' he said, as he walked back out.

That's easy for him to say. I needed recovery time.

So I grabbed a few hours on the sofa before I had to go back out again.

I'd run out of orange juice by the time I was just about able to stand and put one foot in front of the other. There was no sign of Tony as I got hold of Zammit to drive me back into town. I was sure he was swerving more than he should, as I felt my stomach heaving and going back down. For that, I told him there was no tip as he dropped me off outside the constabulary HQ.

It was stuck out on the edge of the old town, close to but also far enough away from the bar strip and the hotels, and a stone's throw away from the shagging car park. It was a grey, pokey office block, four stories high, with broken blinds hanging down, leaning on plant pots and piles of files. Once I'd got past reception and was walking up the stairs to see Spiteri, Vella was walking back down. He pretended he didn't see me, keeping his head down and scrolling through his phone.

Spiteri was at the top of the stairs and told me to follow him. He looked way too serious for dropping off a bunch of passports. That's when I wondered if I should have brought a lawyer with me.

We were on the third or the second floor as I looked around the open-plan office and noticed all the desks had very large VDUs, probably 1980s style and about as efficient as a pocket calculator. There were a few constables hunched over their keyboards, punching one handed, with one finger, all the latest crime figures, which added up to about half a dozen – apart from the odd the murder I suppose. Spiteri had a desk in the corner so he could keep an eye on his constables in case they all went off to lunch together. I carried on looking around his shitty office as he told me to sit down.

'Listen,' I said, 'if it's new computers you want, I know a guy called Sinclair who can do a job-lot for you.'

'If you are referring to our capital investment programme, Mr Mason, we will always consider donations, as long as they are from reputable sources.'

'Oh well, you're right then, that rules me out.'

'Do not worry, Mr Mason, I have also ruled you out.'

'You mean I'm free to go?'

Spiteri ignored me and started tapping on his clunky keyboard. I got distracted again and counted only three other constables on the floor. If this were the combined police force on the island, they could just about keep up looking for stolen bikes and fines for littering on the pavement. The idea they could deal with a murder investigation that looked like some mob job was a joke.

Perhaps that was why Spiteri was in such a bad mood.

'So,' said Spiteri, clicking his mouse like he had made some important data entry, 'how is the little boy?'

Jesus, how does this guy know everything?

'He's good, thanks.'

'And so this is the reason why you stayed away from the police station yesterday, and why you have now arrived with the documentation today?'

'That's right.'

'You must have been upset, seeing a child in your care acutely ill, with their mother and father so far away.'

'It's just their mum,' I said, wondering where Spiteri was going with this.

'And you are still in touch with the mother, especially when things like this happen?'

'I tell her what I can, but it's not easy. She's not herself, you know, so I must be careful with what I say.'

Spiteri paused. I could tell he had some line of inquiry he wanted to follow and was just working out where to start.

'Last night…' he said, searching for a piece of paper on his desk in front of him, before he started his sentence again. 'Last night, we had a report of a theft from the presidential garden.'

I nodded, showing the same concern I would for a mosquito drowning in lager.

'And...' continued Spiteri, 'we had a report from one of our constables that you, Mr Mason, were seen in the bar area at around midnight. The constable said...'

Spiteri moved a few bits of paper around then found the quote he wanted.

'Mr Mason was intoxicated, loudly shouting the name Schmidt and Diablo, accusing the constabulary of conspiracy in the killing of the journalist Garibaldi and claiming that our prime minister, Mark Grech, liked to... bum fuck lady boys with the president's wife in a sandwich. Was this because you were upset, Mr Mason, by the little boy falling ill?'

'Could be,' I said, nodding wisely. 'If it was me.'

'Are you saying it wasn't you?'

'I don't know, I was drunk.'

'Then it was you...'

'No, I was drunk.'

'And therefore, you were so drunk,' added Spiteri, 'you cannot remember the behaviour that I have just recalled for you.'

I leaned forward and whispered, 'I don't think it will have much of a chance in court, do you?'

Spiteri got all frumpy.

'Mr Mason, I am not trying to charge you with calling people names, however offensive. I am alluding to the fact that you were in a state of mind, or lack of it, whereby you had got it into your head to steal flowers from the presidential garden. And that is a crime, even if it may seem trivial.'

'I suppose you're going to tell me it made the front page.'

'Yes, it did!' screamed Spiteri, banging his fist down on

what looked like the local paper.

'Well,' I said, keeping calm, 'it's good to know the constabulary has got its priorities right. After all, I can understand why you would be angry about stolen hanging baskets from the presidential garden. I mean, it's not like some guy has been assassinated for writing stories about how corrupt everything is on this island. It must a boiling inferno in here, with so much raging and anger and all the injustice of it because the petunias have been kidnapped.'

'That,' said Spiteri, who knew he'd made an arse of himself, 'is a very serious crime, which we take extremely seriously, and, I might add, where you also happen to feature.'

'Yeah, that's me all over… always trying to help where I can.'

'You are not helping, Mr Mason,' said Spiteri under his breath. 'Shouting out libellous accusations in a public thoroughfare, in what is a volatile political environment, is not helping. And it also does not help if you go gardening in the Presidential Palace at one o'clock in morning!'

'How am I not helping?' I said, all innocently.

'You are not helping yourself,' said Spiteri, pointing his finger at me.

'I'm sorry,' I said, doing my best to apologise, pretty sure Attard had been jumping up and down on Spiteri's head for my minor misdemeanour.

'However,' he said, 'as much as you should be locked up for being a fool last night, I am not without leniency. And I also think you do care about that boy, even if your relationship appears to be… acquired. It is for that reason only – that you appear to care – that I am not punishing you for this indiscretion.'

Which sounded like he had others.

'So,' he said, thinking he had laid the law down for me, 'do you have the passports?'

'Yeah...'

'And can I see them, please.'

I pulled mine and Tony's out of one side pocket and the kids' nice new shiny ones out of the other. He didn't bother looking at mine or Tony's and went straight for the kids. He started feeling the outside of them with his fingers, flicked the pages like a pack of cards, examined the photo page and angled it against the light. He then placed them in front of him on his desk.

'Are the children's passports the ones they had on them when they first arrived on the island?'

'Yeah...'

'And have you been holding them since they arrived on their holiday?'

'Yeah... just in case they got lost.'

'And so they have been in your possession and they have never at any point been damaged and replaced?'

'Yeah...'

That's when Spiteri took a deep breath, like he needed a load of oxygen to think.

'Now, a few minutes earlier, you were trying to demean the constabulary's investigation into the brutal killing of Mr Garibaldi. However, I must now tell you that as part of the investigation, we have designated you and your friend Tony as persons of interest in the case. It is a bit of a technical term, a legal phrase, but are you aware of its meaning?'

'I get the meaning,' I said.

109

'Are you sure, Mr Mason? The legal process is different here, and these technicalities have some nuances and can easily be misunderstood.'

'Oh no, Inspector, wherever I go, the law is the same. I don't see any difference. Just like in London: all the crooks look the same, they just don't look like crooks, and all the villains look the same, they just don't like bullshit.'

Spiteri got my point, so he carried on explaining.

'It is a fast-moving case, Mr Mason. We have dedicated all our resources to solving and capturing the culprit or culprits, and in such a complex case as this, there is always new information that comes to light.'

'I'll make a statement now if you want,' I said, as I couldn't be arsed having to deal with this BS again.

'That is not currently necessary,' he said. 'A person of interest, if you wish to know, is not a suspect. They could just be a witness, but they could also have other things we need to know, that perhaps even we don't know for sure what is.'

'But it gives you control.'

'Yes, I am afraid it does. Which is why, for now, I will be retaining your passports – yours and your friend's and the two children's.'

It was now my turn to get angry, but I didn't slam my fist on his desk.

'How long is this going to go on for?'

'For as long as it takes to get to the bottom of who killed Mr Garibaldi.'

'And you seriously think that even if you solve the case, you'll be allowed to arrest anybody who was involved in it?'

'Whatever you may think of us, we do know how to do policing, and if there is one thing police are good at, it is

110

solving murders.'

'You can solve as much as you like, but from what I've seen, the only thing you're going to convict is the piss raining down on you from a great height. Give me a badge and I'll go and arrest the bastards who did it, because all you have to do is walk up to the top of the hill and ask if Grech is in.'

However, Spiteri wasn't going to bite.

'Slander and defamation are not going to solve a serious crime, Mr Mason. You are falling into the trap of the popular myth on this island, that everybody who dedicates themselves to public service, and to the service of the people, is somehow corrupt and unworthy.'

OK, I thought, this proves he's on the payroll.

And that's when I knew Spiteri was never going to prove anything, because truth would crawl under a rock as soon as it saw the light of day.

'There is one more thing,' he said, searching his desk for another piece of paper.

'Let me guess,' I said. 'Vella has legal BS on The Seashell and you just want to share this information?'

'You passed him on the way in,' said Spiteri, as he found what he was looking for. 'However, I do not need to inform you legally of this repossession order. You will find it outside the premises that I regret will be closed.'

'You know,' I said, puffing out my cheeks, 'I ain't feeling the love here, Inspector.'

'Well, I will put aside my inspector's hat for just one minute. I have no side in this, but if I were you, now would be a good time to acquire a lawyer. And I would also suggest this cannot be any old lawyer because your battle is not just a legal one, it is also political. Therefore, you should make an appointment to speak to Mrs Cini, not just because she is those two things, a lawyer and a politician, but because she will also find you… interesting.'

'What… in a blind date kind of way?'

'Good afternoon, Mr Mason, and please try to avoid drinking, at least until you have recovered.'

I should have puked all over him, but it wasn't until I got outside that I started to retch, and not just because of all the alcohol I had poured down me – it was also something to do with the foul stench of wealth and privilege getting right up my nose.

12

I slept for two days. On the third day, Tony knocked and came into my bedroom and told me off.

'Jesus, what an effing state.'

'I've been ill,' I said. 'I must have got that virus off the kid.'

'Not the drink then,' said Tony, standing in the doorway.

'Perhaps the drink and the virus,' I said, putting my hand down my pants and scratching my bollocks.

'I don't know why you do it, Steven. You ain't got no tolerance for drink. There's some that can and some that can't, and whatever you think, you ain't a drinker.'

'I do know that, Tony,' I said, sniffing my fingers.

'And what you're doing there, mate, is pretty disgusting.'

I smiled at him.

'How is he, Zain?'

'He's doing all right. I've taken Sonia up to see him a few times. They're very tight those two, been through a lot together.'

'Yeah… anything else happened?'

'Not much. Grandad thinks you're on the case and all that but I can't keep lying to him.'

'It don't matter. He knows you're not telling the truth.'

'Thanks,' he said, pissed that I didn't think he was any good at lying. 'Anyways, it's your head on the block, not mine. I'm just the delivery guy, you're the one who's supposed to get this bloody Medusa thing. Seems like a lot of effort for nothing.'

'Depends on what the going price is for an artefact, but whatever, Grandad is going to lose on the property.'

'Well, you're going to have to tell him that because he wants you to get hold of Borg, pronto. And he's raging about some fish and chip shop. Can't see how there's much money in cod and batter?'

'Tony, The Seashell is a restaurant. Plus, it's Grandad who tells Borg what to buy. I just hold the money and get it flushed down the toilet. I have nothing to do with the rest of it. So buying a restaurant, or any of these villas, ain't my decision. All I do is turn up and sign bits of paper and try and look like I know what I'm doing.'

'Sounds boring…'

'That's not the point, Tony. I'm here to get away from things.'

'You mean because of your brother and stuff?'

'Yeah, especially my brother.'

'Well, I suppose that's what happens when people get killed.'

'Yeah, something like that…'

I was just about to tell Tony that all I did to my half-brother was put him out of his misery and bury him in a hole, when a small face poked her head around the corner.

Sonia looked at me and then put her eyes down on the floor.

'All right, sweet pea,' said Tony.

She nodded silently.

'Have you been ill,' she asked, looking through Tony's legs, 'like my brother?'

'Yeah, dodgy tummy,' I said. 'But I'm feeling better now.'

She looked sheepish.

'I tell you what,' I said, 'how would you like to do me a little favour?'

Her face brightened – she looked up for it.

'It's a bit naughty,' I said, 'but it's not going to get you into any trouble. Well, if we don't get caught.'

'What is it?' she asked, still around Tony's legs.

'I'll tell you what it is in a minute,' I said. 'But only if you can pass a special test for me.'

'What kind of test?'

'It's a reading test.'

'Reading?'

'Yeah, Tony, can you get a book or something? I want to see how good our Sonia is at reading.'

'Steven, what are you up to?'

'Just do it, Tony, will yer.'

Tony walked away and Sonia wanted to follow him.

'Heh,' I said, 'I hear your brother's getting better.'

She didn't say anything and didn't want to give me eye

contact.

'You and your brother,' I said, 'you're a couple of tough nuts, aren't you? That's good because you're going to need each other. You know, I think your mum would be proud of you because you're both still fighting.'

'There you go,' said Tony, who handed her a magazine.

'Cheers, Tony,' I said. 'So, Sonia, can you just read the words for me on the front page?'

She looked at it for a second or two.

'It says: Playboy... entertainment for men.'

It was my turn to be the parent and I gave Tony a serious look.

'What?' he said. 'It's the birds and the bees. They all do that now. My kids tell me things that make me legs go funny at the knees.'

'That's no surprise, Tony.'

Then Sonia started laughing.

It was good to see her laugh, as she pointed at the "boobies".

'OK,' I said. 'We recon at twenty-four hundred hours.'

'What does that mean?'

'He means,' said Tony, as he steered Sonia out of the room, 'that you're going to have a late night.'

Come midnight, Tony was back into old mother hen mode as he tried to put his foot down about Sonia going with me to raid Borg's offices. But the way I saw it, I told him, they help us so we can help them, and I needed Sonia to help me so I can find Borg. In fact, all things led to Borg, as far as I was concerned, and that would help us find Schmidt and get hold of the Medusa. It would also mean, I pointed out to Tony, he would get back home to his real family instead of making one up in my villa.

That pissed him off but it also shut him up, as I got Zammit to pick us up. I had dressed Sonia like a little ninja, all in black from head to toe; I liked the look. Zammit did his usual flying through the lanes at the speed of light.

Then Sonia asked me an awkward question. 'Have you got our passports?'

I could see Zammit raise his eyebrow as I turned around to face her sitting in the back seat.

'I'll be honest with you, kid, that Inspector Spiteri, who came to see us, he's decided to look after them for a bit – mine and Tony's and yours and your brother's. But don't you worry, the sooner we find Schmidt the better because I think that will sort things out for all of us.'

I could tell she wasn't happy with that.

'You have lost them again,' she said, like I was useless at looking after things.

That was when Zammit came to my rescue.

'They do not come cheap, Sonia,' he said, looking to spit at a poster of Grech. 'So perhaps you should thank Mr Mason before thinking he is an idiot.'

I looked at Zammit.

'That's the way kids think,' he said. 'We are all stupid to them. Even my own daughter thinks I am an idiot.'

I looked back at Sonia, but she was staring out of the window, thinking I was an idiot.

When we got into town, I had Zammit park up and then me and Sonia wandered around a few side streets until we found the back of Borg's offices. As it was a small business district, there was no one around to ask why I was getting a little girl to stand on my hands and jump on some bins. There was a small window where I had stuck my leg through when I was off my head – that's as far as I was going to get, but Sonia would be a perfect fit.

'What do you think?' I said, as she lifted up the flap of the window.

'I can do it,' she whispered.

Which made me whisper back, 'Good girl. OK, see you on the other side.'

Sonia then slipped like a snake through the window.

I walked back to meet up with Zammit hanging about in front of the shutters.

'She's a professional,' I said, as we both looked up and down the street.

'You think she's done this before?'

'Well, she's probably had to crawl around 'cause of the bombs and shit.'

'That's military training,' said Zammit, as he sucked hard on his weed.

'Handy…'

We waited, hoping her skill at reading adult magazines meant she could follow the instructions on opening the closed shutters. Just as I was getting worried, and thinking I was a nasty little Fagin, we heard the key in the door and then the key in the bolts. We quickly had the shutters up and down.

'Nice one, Sonia,' I said, as we struggled to see anything in the dark.

I pulled out a torch and shone it around.

We were standing in his little reception area.

'You two look down here,' I said. 'I need to go upstairs.'

'What are we looking for?' whispered Sonia.

'Photos… any photos of Borg,' I said, grabbing the

picture frame of him off the reception desk to show them. 'And Sonia, it's bingo if he's in one with Schmidt.'

I left them to get on with it.

Upstairs was Borg's little campaign room, where he did all his deals, juggling legit with illegit, playing people off against one another, looking for leverage, currying favours, and always pushing for the best price and top commission. He was a clever git, I'll give him that, but this time he'd really come unstuck. In fact, he must be so deep in the shit I'd be amazed if he could even breathe right now.

I went straight for his filing cabinet and used a knife to wrench open the drawers. I pulled out all the title deeds on the deals he'd done for Grandad. I found The Seashell to take with me because that was the one that was heating things up.

Downstairs, Zammit and Sonia were sitting on a sofa.

'Did you find anything?' I asked.

'Just this,' said Zammit, who handed me a photo.

I shone the torch.

'What is it?' I asked, looking at a photo of Borg sitting in a hole with a trowel in his hand, smiling away with a bit of pottery in the other.

Zammit piped up.

'It is the dig,' he said, keeping himself comfortable by staying on his arse.

'What's a dig?' asked Sonia.

'They dig up the past,' he said. 'And then put it behind glass.'

'Is this on the island?' I said, turning it over to see if there was anything written on the back.

'Yes, you need to go south east and you will find it on top of the cliffs. You can go and look. They will have put their tools away now – they do not dig out of season. Then you can see.'

'See what?'

'To see if he is hiding.'

'What, in a hole?'

'Perhaps, if he is dead – if they have put him in a hole,' said Zammit, who liked his own sense of humour. 'But also, you can hide up there, if you know. But not many know, and not many would do it, unless the person was very scared.'

'Well, I reckon Borg is running away from half the island,' I said. 'So, where is he?'

'If you go there, you climb down the cliff and there is a place where the human monkeys lived. If Borg likes the past, then he would know about this.'

'And how comes you know?'

'Because anyone who dares can go there, so when I was younger I would go there.'

'Well, it looks like his hobby has kept him alive if he's hiding on a cliff,' I said.

'Take rope,' said Zammit.

'I'm not going to hang him,' I said.

'No, perhaps not, but you will need it… to climb down.'

13

It was cloudy when I left the villa early in the morning with some rope, a rucksack and a compass heading south east. I was going cross-country, but you're not talking about walking through green fields and hedges – this is rock, dust and stone, and bone-dry bushes.

By going inland, I was coming across a few abandoned old stone buildings and the odd half-built new home – projects the locals would spend a generation on, adding breeze block walls and steel girders whenever they had any loose change. But there was not much life out here in the middle of nowhere, away from the coastline, just lizards and stray sea birds, flapping above my head trying to catch the warm air current. After a couple of hours, Zammit had said I would know I was going in the right direction if I got to an abandoned film set. I'm no great navigator, but I made it there by mid-morning.

Well, all the film stars had gone. They'd made some big western and it had won loads of Oscars and things like that. I'd never seen it – westerns aren't my thing. I walked down the middle of the old set and you could look through the windows and see all the struts keeping the facades up. It was all false. Weird, I know, but I just don't like films. I don't get it – they bore me stupid. There was a saloon at the bottom of the set and they'd built some of the inside. I sat in a chair where the Hollywood actors must have done their thing. That got me thinking about playacting, pretending, being someone who you're not. It's a strange way to be. How could you ever know who you really are if you're always being someone else? You're like, trapped. Your mind and body must be going crazy trying to work out who you are each day.

That also got me to thinking about Schmidt. No one normally gets under my skin, but this guy, he was acting, playing some big part and trying to freak me out. And, unless he does that kind of thing to get off on one, I couldn't see what was in it for him. Why pick on me? Most people, if they saw me or knew anything about me, would keep their distance. Like, that would be the sensible thing to do. But not this guy. He was well into it, laughing and joking, like he got a kick out of playing with me. Perhaps he was just a crazy guy and he couldn't help himself. But there was one thing about him that put him way off beam and out there with the crazies: there was a presence, like you could feel him before you could see he was there – once at the garden party, once in The Sapori. And if you have that kind of power then you're not just some messenger boy, some mule – you're into all kinds of things and capable of anything.

I left the saloon bar with a salute and had a look at one more fake thing to the place: a graveyard. They'd done it up old western style, with the body mounds and wooden crosses. There was even a bunch of made-up names for the dead, except the one that said "Brad Pitt". It seemed only right and proper I should leave my mark so I found a deep six-foot trench to piss in. It took me back to the hole where I buried my half-brother Greg, who was half-dead anyway by the time I shoved him in with the people he had killed that night. He'd got what was coming to him. All I did was make it final.

I checked my compass and looked south east again. I would have carried on marching but for something that made me turn and look back at the old film set. The sun was up and I was blinking, using my hand to cover my eyes, to see if there was anyone. But there wasn't anything, just the sound of the heat and the buzz of insects. Nothing really, but just that feeling again, a presence, and not a good one. It felt like Schmidt – he was there for sure, hiding and watching – but there was just no way of telling unless he wanted to show himself.

That gave me an uneasy feeling in the gut of my stomach as I walked the rest of the way to the archaeological site. Suspicion, or paranoia, was creeping up on me. I was turning my head back to check on what was behind me, wondering if some freaky drag act in a devil's mask was about to fly out of the heat haze and whack me over the head with their handbag. Then I wondered if I should go to church and make a confession. I think that's what the Catholics did and there were a few churches around on the island. But would telling a priest that I'm not just a naughty boy, but a very naughty boy, change anything?

The only thing that stopped my crazy thoughts was getting to the archaeological site. It was mid-afternoon by now and the holes that Borg had been standing in were covered over with tarpaulins. This was squared off by metal stakes and orange string. There was another stake in the ground that propped up a large information board. The EU had funded the dig, with lots of other organisations with letters and my old mates from the Global Venture Capital Group – good to know they cared about the past as well as the future of the island.

There was a load of waffle about how important the site was and how this was possibly one of the few places where Neanderthals clung on before they were replaced by homo sapiens, which I guess means us. And, for stupid people like me, there was picture of a bunch of thick heads cooking soup and cutting the leg off a dead animal. But the interesting bit was at the bottom and in small print:

DANGER! PLEASE DO NOT TRY TO TRAVERSE THE CLIFFS TO ACCESS THE CAVE SITE – IT IS

EXTREMELY DANGEROUS AND REQUIRES
SPECIAL PERMISSION FROM THE ISLAND'S
DEPARTMENT OF ENVIRONMENT.

Christ, I thought, Vella has his fingers in everything. I looked over the edge of the cliff and then had to lie down to get a good idea of what I needed to do. Zammit had said it was about five hundred feet above sea level, and I needed to drop about fifty feet down to get to the cave. That's when I wondered what the hell I was doing. Still, I had got this far, and if anything, I would probably get one of the best views on the island.

Zammit had told me about the footholds to use, which I spotted over to my right. He said they'd done it once as kids and then had a few parties down there as teenagers before he got married. I tied the rope around one of the poles that marked the site above the cliff, tied the rope around my waist and eased myself down the cliffside. The wind was strong and the sea was a deep blue below, and if I fell, it would be fatal.

There were small ledges and tufts of grass and I used these to hang onto as I made my way down. I had to stop a few times, just to steady myself, looking out to sea and admiring the richness to it, the shiny blue sheet that just rippled now and then. Zammit said the hardest bit was getting into the cave. I had to trust myself, trust the rope would hold and swing out because the cave entrance couldn't be seen below a ledge covered in thick grass. I wasn't keen on throwing myself and swinging like a helpless lemon. I tried my best to look down and into the cliffside to spot how close I was. And that's when I slipped. The wedge of grass gave way and I shot out like a bullet, heading towards the bottom of the rocks below. Then the rope pulled at my waist and rose up to my armpits. I screamed out as the rope gripped and tore into my flesh. I was in shock, praying my weight didn't pull the rope lose from the metal pole above. I was dazed. I didn't do anything. I just swung, helpless.

And then I heard Borg. 'So, Steven, I suppose you are going to tell me you were just hanging around and decided to drop in?'

I was winded and could hardly breathe. I was twirling around like a spinning top – sky, sea, cliff, then sky and clouds and Borg. He smiled, perched on the edge of the cave entrance, his fat cheeks making him look like a bald, hairy-chested toad, with small round eyes that looked ready to pop.

'You don't mind,' he shouted, as the wind whipped around my ears, 'if I leave you outside for a bit? I just have some tidying up to do, as you can see.'

He then turned and moved back into the cave, which was littered in tin cans. I grabbed hold of the rope and felt the tension loosen. But I was stuck, swinging gently in the wind, needing Borg to help me if I wasn't going to rot here and drop. He came back with a shopping bag and started picking up the litter, like he was out in the park and a responsible citizen for the day.

'Heh, Borg!' I shouted. 'You do know you're supposed to help your clients!'

He ignored me and carried on with his tidying. I was like an effing fly stuck in water – alive but with no way of escaping by myself. And all the time, the rope tightened and cut into my chest.

'You know, Borg!' I shouted. 'This ain't going to do you

any good, leaving me like this.'

He turned his back on me as he carried on, bent down and chucking all the rubbish in the bag. As he looked busy, distracted, or insane, I stretched out my hands to work out the distance to the edge of the cave. About another arm's length, I reckoned. I would need to swing, get in motion, hope the rope would hold me and dive across. And I was running out of choices because this rope was stinging as it cut into my chest. Then Borg raised his head, like he had become aware of me again. He moved towards me and stood with his feet on the edge. I could almost hear him breathe in the breeze around my ears.

'That's what happens when you receive unexpected guests,' he said. 'You need to rush around and make sure that the place is tidy enough to let them in.'

'That's me,' I said, smiling, 'the unexpected guest. So why don't you give me a hand then?'

I put my arms out hopefully.

But he didn't seem keen on helping.

'However,' he said, 'unexpected does not mean they are people you should let in.'

Shame...

'I had to tidy though,' he said. 'I feel ashamed. I love my history, Steven, and I have been as bad as those teenagers who regularly trash this site.'

'Well, it looks nice and tidy now,' I said, thinking the best thing to do was to humour the mad bastard. 'Trust me, Borg, I won't do anything to you. That's not why I've tracked you down. Why don't you just pull me in and we can talk?'

But it didn't look like he was going to.

'Now, let me guess,' said Borg, 'knowing the kind of

125

person you are, Steven, you would have broken into my office, snooped around, maybe removed some papers relating to land deeds and purchases. And then, in discussions with that taxi driver of yours, calculated this would be a good hiding place for someone like me and would enable you to initiate your interrogation.'

'That's not why I am here,' I said, lying.

'Why are you here then, Steven?'

I was going to say he knew exactly why and to stop playing games, but I had to reach up and grab the rope above my head to relieve the pressure on my chest.

'I can see you are in some difficulty, Steven, so I shall tell you why you are here and what you need to know.'

'Get on with it, Borg!' I shouted, feeling the tension of the rope bite even harder.

'You know, Steven, I have lived on this island for over twenty years. I have become a fixture, accepted by everyone. Then there was a turning point, a point when things went from very good to very bad. And do you know when that started, the point at which my comfortable, sustainable, fulfilling world was turned upside down?'

'It's not me who's caused you all this trouble.'

'Perhaps, but it is the point at which it started.'

'Look, buying property for us, for Grandad, is not going to cause your world to collapse.'

'You're right, it shouldn't, and yet it did.'

I was getting angry now. The rope was making it hard for me to say anything.

'Borg, for fuck's sake, you need to help me!'

'But I don't think I can, Steven. You have brought certain things to light... and you have brought certain people into my

126

life… who I would never ordinarily have had the displeasure to engage with.'

'That's bollocks! You and Vella would have done a thousand deals, with or without me.'

'Ah… The Seashell. I imagine there are some problems with that right now. But you needn't worry, the deal is a legitimate one. Vella just couldn't help himself when it comes to cash wafting under his nose. He must be trying to get it back with our friends from Global Venture Capital Group.'

'Repossession…'

'Well, let's not mince words, Steven, and call it what it is: corruption. It is everywhere now. It is like a way of life. It has become global. I am just a small trader in comparison.'

I tried to pull myself up again on the rope, as it carried on cutting into my skin.

'Is that why they blew up the villa,' I said, squeezing out the words as I held on to the rope, 'because of The Seashell?'

Borg laughed and shook his head, like I had said something stupid.

'I am just a pawn, you know, a disposable little chess piece. You need to look at all the pieces on the chess board, Steven, to understand the game.'

'Look, I'm after Schmidt, that's all I want!' I said, beginning to swing uneasily in a sudden gust of wind.

'All the pieces, Steven, you must look at all the pieces. They interact with one another. But if you are not a good chess player, then you are at a bit of a disadvantage.'

'That's me,' I said. 'I was never very good at stuff like that.'

He nodded, like he would help me to understand a few

things.

'OK,' he said. 'Let's see what you should know. The villa, as you mentioned, I am afraid was something rather unpleasant. The journalist, Garibaldi… only the people liked him. The powerful were less inclined to his type of journalism. You see, things were starting to come out, like sewage seeping out of a broken pipe. But rather than fix the pipe, they decided to blow it up.'

'Who?'

'The constabulary, of course!' said Borg, laughing. 'They were the ones who told me to put him somewhere out of the way. I became his friend – he trusted me. I said, I have a nice villa for you whilst you wait.'

'What was he waiting for?'

'Indeed, Steven, what was he waiting for that meant he had to lose his life in such dramatic circumstances?'

'You tell me?'

'Our friend,' he said.

'What friend?'

'Max Schmidt.'

'You know Schmidt?'

'In a way, if anyone can really know that kind of person. But Schmidt is who Garibaldi thought he was wating for at the villa. And yes, I know, you had gone to the Leninsky Komsomol to pick up something from Schmidt, a small artefact I believe. But Schmidt was never going to give that to you because he is a greedy man who understands one thing and one thing only: the true value of corruption.'

'Look, I can't stay like this,' I said. 'I need to know what you know and I need to do that without hanging off a cliff.'

'You're right, your position is a rather untenable, but then so is mine. We both have no hope.'

'Why?'

'Because of Schmidt.'

'You mean Schmidt is behind everything?'

'No, he is not so powerful, but he is omnipresent. Do you know what that means, Steven?'

'Like God?'

'The opposite, I think. Schmidt is not a god but an opportunistic devil. I suspect he is peddling something now to the highest bidder.'

'The Medusa?'

'That's what he has in his possession.'

'But how much is it worth?'

'That depends, I think, on who you are.'

'What are you trying to say, Borg? Why did Garibaldi want the artefact?'

'Honestly, Steven, I don't know, and to some extent I don't care.'

'Then why are you hiding? What are you afraid of?'

'I thought I was afraid of dying. That's why I came here. But if you look out to sea for long enough, there is an inner peace, a way to find acceptance of the inevitable.'

'You look healthy to me,' I said, pulling again on the rope to ease the pressure. 'Look, why don't you just tell me what Schmidt looks like? If he's the one causing you trouble, I will find him and sort things out for both of us.'

'Have you not seen him?' said Borg, edging his feet further over the edge. 'I think you have seen him, probably in one of his many disguises. That is why nobody really knows who he is. But I have seen the real Schmidt, and trust me, the face of evil is average, until it is transformed into the devil.'

'So, he looks like an average bloke?'

'You still don't understand, do you, Steven? Schmidt will know I am here now. He will have followed you and when you are gone, whether that is down there or up here, like a naughty little angel, he will do what he must.'

'You're afraid of Schmidt! Has he said he'll kill you if you talk to me?'

Borg edged another few inches forward.

'Just remember, you cannot fly without wings,' he said. 'If only I were like Pegasus.'

Then he jumped straight at me, laughing like a crazy man.

He grabbed hold of me, pulling on my t-shirt, his sweaty body and stinky breath pulling the rope down.

I did my best to hold on to him.

'You crazy fuck!' I screamed, as the rope was slipping.

Then Borg was up close and personal, in my ear.

'You will be better off dead, Steven. Fall with me now. You do not want to live a second longer. Schmidt is all evil. He will torment you, haunt you and take you down into the bowels of hell, laughing as he goes.'

The threads were coming apart.

We dropped a few feet.

The threads were coming apart.

'Goodbye, Steven. It was a pleasure doing business with you.'

And Borg let go.

14

I didn't waste time looking down at Borg. I started bending and straightening my legs like I was on a swing, trying to get myself moving towards the ledge. I stretched my legs high and back again, pushing to grab hold of the tufts of grass sticking out of the cliff edge. As soon as I felt my arms could reach across, I had a go.

I missed.

I lost momentum.

I had to get it going again, only this time I needed more swing. But the more I got my body swinging, the more the rope started loosening and the thread fraying. I gave it a few more goes but kept missing.

I needed a rest.

I swung in the wind, wondering if I should pray or just wait to fall and land on Borg. I watched a few seabirds circle above my head. They were laughing, telling me I can't fly. I got a bit of energy and got my back into it this time, swinging my legs up and down. But the rope unravelled a lot more. There was not much thread left. I knew I had one last chance before I ended up joining Borg. One, two, three… and as I reached out, the rope snapped.

I fell and my face hit the cliff. I felt the crunch grind into my body and my hands reach out to grab the grass sticking out. But it was my legs that somehow found a footing. My boots seemed stuck on something solid – a small ledge. It gave me balance.

I pushed up and put one arm on the spot Borg had jumped from, grabbed hold of some rock poking out and pulled myself up. As I heaved, I scraped my flesh but landed on my stomach, my legs hanging off the edge and sticking out in mid-air. I ate some gravel and hoisted myself forward so all my body was in. I just lay there, breathing at a hundred miles an hour, the adrenaline pumping around my body like I'd had it rammed up my arse.

So I had to let it out: 'Jesus fucking H Christ! What the fuck! You crazy fucking bastard, Borg, you crazy fucking bastard!'

Then I realised I had the rope still tied around me, with the end of it hanging down over the edge. That freaked me out. So I pulled it in, just in case there were some little red devils who wanted to drag me back down again.

That's when I started laughing out loud to myself, like a crazy guy. I don't think I'd ever come so close to dying. Plenty of times things had been nasty, blades and shit like that, but never anything as bonkers as this. That was one mega head-fuck, no two ways about it. I thought I was going to go down with him, the Falling Man and all that shit, all the way down to the rocks below and the bottom of the sea.

I turned myself around, still on my stomach, and looked down to where Borg had landed. I couldn't see properly with bits of cliff jutting out. All I had was a view of the blue sea, the bent horizon and the sun. But there was no way anyone was going to survive that kind of fall. And anyway, he wanted to kill himself, so if the rocks hadn't smashed his body, he can drink the sea and drown. One way or another, he had been on suicide watch, and I had given him the excuse to pull the switch and finish it all off.

With Borg having made himself persona non grata, I undid the rope and gave myself the once over. There were grazes but it was the rope burns across my chest that had made their mark. It was painful, the bruising and the burning, and it was going to get a lot worse once the adrenaline wore off.

However, I did need to find a way to get out of the cave and get back up top. I looked around and there was all of Borg's stuff: a few shopping bags, a camping gas ring, a sleeping bag and a rucksack. I went further into the cave and it narrowed for about twenty feet or so, until I hit a dead end.

That was it, no other way out. I checked for a phone signal but there was nothing out here on the cliffs. Tony and Zammit knew where I was, so I had the option to wait it out, but I would be better off finding a way to climb back up. No panic, I thought to myself. I was alive and that's what mattered.

I walked back to the cliff edge and sat down to take in the view. It helped me relax and think again, about what had just happened and what had got into Borg's head. And, as far as Borg was concerned, it was Schmidt who was in his head, giving him the heebie-jeebies. He had put the hex on him and Borg could see no other way out. He must have known he was going to die, killed either by the constabulary or by Schmidt. And that's because of what he knew, and definitely because of what he knew Schmidt was up to. His thinking must have been that he'd rather do it his way, when he was ready, than give the satisfaction to the assassin, or assassins. And there was some sense to coming out here, spending his last days thinking about everything, before he was ready to jump. I was just the trigger, with people behind me queuing up to push the helpless Borg over the edge.

At least I'd got out of him a few nuggets before he leapt to do business with his creator. It was clear this Medusa was

133

not just an ivory thing for collectors. But I couldn't see what a journo was going to get from an artefact, when all he wants is dirt on people at the top. If the Medusa had another value, it should have something else attached to it because people were prepared to kill or kill themselves over the effing thing. And then there's Schmidt, creeping around, and I was sure trying to get the best price for it. That was good news for me because I could still track him down. The only problem was, it felt like he was tracking me.

Then, just as I was thinking about giving it a go back up the cliff, a rope slipped down in front of me. I must have ESP or whatever that telepathic shit is. Tony and Zammit had heard my mind calling out: get off your arse and do something! I was in no mood to hang around and tugged on the rope to make sure it was secure. It would have been nice to hear a friendly voice up top, but I took it for granted it was one or both of those two. I used the rope to ease myself out of the cave and was nifty in scaling the cracks and ledges to get back up top again.

And that's when things got weird.

I looked around the site and there was nobody, not a soul, no sign of life. If it had been Tony or Zammit, I would like to think they would have hung around, even if was just to call me an idiot. If it was a stranger, then they must have x-ray eyes and like to carry fifty feet of rope around because they're members of International Rescue. Not impossible, but seriously not likely. So, I either had a guardian angel who liked to drop in now and then to keep me going until judgement day, or as Borg had so freakily said, Schmidt had followed me and was keen to save my bacon. But why help? Why not just get rid of me? It was in Schmidt's interests to see me disappear, but why does he want to keep me alive and well? Perhaps Borg was right: I was dealing with a crazy fucked-up guy, someone who got a kick out of playing games, a little devil – a diablo. But I just couldn't see any reason for keeping me alive because if I were Schmidt, I would certainly want to see me at the bottom of a five-hundred-foot cliff.

I checked for a phone signal and there was nothing. It would mean walking until I got to the nearest main road, or it would mean walking all the way back to the villa. But I was aching, creaking, and all I wanted to do was lay down and rest after the day's excitement. I spent a good few hours just lying flat out on my back, watching the sun go down, the sky go red, listening to the birds squark and the insects chirp away like manic sex fiends. Then the light went dark and the temperature got cooler, and for whatever reason, I decided to just roll under a tarpaulin. It was warm and sheltered and I liked it under the covers, with sleep running all over me, knocking me out.

It was only later that I had a strange dream.

I was following a river of fire and blood, with ash floating down like snow over my head. I looked up and there was a tall black mountain spouting ash like a volcano. My hands and my feet were covered in shiny grey crystals. I could feel a pressure in my head, pounding and throbbing with a thumping, whooshing sound, swishing and gushing, like my ears were trapped in a giant seashell. Then I noticed how black and soft the ground was. I bent down. It felt like warm sand. Then a red devil ran up to me and started laughing in my face. It was screeching and catcalling, like some effing hyena: the diablo. It carried on grinning, its cheeks pulsing like a demented red traffic light, its eyes spinning around like a firework on a fence post. It grabbed my hands, tied my feet and started pulling me along. I could feel my skin beginning to rip, my back and my chest burning. It had great big feet and a massive tail, which kept slapping me in the face. I could feel deep cuts opening my cheeks. There was blood spurting from all sides and there was blood pouring down the black mountain. A dirty red blood was lapping up against me, a sick gooey glue sticking to my body. I tried to hold the red devil back but that bastard kept on dragging me up towards the black peak. Then it started singing:

> *'This devil hates to hear complaints*
> *From robbers, thugs and reprobates,*
> *Who lie and cheat and fornicate,*
> *And kill their older brother.'*

And then I knew it was Schmidt. It was him pulling me up the mountain. I was screaming, 'I know it's you, I know it's you!' I started wriggling, trying to stand up. And just as I thought I had got hold of the rope and was about to pull him back, my body flew into the air, catapulted on a giant line of elastic. I was flying and could look down on everything below. I travelled like a bird, soaring and sailing through the wind and the clouds. I was free of all the things that held me down on earth. I flew over the mountain and could see red-hot veins of lava flowing down. But I was falling, falling into the hole where all the lava was pouring out.

I knew I was going to hell.

As I got close, the heat was burning my body. But then I felt a thud on the back of my head. I turned around and there was an intense bright white light. I ran towards it, as fast as I could. The light got brighter and whiter. I felt free. It felt like I had escaped and I could go anywhere I wanted. I was feeling good about myself. I had avoided hell. I wasn't going to die down there. I had a way out, a way of surviving. And I had power. No one could see me. I was an invisible ghost, a fly on the wall, watching life go by – watching people cry, laugh and play, love, hurt and hate. But then I felt myself being sucked down again, my feet being held and pulled. The white light was going away. I was heading back down, falling into the hole, falling back down into hell. I was throwing my arms around, trying to fight my way out.

So I fell on my hands and knees.

Then my head flowed with thoughts.

Perhaps I shouldn't live. What had I done with my life? All I had done was bring pain and hurt. All I had done was wait to take advantage of people. Wait to take. Wait to steal. Wait to make money. Are people just things to be used? Is it right I keep everybody at a distance? Are people like meat, who always go rotten?

I lifted my head. The rivers of fire had gone. There was just darkness and a pale shadow, flickering at first, jumping around like a jack-in-the-box. It was turning into something. It was someone I knew. They had a heavy limp. They were slowly walking towards me. Dragging their foot, breathing heavy. I didn't want to look. I bowed my head. I was afraid and ashamed.

'Heh, little bro,' it said, 'now you know what it feels like. Now you know what it's like to die.'

I was shaking.

I was ready to say sorry.

I was ready to beg for his forgiveness, but he was walking away, limping back to hell.

I started screaming, 'Greg! Greg!'

But he wasn't going to help. He wanted to punish me and see me suffer.

15

I crawled out from underneath the tarpaulin after I had that dream. The ghosts and demons had crept up on me, and I was shaking because of the nightmare and the cold. I brushed off the dirt, the ants, the spiders and things that had two heads, twelve legs and spoke Klingon. I wasn't hanging around, as I took one last look at the archaeological site. I suppose it had proved that suicide is dangerous and spooks come out at night to put the shits up you. I was also tempted to see if my half-brother was under the tarpaulin but slapped myself, picked up the rucksack and headed off looking for a main road.

Seeing as I'd walked south east yesterday, I set the compass for north west and hoped I'd hit the tarmac soon. As I walked back over the dry earth, I felt like a lizard, desperate for the sun to come up and start warming me. I was also parched and drained what water I had left in my bottle.

Oh well, things had to get better, and then they did.

The first bit of good news was getting a phone signal. The second bit of good news was climbing over a busted stone wall and landing on the tarmac road. The third bit of good news, which even managed to cheer me up, was the sun coming over the hill and getting those first rays on my scratched, grazed and bruised body. I soaked it all up until I thought it was time to make the first of a few calls.

It seemed to take Zammit for ever, and I was cursing him until he found me. He did his job by not asking me questions, until he couldn't help himself and asked about Borg. I lied and said there was nothing. I knew Zammit didn't believe me, but then it was not his job to know anything about Borg. He then tried to tell me stuff about the site and how it was haunted by human monkeys at night who were hunting for prey to feed their dying tribe.

I said I hadn't seen them.

'But what did you do... out there, in the cave and on the cliff?'

'I slept under the stars,' I said.

'You had some deep thoughts?'

'Yeah.'

'And do you know what you have found?'

'I think so.'

'And?'

'I'm going to become a nun.'

Zammit was trying to work out if this was possible when I shouted at him to stop. I threw open the car door, jumped over another stone wall and after a short trip across a field, threw myself into the sea. It was cleansing, cooling and desperately needed, to get the stench and dirt of yesterday washed away. Then the pain of the sea salt stung the grazing and bruising that covered my chest and legs. I hauled myself out onto a slab of volcanic rock and pulled off my soaking t-shirt and shorts. As I sat there, I had a quick inspection of my body parts and winced and groaned as Zammit walked up behind me.

He took one look and said, 'I will drive you to the hospital.'

It meant I turned up in my underpants, with my clothes in the rucksack, and Zammit disappeared into the distance.

With the genuine excuse about rock climbing as the cause of my injuries, they disinfected me and put some plasters on, and I chucked a load of pain killers down my gullet. I asked after Zain and found out he had been discharged in the morning, picked up by Tony and Sonia. That was good news and saved me having to visit the kid looking like a first aid dummy.

After spending the rest of the afternoon sitting in a wheelchair and eating crisps and drinking fizzy drinks from the vending machine, I made myself presentable by borrowing some clothes off a male nurse.

I had one more thing to do before I got back to the villa, and that was to go and see this Mrs Cini.

I wouldn't say they were cheap offices for a lawyer, but neither were they plush. They were in the shopping mall, where I had bought the kids their toys, in between a supermarket and a jeweller. The office was a shop window plastered with posters about elections and stuff. Inside, about half a dozen flunkies beavered about, making lots of noise, answering the phone and filling up envelopes. It was like a campaign room, with the name Cini on everything.

I kept looking at the clock and waiting for someone or something to appear. By about five, I was fed up and ready to go, when I got a shout from an acne-cursed teenager. I shot up a narrow set of stairs. There was a door with a picture of a guy and girl, so I knew that was for pissing in. Another was all glass with the name Cini engraved and some fancy-looking letters after it.

I kind of knocked and walked straight in.

She looked up from her desk, startled by my unannounced entrance. And then I was looking at her hazel-lit eyes, liking the deep brown Mediterranean skin and her shoulder-length black hair.

'Sorry,' I said, which was not something I normally said.

'No problem, Mr Mason, please take a seat. I'll be with you in a minute.'

There was only one seat – an old hard-backed plastic chair. The rest of the place was wall to wall shelves, full of A4 boxes with reference numbers and legal jargon written in black marker pen. Behind her was a large window that looked out on rusty guttering bolted to the brick walls.

She dropped her pen and then looked up at me again.

'OK, so how can I help you?' she asked.

Usually, my words came out a lot quicker, but I was thinking about how good-looking she was, which was stopping my brain from getting into gear.

'Mr Mason?'

'Sorry,' I said, 'just taken a load of painkillers.'

'I see… please… take your time,' she said, looking at me with a kindness that I hadn't seen for a while. 'Have you had an accident? Is that why you have come to see me?'

'Eh, no,' I said, starting to get a grip. 'I have some legal problems.'

'Yes?'

I decided to start with property, rather than possible murder charges.

'It's a restaurant called The Seashell.'

'I know it.'

'And there's a repossession order to shut it down.'

She smiled, like she knew.

'Do you mind if I ask you a slightly different question?' she said, brushing her hair back.

'Go ahead,' I said.

'How much do you know about politics, and specifically politics on this little island?'

'Well, I got invited to a garden party. I said hello to the president just before his bedtime and made sure he was nice and comfy. Then I spoke to that guy, Grech. He talked to me about marrying ugly women, which he said keeps everyone in their place.'

'That sounds like Grech,' she said, laughing. 'He likes to use the folksy pitch to justify doing things for the benefit of the few, at a cost to the many.'

'You're not a fan then?'

'No, Mr Mason. I am, to use a sporting term, on the other side.'

'That doesn't sound good,' I said, 'because I think they only listen to people who are on their side.'

'Anything is possible if you have the people with you.'

'It's not people I need, but the law.'

She sat back in her chair, like she was going to tell me there was nothing she could do.

'OK, Steven… do you mind if I call you Steven?'

'No.'

'So, I will be honest with you. I do know some things about you, and from a legal point of view, I will not get involved with the difficulties you have with the Department of Environment. That is not to say you do not, I am sure, have a very good legal case, but you will need to find a lawyer who is prepared to work with English gangsters.'

I wanted to like her because I found her attractive, but now she was just being rude!

'Well, you know,' I said, 'I need to get the restaurant open, or the money back, plus a load more money for all the hassle.'

'Did you know, Steven,' she said, sounding like she was going to give me a speech, 'that restaurant has become a symbol of resistance for the people on this island? You may or may not be aware, but the people are very angry about the amount of unchecked, rampant development along the coastline. It is a scar, an ugly distortion of the environment, rapaciously putting profits before the needs of the people. The Seashell is part of our island history. The building's origins can be traced back two or three hundred years. Families have been going there for generations – wedding receptions, birthday parties, social events. We know what the repossession order is all about, Steven, and the intention to ensure the land and property rights are handed over to Global Venture Capital Group.'

'Then you need my help, don't you?'

'I have two roles in my life, Steven. I am a lawyer and I am a politician. In fact, although you do not see my poster as much as Prime Minister Grech, I am Mrs Cini, leader of the official opposition. Therefore, whilst you formally hold the land deeds of The Seashell, because of who you are, this is a case where I cannot get involved.'

'What can you do then?'

'What I can do is offer some discreet advice and put you in touch with a lawyer who is…'

'Used to villains?'

'Are you a villain, Steven?'

'You seem to think so.'

'And does that matter to you, that I think you are?'

'That depends.'

'On what?'

'I don't know…'

I scratched the back of my head.

It was awkward for a few seconds, then she got back on track.

'The point I am making, Steven, is that it would help if you do not give in to the pressure to sell, that you fight your legitimate legal case whilst the people make their feelings and protests known. The Seashell is a symbol of resistance. There is a lot of anger towards Grech and his clique, not least for the killing and silencing of the journalist Garibaldi, which everyone knows is a consequence of the corruption that lies at the heart of this government and their ties with big business.'

'You seem to think I care…'

'There is a mutual interest, but yes, I am trying to appeal to your better nature.'

'Even if I am a gangster.'

'Well, Steven, from what I have heard, I believe you to be a good man, who happens to have a career in criminality. Whereas a man like Grech is not a good man and is also a criminal.'

'Do you mean I'd make a better prime minister?'

Cini smiled.

'Well, that happens to be my ambition, but you get my point.'

She then pulled out of her desk drawer a business card and

handed it to me.

'You can contact my colleague anytime. He will be a perfect fit for your needs – in terms of property issues or other.'

'Thanks,' I said, checking the guy's name.

'And regarding the *other*, Steven,' she said, which could only mean murder, 'we know Mr Garibaldi was killed staying in one of your properties, a villa, which had been provided by your agent, Joseph Borg. I also understand there is another suspect in the case, a Max Schmidt, who the police are interested in.'

'You can add me into the mix if you want.'

Cini took that as new info.

'Are you involved?' she asked seriously.

'Not really,' I said.

'That sounds evasive.'

'It means nothing is simple, but I didn't kill Garibaldi.'

'No, I do not believe you did. However, that type of killing has far more meaning than just taking another man's life. There are ripples and effects that go far beyond the borders of our little volcanic rock. It is a warning to all who would seek to reveal the stench that pervades the world of politics and business today. The art of power, you see, has become a blunt instrument. There is no veil to behave discreetly. Today, power is demonstrated in the explicit use of the hammer, for all to see. And those that dare to challenge this, who dare to shine a light on this new world order, are extinguished, to provide another lesson to us all. It is the equivalent of the guillotine, a new type of terror – unfettered, unapologetic, unbound.'

I laughed.

'Do you find these things amusing?' she said, all offended.

'No, I was just thinking, you sound like a politician.'

'We need politics, Steven. It is not something to be ignored or dismissed. It is how society is run. If you abdicate interest, then you only have yourself to blame if someone shoves you in the oven.'

She was all preachy, but I liked it.

'Can I ask you something?'

'Of course…'

'Is there a Mr Cini?'

'Why does that matter to you?'

'I'm just nosey.'

I was thinking she wasn't going to tell me, then she said, 'Yes, but I don't know where my husband is. He left a long time ago. As far as I know, he could be dead, or he could be happily married with two children and a dog. He could even be President of the United States for all I know. After all, anything is possible in the land of dreams and delusion, don't you think?'

'I've been there,' I said.

'America?'

'No, just the dreams.'

That's when she looked at me, like she was waiting for me to say something about myself, but I couldn't really think of anything that would impress her.

'I'll go then,' I said, standing up and squeezing myself around to open the door.

'Of course,' she said, looking a bit embarrassed.

I stood in the doorway. I was going to say something, but it seemed like she would only throw it back in my face.

'Just so you know, Steven, I find cynicism unattractive.'

'Well, there's not much I can do about that.'

'Why don't you try,' she said. 'Tomorrow, we march from The Seashell. You should join us. These experiences can change a person if you take part in it.'

I nodded, taking one more good look at her.

I hated politics, but maybe I had to think about it if I wanted to get out of the shit I was in.

16

I was late for the party, not that I knew there was a party, but that's what was going on when I got back to the villa. There was a banner hanging up outside:

WELCOME HOME, ZAIN

I was in a mood and that pissed me right off. He didn't have a home, just like his big sister. I didn't fancy going in and being ice-cream happy, so I went around the back.

The flowers I'd planted were bent over – too much sun and no water. That was Tony's fault, I decided. I found a bucket and gave them a nice drink. Then some kid came flying out the back, got frightened when they saw me and ran back in.

A minute later, Tony came out.

'How'd it go?' he said.

'Borg's dead.'

'Yeah, you found him then?'

'Yeah, then he died.'

'You killed him?'

'No, he killed himself.'

'Did he say anything?'

'Yeah, he thinks I'm fucked.'

'You've been fucked before.'

'Yeah…'

I then threw the bucket as far as I could. It flew over the outhouse and bounced around a bit.

Tony kept quiet.

'Trust me, Tony, I've been to a very dark place. I slept out there under a tarpaulin… it was trippy.'

'Yeah, and which way were you heading… heaven or hell?'

'I think we both know which way I'm going.'

'Yeah… did you get in touch with Greg then?'

'Why did you say that?'

'Well, you know, the Greg thing… it's not easy to get over… him being your brother.'

'Half-brother…'

'Well, at least you know one thing…'

'Yeah?'

'That he's dead.'

'I know he's dead, Tony, but I don't need the bastard somehow fucking with my head.'

'OK, just trying to help you, mate.'

I let myself cool down for a few seconds and then got back to business.

'Schmidt's playing us,' I said. 'He's got the Medusa and he's trying to flog it.'

'I think that's what's called stating the bleeding obvious,' said Tony.

'I know.'

I looked at the depressed flowers.

'You could have watered them,' I said.

'You don't water flowers in the day. It's too hot and just evaporates. You need to water them like you've done, in the evening when its cooler.'

'I suppose you know all this because you've watched a video?'

'I've got an allotment where I grow my veg.'

'No garden?'

'Come off it, you know where I live – in a flat on the estate. And I would like to go back.'

'I reckon you will, Tony. Give it a couple of days and I'll have it all sorted.'

'How?'

Then I was I honest. 'I don't know, but even if I stood here naked with a flower up my arse, I reckon things will come my way.'

'That don't sound like too much of a plan, mate. You know, Grandad, he won't be happy with what I've got to tell him.'

'Yeah, well, it will be better coming from you. But make sure you tell him it wasn't me who killed Borg – it was suicide.'

'How do you know it was suicide?'

'Because he jumped on me and then he let go, or else it would also be me at the bottom of the sea.'

'So, you tried to save him?'

'No, I saved myself, but Borg just wanted to die – end of.'

'Did he say anything about Schmidt?'

'Yeah... he was coming for him, so he wanted to do himself in before Schmidt got to him, or the constabulary.'

'You mean Grandad ain't got no one to manage the properties and Schmidt is an effing psycho killer?'

'Yeah, that about sums it up nicely.'

Tony gave me a dad look.

'You know, mate, this is all getting out of hand. Plus, the kids and all.'

'You don't say.'

'Listen, you brought the kids back, Steven.'

'I can't roll back time, can I, Tony?'

'That's not what I mean.'

'Then what?'

'I don't know, maybe we just need to keep it simple, keep our noses out of stuff that goes on here. Just carry-on fishing for Schmidt – he's coming up to the surface. Then you get the hold of the Medusa, give it back to me and I can go home.'

'Tony, trust me, if I could keep it simple, I would.'

He let out a big sigh.

I didn't envy him having to explain these things to Grandad.

'How's the boy doing?' I asked.

'He's good. Still don't say nothing, but he is playing and smiling.'

I nodded.

'Listen,' said Tony, 'stay out here for a bit, cool off, and then come in. The kids are all right, you know. That Zammit is here with his kids. It's nice – reminds me of my own family.'

'The thing is, Tony, I don't know what a normal family

is.'

'Listen, mate, there ain't no normal families out there. It's just people.'

That was easy for Tony to say because he came from a normal family.

'Look,' I said, 'don't take it personal, but there's something else I need to do tonight – all part of the plan.'

'Is that the plan where you shove a flower up your arse?'

'Hopefully…'

'Well,' said Tony, as he turned to go back in, 'remember to water it at night.'

'OK,' I said, smiling. 'I need to get going.'

And that was it.

I started up over the hill, with my chest sore as hell, and chucked a load more painkillers down me. Once I'd got to the burnt-out villa, I followed the lanes for a bit until I got Cini's place. She had a house, smaller than my villa and out of the way. There was a brick stone wall around it and a large iron gate. I was going to be polite so pressed the buzzer on the intercom.

She could see it was me.

I didn't say anything.

It was her decision.

I waited, for a good minute.

I thought she wasn't interested, so I started walking, but after a few yards, I heard the gate click. I turned back and curved my way around the driveway and a green lawned garden. She also had a proper front door and stood there waiting as I got close.

'I thought I'd come and see you,' I said, wondering how she would react.

'And why's that, Steven?'

'I like you,' I said.

'Yes, and what do you like about me?'

I wasn't going to tell her that I thought she was well fit for her age, but it's basically what I thought.

'I like… the way you look at me.'

'And what way do I look at you?'

'You look at me… like you like me.'

'So because you think I like you, that is the reason why you have come to my home, unannounced?'

'I was in the area,' I said, looking around the valley.

'If you can find out where I live, then I am sure you could have phoned me.'

'Well, you know, I only just thought about it, as I was walking along. I'll go if you're with someone, or family or whatever…'

'You amuse me, Steven. For a gangster, you are not very confident with the female sex.'

'Well, I've got this far…'

'Yes, you are close to my door, but do you have the confidence to come in and meet other people?'

'No, I don't want to see anyone else. I'll leave it.'

I was about to go when she laughed.

'There is no one else here,' she said, leaving the door open for me to follow.

I went in and shut the door behind me. I looked around a large open room, with low light and fancy artwork all over the walls. She had a bottle of plonk on the table.

'Would you like some wine, Steven?' she said, as she picked up her glass and sat down on the sofa, pulling up her legs.

'Nah, I'm trying to keep off the sauce for a bit,' I said, walking around to look at the paintings.

'I can understand you might need to do that.'

'Yeah?'

'Well, you don't want to go around this island every night defaming Prime Minister Grech.'

'I don't know, he must be used to it, people calling him names.'

'A man like Grech has the ego of a spoilt child. He never forgets who slights him and he plots revenge, however minor the perceived offence.'

'Tell me, then,' I said, still standing. 'If everyone hates him, why do people still vote for him?'

'Unfortunately, not everyone hates Grech. And without being too political for you, Steven, voting for Grech doesn't mean those people like him. They just think they will get a crumb or two thrown their way.'

'That could still be a lot of crumbs.'

'Well, in the end, he only cuts a slice of the cake for the chosen few.'

Having done the brief tour of her gallery, I sat down on a chair so I was facing her, looking at her smooth brown legs and those hazel-lit eyes.

'I like the paintings,' I said.

'Thank you. They are all by local artists. We might be a small island but we put a lot of energy in the creative arts, as well as politics of course. You see, we are a strategically located island, with hundreds of years of history. All Europe and the Middle East has passed through here. So, although we are small, it makes us global. That means we are not that different from all the other things that are happening in the

153

world, but perhaps because we are small it is more… intense. Grech is just the same kind of beast that you can find in Russia, China or the Philippines, or perhaps even in the land of dreams in the Disunited States of America.'

I didn't say anything, just in case I put my ignorant foot in it.

'Am I boring you, Steven?'

'No.'

'That's the thing you see, politicians like me love to talk, and we always end up talking about the same things.'

'Yeah, I know people like that, but they talk about football.'

She pulled her legs up again on the sofa and sipped her wine.

'You should tell me what you are thinking, Steven.'

I thought about it for a second and then decided it was better she know for sure why I was here.

'OK. I was wondering if you wanted to have sex with me?'

'No,' she said, keeping her gaze on me. 'I do not want to have sex with you, but I would be happy to make love.'

'Same difference…'

'Well, we shall see. And call me by my first name, Sefora. Do you think you can remember that?'

'I'll try…'

'Yes please, do your best.'

17

For all the things I didn't like about the island, there was still nothing better than catching a bright blue sky, without the heat, and just the thin breeze. I could never get anything like that back on the estate, which kind of made me happy I was still here, even if things were going seriously pear-shaped.

I had got up early, with Cini still asleep, and I didn't fancy going back to the villa. I headed down into the old town and found the patch of volcanic rock where I was wasted and puked up. The sick stains were still there so I moved away and perched on the edge. The sea was about half a yard beneath me – a rich sweet blue, a clean white froth licking at the edges. And across the sea was the inlet into the old harbour, banked by great big fortifications, built when the knights were raping and pillaging in the name of God and Christianity. It had grandeur, size, status. You couldn't help but be impressed with the statement they had made: they were here to stay and were going to defend what they'd got. Not that Zammit would have any of it – racist history, he would say, and he was probably right.

Still, there were times when you couldn't beat being out here. It wasn't like back home, with the sea cold and dirty brown, full of seaweed and plastic. There was something pure about the Mediterranean, something grand, old and deserving respect. All we had back in England was a bunch of rocks in a circle, and most of them had fallen over. But out here, things were still standing from hundreds of years ago, like they had just been built – unless someone was running around all day fixing the bricks and mortar. I suppose the

German bombs in the war must have done some damage, but it was still in good nick – nice and proud, full of history that wasn't going anywhere.

But behind me was a load of old shite, great big hotels that stretched all the way along and was going to carry on stretching all the way down to The Seashell, probably until the whole island was like a ringed fortress of faceless hotels. I could understand why the locals were so vexed about it.

Still, they had Cini on their side, and she was going for it, ready to bring down the incestuous bunch of turds who ran the show. She would also want to get rid of the likes of me because you can't get rid of a load of gangster businessmen and still have the genuine article-type villain doing business, however good they were in bed – making love or having sex.

But for now, I couldn't give a monkeys.

I lay back down on the rock, shut my eyes and let the sea do the talking in my head, just for five minutes, or however long it took to rest my aching body.

I must have been off the grid for a good few hours because when I checked the time, it was getting on for midday. Also, Grandad was right about one thing: I should always wear a hat. The sun had come over and it felt like a nuclear power station had given me a good old Sunday roasting.

I bought a new hat and then strolled down to The Seashell to see how the revolution was going.

They had sectioned off the whole of the restaurant with wire fencing, but what surprised me was the size of the crowd that had come out to protest. A hundred, maybe two hundred, were in front of The Seashell. I stayed at the back because Cini was there stood on a crate, using a megaphone, telling everyone that the repossession of The Seashell was illegal.

Not that she went on to say it belonged to me, the English gangster, or Grandad, the hard bastard English gangster, but it belonged to the people because of its history, because it was a symbol against the rampant corruption polluting the island, destroying the heart of an island, for the sake of profit and greed. But if that wasn't bad enough, they were now killing journalists who tried to tell the truth about what was going on, about how people like Grech, and the big global companies, think they can do what they want and get away with it. Power was a bullet in the head, murder on the streets, because power was violence and barbarity. They treated the people as if they were ignorant, stupid and powerless, but it was the people who had the power to change things and that's what scared the bosses.

She had the crowd clapping, nodding and agreeing.

But, she said, voting for an alternative, voting for her party, voting for her, was the best way to hold the powerful to account. This is what she did, she said, every day in parliament, in her practice as a lawyer. And by holding rallies like this, they were showing the authorities that the people knew what they wanted and they were not going to back down. This, said Cini, was the start of her anti-corruption campaign, to hold the government to account for all its mishandling of the due process of the law, for its failings in finding the killer or killers of Garibaldi, the brave investigative journalist who had given his life for truth and justice.

There was a big roar from the crowd, like someone had scored a goal. Then I felt a tug on my shirt and a little old lady said, 'They're greedy. They want more – more, more, more. It's like the mafia. They do whatever they want.'

And an old man, perhaps her husband, said, 'It's an orgy of construction, a frenzy – it's construction on steroids.'

'You need to see with your eyes,' said the little old lady, pointing at her face. 'Open them – they are destroying everything for money.'

I nodded, like I cared, as Cini was back to telling everyone how important it was to vote for the right people at the next election, to vote for her party and to vote for her. And she thanked everybody for turning up and showing their support. This was the new beginning – how they would show Grech his days as a pompous arrogant king were soon going to be over.

Fair enough.

Cini stepped off the crate and the people were clapping as she started moving through the crowd shaking their hands. As she got closer to me, she made a beeline in the other direction. I have this effect on women, before and after I've slept with them.

I thought that was it and started to make my way to the front to check out what this repossession order stuck to the fence said. As I got up close, I noticed a few security guards behind the wire looking back at me. I smiled back at them.

The repossession order was in English, with legal sections and articles that all added up to one thing: Grech, Attard and Vella were making sure nothing stood in the way of Global Venture Capital Group, or any other of the big developers that were building glass concrete temples. The only thing in my favour was, having grabbed the land deeds, I had something to show a lawyer. But there was no way I could see Grandad going to war over this, not unless he was going to ship all his crew over, which would then turn into a bloodbath. It will be a bitter pill for him to swallow, but he will have to cut his losses, pull out and find some other dodgy lump of rock to funnel money into.

It kind of made running after Schmidt seem like a bit of a sideshow, another deal gone wrong, unless the exploding villa, the restaurant and the Medusa were all linked together. And if that were the case, I could see myself having to be the gangster everyone thought I was.

I was about to call it a day when Zammit appeared out of nowhere and just like Cini, grabbed the megaphone and got up on the crate. Only this time, I couldn't understand a word he said because it was all in local Arabic. But Zammit was in full swing with whatever he was saying and the clapping had turned into shouting. He had got the crowd going and none of this lot seemed like they were going to wait to vote to make things happen, because they weren't wandering off to have their lunch, they were turning around and heading back up the road into the old town.

As I watched the crowd go, I got clocked by the manager of The Seashell. He was on me double quick and had desperation written all over his face.

'Mr Mason, where have you been? Where is Mr Borg? I have been trying to speak to you and to Mr Borg, but both of you do not return anything.'

He was right, but my general rule is, I never reply to anybody, and Borg was resting on the bottom of the seabed.

'Yeah, I know, but don't worry,' I said, 'I haven't sold the place.'

'Oh, that is a relief… some, anyway. But what can we do? Are you fighting against this?' he said, pointing to the repossession order.

'Yeah, and we've got an army,' I said, nodding in the direction of the chanting crowd as they followed Zammit up the hill.

'But there are staff, Mr Mason. They will need to be paid. This was all the things that Mr Borg would do for us.'

'It's something I'll get sorted,' I said, deciding I would also follow Zammit's popular front. 'Just hang in there.'

He wasn't happy, but there was nothing I could do for him right now. I left him staring at The Seashell, like he'd had his favourite toy taken off him for no reason.

I caught up with Zammit's march and strolled along behind the crowd. I had no idea where we were going, but it had a bit more promise than Cini, even if she had my vote at the next election. There were chants that had Grech in it, something to do with liars and profit and greed. I could have come up with my own chants but these would have been more like, 'Here we go, here we go, here we go,' so I left it to the locals.

Then we stopped outside the constabulary HQ. There were no constabulary outside or in the reception area. Zammit jumped up onto the steps and took hold of the megaphone. He started raging again, giving the crowd what they wanted to hear.

Once Zammit had finished, the mood changed. All the chanting had gone and the whistling started. And OMG, did they hate the constabulary! There were different groups of chat in the crowd: plotting, planning, pushing and just angry. It was a good brew and just needed a match. I moved around the side of the crowd, which got Zammit's attention. I gave him a look and he smiled back at me, like a big Cheshire cat.

He knew, and I knew – this would be a good moment.

There was enough rock and stone lying around to find something nice and heavy. I lobbed it over a few people and it smashed against a glass window. The noise made everyone stop for a few seconds. I couldn't tell if it would spark a riot or get everyone backing off and going home for a nice lie down and siesta. But the answer came when another rock was thrown.

And that was it, the whole place kicked off.

With my deed done, I slipped back behind the crowd and watched the windows being smashed. Once the glass had gone, people were stepping into the reception and looking around, happy and confused. After all, this was the HQ and there was nobody about – no constabulary.

Well, they were either waiting upstairs and were going to jump on us with batons and tear gas, or they had some warning of what was going to happen and had realised that half a dozen plods were not going to stop this lot throwing stones and smashing windows. I pushed through the crowd because they didn't look too bothered about doing much more and I grabbed hold of Zammit.

'Come on,' I said, 'I need to look upstairs.'

He looked at me like the deal was to smash some windows and go home.

'Yeah, come on,' I said. 'Now's your chance to check your file. Is there anyone up there or have they all runaway?'

'No,' said Zammit, 'they have all gone to lunch. We are not meant to go any further.'

'Rubbish!' I said, pulling him by the shirt so it looked like he was leading the way.

Well, whatever was arranged, I wasn't going to look a gift horse in the mouth. As soon as we were up the stairs, others started to follow. I didn't waste time and headed straight for Spiteri's desk. I couldn't find anything to wedge open his drawer so gave it a few good kicks. That's when someone came over and had a neat little crowbar in their back pocket. It sprang open. I was in luck. Four passports, lying there ready to be repossessed.

Other people headed for the filing cabinets or were randomly trashing the place. As I tucked the passports in my back pocket, keen to vacate the scene, a guy came over, sweaty but looking a lot calmer than the rampaging locals. For a second, I thought he might be some responsible citizen who was just going to let me know he had seen what I had done.

But he kept it simple.

'There is someone at The Seashell. They will tell you where Schmidt is.'

And then he turned and went.

I didn't believe him, I didn't trust him, but he knew I couldn't say no.

I found Zammit with his head buried in a file.

'Heh,' I said, tapping him on the shoulder and handing him the passports. 'Put these in your pocket. I'm going back to The Seashell to check on something. If you can't get me on my mobile in an hour, you need to come find me.'

'Bastards!'

'Is that your file,' I said, looking at a long list of minor convictions. 'You know, you should work something out with your brother. You can't have him on the inside and they've still got all that crap on you.'

'What can he do? He must put the food on the table like me.'

'Yeah, but I bet he has a big fat pig for dinner and you eat rice and chickpeas.'

Zammit didn't say anything. He got back to looking at what a naughty boy he had been and I headed off.

The crowd outside had thinned, and there was a guy with a few cameras tied around his neck, clicking away. He was going to put me in the picture, so I gave him the grievous look.

'How did all this happen?' he asked, picking his way through the broken glass.

'It was the constabulary,' I said. 'They started it, harassing everyone and then ran away when people fought back.'

'You mean there is no constabulary here?'

'Yeah, I reckon they've gone to lunch. They'll be just finishing off their pudding, so you won't have long to wait.'

'So, who's inside?'

'Eh… some guy called Che Guevara,' I said, as I left him to think about his story for the local newspaper.

It didn't take me long to walk back to The Seashell.

I was right to be suspicious. The security guards had gone or were having lunch with their mates in the constabulary. I sat down on the roadside kerb. The sun was now blazing hot. With a no-show for Schmidt, or whoever it was who was supposed to be meeting me, I was planning on heading back to the villa. That's when I heard the huffing and chuffing of the hydraulics of a great big truck loader. There was a small excavator on the back, and it turned in down the slope and parked up right in front of me.

This had nothing to do with Schmidt then, I thought, and everything to do with pulling down The Seashell. I got up, about to phone for a lawyer, when both cab doors flew open and three guys were on the pavement looking straight at me.

They were all meat, vest and hard hats.

'You!' said one of the meat heads.

'Yeah? You can call me Mr Mason.'

'OK.'

And that's when being casual and polite didn't work.

They jumped me, buckled my knees and had a hood over my head before I had a chance to ask for a cup of tea and a biscuit. After that, I was used as a footrest, rolled up in a heap on the floor of the cab.

Had I known they were going to bury me alive, I might have done a load more to get out of the situation. But hindsight is a wonderful thing, especially if you can travel back in time.

But it looks like I'm stuck in the underground bus stop waiting for the 666 to take me to the hot tourist resort called Hell.

Plus, I don't think I can breathe.

Ashes To Ashes

1

'Motherfuckers!'

'Heh, mate, what are you doing down there?'

'Motherfuckers!'

'You're like... white as a sheet... you know... Dracula kind of white.'

'Shut the fuck up, Tony!'

'OK, I get it, you need some air. But just so you know, mate, I have saved your life.'

That was it, I couldn't talk. I had to use my lungs to breathe. That's all I wanted to do, breathe in great big buckets full of air.

How I love air!

'You know, that's real mean,' he said, with his feet straddled across the rims of the coffin. 'I mean, that's a really mean thing to do to someone. How long have you been in there?'

'Long enough,' I said, breathing more great big gulps of air and staring up at Tony's bollocks.

'Did you know that if someone is buried alive in a coffin,

they have five and half hours left to live?'

'You're not the first person to tell me that,' I said, gripping the edge of the coffin, like I was hanging on to a swaying ship. 'Anyway, how did you find me?'

He pulled out his phone, as he used one hand to balance himself in the hole.

'I got this weird text,' he said, trying to show me the message.

I couldn't read it.

'My eyes,' I said, struggling with the dim light.

'Oh yeah, right. Well, it says: Because the devil understands your friend, you have until seven. Go to where the West is fake and look where death is buried.'

'Cryptic…'

'Yeah, that's what I thought – like a crossword puzzle.'

'And you don't know who sent that?'

'No. I got hold of Zammit. He said you were over at The Seashell, but you weren't there. Then, you know, my old antenna started going, and so I walked all the way out here, looked around and found another message.'

I looked up, all six feet.

'Yeah, you ain't going to be able to read it upside down,' said Tony.

There was a wooden cross casting a shadow over both of us.

'You mean, they marked my grave?'

'Kind of…'

'You mean, with my name?'

'Nah… it says:

'HERE LIES POSEIDON

DEEP UNDERGROUND
A FISH OUT OF WATER
WAITING TO BE FOUND'

'Schmidt...' I said, spitting out his name.

'His English is good,' said Tony.

'Well, I'll give him something to sing along to when I find that fucked-up fucker.'

'Poseidon,' said Tony, still on the track of all things Greek, 'was the father of Medusa's children – that was the clue.'

'Yeah, but it's not like you're going to miss a shiny coffin at the bottom of a pit.'

'Heh, mate, if they'd put earth on top of that,' said Tony, who wanted a bit more credit, 'you'd be dead.'

'I thought they did,' I said. 'Looks like they just threw some dirt down on the lid.'

'Wow! They wanted to make you suffer.'

'Tony...' I said, holding my head because he was making it explode. 'Just get me out of here.'

He stretched out his hand so I could sit upright in the coffin. I should have waited to let my head get back in order but I was desperate to get out. Tony hauled himself back on top and then gripped my arm to help pull me out. I sat there, not moving, trying to get my head in gear.

'It's going to get dark,' said Tony, 'and we got to walk. There ain't no buses.'

'Phone Zammit,' I said, struggling to get some blood moving in my legs so I could stand.

'He ain't coming, they locked him up.'

'What!'

'No worries, he gave me the passports.'

'Something's gone right then,' I said, as I wobbled about on my pins.

'See, life ain't so bad, is it,' said Tony, as he helped me keep my balance.

'Shit... that feels good,' I said, letting the dipping sun go right into my eyes.

I felt calmer with the warm light.

'Strange, this place, isn't it,' he said.

'You don't suppose the saloon bar is open?' I said, licking my lips.

'No need,' said Tony, as he pulled out a bottle of water from his rucksack. 'Here, you must be dying of thirst.'

I gulped it down.

'I love westerns,' he said, 'but I don't think I've seen the one they made here.'

'Who gives a fuck, Tony.'

'Do you know who my favourite actor is?'

'John Wayne,' I said, exercising and flexing my body to get the blood circulating.

'Clint Eastwood,' he said, like it meant something to me. 'He's the best. He ain't got no morals in them spaghettis, but he always does the right thing in the end. Just like you, Steven.'

'What's that mean?'

'Nothing, mate. You know me, always talking out me arse.'

'For once, Tony, I think you're right.'

'Cheers...'

'Still, shame the saloon bar ain't real. I could do with a proper drink.'

'That's where I put the kids.'

'You what?'

'Childcare, mate, you can't get none.'

He had a point, what with Zammit locked up.

'Right,' I said, feeling my muscles coming back to life. 'Let's get them and then get going.'

Tony had spun the kids a story that I had fallen down a hole and that's why they had come out here to help me get back out again. It wasn't too far from the truth, and after a lot of questions about fire engines and ambulances, we headed back towards the villa.

Zain was up on Tony's shoulders and Sonia was walking by my side. I think she had got over the whole blaming me thing, for her mum and whatever else she thought I should be guilty of. She was talking to me like I could be her older brother, or maybe her dad. And being buried alive was really playing on her mind.

'Was it dark?' she said.

'Yeah…'

'Were there worms?'

'No, no worms. They put me in a coffin.'

'Like a box?'

'Yeah.'

'So, it was dark?'

'Yeah, but it didn't matter because I shut my eyes.'

'Were you lonely?'

'Not really, I was just thinking.'

'What did you think about?'

'Oh, you know, how I ended up in a coffin.'

'Do you know?'

'Know what?'

'Why they put you in a coffin?'

'That's a good question, Sonia. I'm still thinking about it.'

We carried on walking for a bit, not saying anything.

Then she said, 'I don't want to die.'

'Trust me, Sonia, most of us don't.'

'But I'm afraid.'

'Yeah, of what… dying?'

'Yes.'

'Is that because your mum and dad are dead?'

'No.'

'Then what?'

Sonia thought about it for a moment, then said, 'Why do we have to die?'

I laughed.

That was a good question.

'No one knows why,' I said. 'It's just one of those things. That's why people like to believe there's another life, after death.'

'You mean like heaven?'

'Yeah, or hell. So you need to make sure you're good because the naughty people go to hell.'

'Are you going there?'

'Who knows, Sonia. It's not my decision to make.'

'You mean that is what God tells you, if you're going to heaven or hell?'

'If there is a god.'

'But if there is not a god, there is no a heaven or hell.'

'Well, I'll vote for that.'

'Can we vote?'

'Not really.'

I could tell Sonia was chewing this one over.

Then she got back on track with what was on her mind.

'I don't want you to die,' she said.

'That's good, neither do I.'

'But I can't stop being afraid of dying.'

'Well, perhaps that's because of what you've been through.'

'No, I've always thought about it, before we left London.'

'That's heavy stuff for a little girl to think about.'

'Why?'

'Because it's the sort of thing you think about when you're a teenager, or when you're old.'

'I don't like it.'

'What, thinking about death?'

'Yes.'

'Then don't think about it.'

'How do you stop?'

'How do you stop thinking about death?'

'Yes.'

'Think of something nice.'

That's when I wondered if Sonia could, after all she had been through.

'I bet there are some nice things that have happened to you,' I said. 'Think about those if you end up worrying about dying.'

'I liked the toys, the ones you gave us.'

'Yeah? There you go then. Did you ever do anything nice with your mum and dad?'

'Yes, we used to go to the park. I liked to go on the swings.'

'Yeah? I bet that's fun, swinging up high in the air.'

'Do you like the swings?'

171

'Nah… makes me dizzy.'

Then she went all quiet on me again.

We carried on walking.

I checked on Tony, who had managed to get Zain off his shoulders. He was still far enough away for me to say what I wanted.

'So,' I said to Sonia, 'do you remember our little promise?'

She nodded.

'And do you still want to go to Germany?'

She nodded again.

'Which means, you know, that you have to leave the island with me.'

Again, she nodded.

'OK, let your brother know, but don't say anything to Tony.'

'Do you want to go to Germany?' she asked.

'I know some people who live there.'

'Are they your friends, like Tony?'

'Yeah, they're nice people, and they like to help people like you who are looking for somewhere safe to live.'

I thought I was going to get a thousand questions about friends, when she screamed loudly.

'Look!'

Sonia had her hand out in front her.

'It's snowing!' she shouted.

I stood there and then, like her, noticed what looked like flakes of snow – but they also didn't really look like snow – floating down on top of us.

Tony caught up. Zain didn't really know what his sister was going on about.

'It ain't snow,' said Tony, in my ear. 'It's ash, from the fire.'

'What fire?'

'The daft buggers burnt down that police HQ.'

'Shit!'

'Yeah...'

'Look, Zain,' said Sonia. 'It's snow.'

And neither me nor Tony had the heart to say anything different.

2

After the we got back to the villa, I had the worst sleep ever, tossing and turning and lashing out at things that weren't there. There was no point trying to sleep, and I sat outside the villa in the cool of the early morning, going over and over in my head everything that had happened since Tony had arrived. With the whole buried alive thing, I knew I couldn't let things ride any more. The ball was firmly in my court and I had to hit back, hopefully right between the eyes of all the bastards who had been playing me, like I was some dumb-fuck-moron gangster who didn't have a brain!

So I had two or three breakfasts and then made everyone else eat breakfast. I then told Tony to take the kids out for the day, around the island or whatever. After that, I was on a mission, and the people I was going to see were going to start telling me what I needed to know.

First off, I focused on Mila, but she ignored my messages and calls, which meant I was outside her place, knocking on her front door. She didn't answer but I was pretty sure she was in her flat because that was as safe a place as anywhere. And, after all, she had an elephant gun.

Just when I thought I would have to jump over the wall and risk getting my balls blown off, she opened the door, pretending she was glad to see me. She was all dolled up and tossing her wig like it was her own hair.

'You know, if you come in, I'm not going to suck your cock.'

'I'm not here for that. Why didn't you answer my calls?'

'When the phone rings, it is a request. If I do not answer, I have not answered your request. It is nothing personal, you understand, but that is the way I manage my affairs.'

'Yeah, and if I pay someone for a service, they have to keep their side of the bargain.'

'I would not say that what we agreed was a bargain,' she said, stepping back from the door. 'However, you look like shit. I will make you some tea. It's proper tea by the way and not your milky English stew.'

I sat down in the front room. For someone who tried to be so glamorous, it was a plain room, like she didn't care about where she lived – she just wanted to be out and about.

Mila kept herself hidden in the kitchen as she boiled the water. I noticed she had the back door shut. She was afraid of something, and that had to be Schmidt.

'Where's that crazy gun of yours?' I shouted.

Mila didn't say anything.

Then, a couple of minutes later, she came back with the tea, without milk, in two clear glasses.

'This is how they drink it in Morocco,' she said. 'You can add plenty of sugar.'

I wasn't going to drink it.

'Do you like films?' I asked.

'Listen, Steven, whatever you think of me, I will not do porno. It disgusts me.'

I laughed.

Mila crossed her legs, like she was a proper lady who was above that kind of thing.

'No, I don't mean porno. Did you know there's a film set on the island out in the middle of nowhere?'

'Of course,' she said, putting her hand to her mouth as she yawned. 'They come here for nothing and tell us this is going to be the new Hollywood, and then they go and never come back again.'

'Yeah, well, I've been there, and yesterday they put me a coffin and left me to die.'

I watched carefully to see how Mila would react. She was cool as a cucumber, trying hard not to react.

'That sounds terrible, Steven. You are lucky to be alive.'

'Maybe,' I said, changing my mind a bit about the tea and taking a sip.

'How did you escape?'

'Well, that's the funny thing about it. I don't think they wanted to kill me because they left clues... clues that rhyme... so my mate Tony could find me. Do you know anyone who would do something like that?'

'Why would I know anyone like that!' she said, trying to be all offended.

'You know Schmidt.'

Mila rolled her eyes.

'Perhaps...'

'Yeah, have you seen him?'

175

'No.'

'Are you telling me the truth?'

'I do not need to lie, Steven. My life is worth more than a lie.'

'Are you telling me the truth?'

'Please, I do not know where he is,' she said, all defensive. 'He is… elusive.'

'He keeps you… he controls you.'

Mila screamed.

'Stop!' she shouted.

'Is he here?'

'No!'

'Then where is he?'

'I do not know,' she said, moving her hands in front of her like she was trying to wipe him away.

'Then who does?'

She moved her body from side to side, breathing deeply, calming herself down.

'I have told you before,' she said, sipping her tea. 'Schmidt is not a man; he is the diablo.'

'That doesn't help. I know you've seen him. I saw him that night, when the fireworks were going off in the presidential garden. He was there, below the cliffs.'

'There you go then,' she said, fidgeting. 'You have seen him and now you can find him.'

'I only saw something in the dark.'

'Then perhaps you did not see him.'

'But I think I did. This guy has a presence – you know when he's there, even if you can't see him. What was he doing there?'

'If it was him, I do not know why he was there.'

'So you're not working for him, helping him, passing on messages?'

'What messages? I cannot pass on messages. I am not a postman.'

'You don't have to be a postman to pass on messages.'

Her fidgeting got worse.

She knew I wasn't going away until I had something to go on.

'If I tell you…' she said, with a deep sign, 'you will not think worse of me?'

'No.'

She breathed in deeply. 'Vella.'

'Yeah, what about him?'

'Schmidt was there to see Vella.'

'But he could see Vella anytime. He doesn't need to sneak around a place like that.'

'He had a message for Vella, which is all I know.'

'OK… what was the message?'

'Medusa.'

'Is that it, one word?'

'I believe you know the meaning of the word.'

'He must have said more than that?'

Mila wanted to leave it there, but I wasn't going away.

'There was a price,' she said.

'You mean there was a price for the Medusa? He was trying to sell the Medusa to Vella?'

'I do not know,' she said, desperate to get out of saying any more.

'So, Vella was buying it for somebody?'

'Yes,' she said, waving her hands in the air.

'And did Schmidt sell it that night?'

'I have told you what I know,' said Mila, trying to remain calm.

'Who did he sell it to? Was it Grech?'

She didn't answer but raised her eyebrows.

Mila knew a lot more, and she probably knew where Schmidt was, but I didn't think I would get much else out of her without things going south.

'I cannot help you anymore,' she said. 'You will need to speak to Vella. He knows more than me, more than anybody. You can also ask for your restaurant back.'

It sounded like a good way for Mila to get out of the little spot she was in, but I was keen on talking to the rat-faced scumbag.

'You can catch him unawares,' she said. 'He does not like that because he always prefers to arrange the meeting. He likes to visit The Sapori, on his way home from work. He is a regular so I know he will be there by six o'clock. He likes to use the toilet, and I cannot think of anything more disgusting, but you English seem to go for that kind of thing.'

I looked at a small alarm clock ticking away on an empty shelf. I had a few hours to wait but I was going to leave Mila to think about things. I could do with a walk, and she wasn't going to go anywhere anytime soon because she looked like she was going to keep her door locked.

'Just remember,' I said, as I got up, 'you're a better-looking woman than most, so don't think your life is over just because you got involved with Schmidt.'

'Steven, if Schmidt were just another man it would not be a problem, but he is obsessed with the devil. He carries with him a book of damnation, *Dante's Divine Comedy*. Not only does he worship the book and the devil, but he also thinks he *is* the devil, and from what I know of him, I would not argue with that.'

'He is just a man. I've met plenty of devils and he is just another one, only he likes to perform and act. He wants you to think he is all powerful and has superpowers, but trust me, only Superman has that.'

Mila stood up, agitated, and put her face close to mine.

'Please,' she said, holding both my arms. 'I know you think you have seen all the horribleness in the world, but Schmidt is not normal. He is on another level, a level I have never seen in anyone else before. You must promise me, Steven, that when you find him, you walk away – do not run after him, do not chase him, but look and turn and go, for your own safety and the safety of all your friends and loved ones.'

'Don't worry,' I said, 'I know how to choose my battles.'

She didn't like that because I wasn't listening.

'OK,' she said, letting go. 'I hope you have superpowers too because otherwise you will die.'

'Well, that's the thing,' I said. 'He's had enough chances but for whatever reason, he doesn't want to see me dead.'

Mila snorted.

'If not you, then he will kill all of those you know, before he finishes you off. That is his torture, his sadism. He is worse than the Marquis de Sade.'

I was going to say there was nothing worse than fear, rather than the reality of the threat, but it sounded way too profound for me.

There wasn't much else I could do to help Mila out of the shit she was in – she would just have to face down the devil herself. But I could see it in her face that fate was not on her side, things had caught up with her, decisions she had made were probably going to be her undoing.

I thanked for the tea and said she was right – it was better without milk.

'When you see Vella,' she said, 'tell him he still owes me.'

'I'll bring back his wallet.'

'There's nothing in there,' she said, laughing.

'OK, I'll bring him back to apologise.'

'You will need a sack for a snake like that. But don't come back.'

'I will need to come back,' I said, letting her know I was not going to leave any loose ends.

'Fine,' she said, sitting back down, depressed it was not going to end for her.

I'd said enough.

I left her crying.

I fancied a walk down to the rocks and a look out to sea, before I got hold of Vella's balls and shoved them down his throat.

3

It was just another empty evening in The Sapori. I found a dark corner, to avoid anyone pointing at me after tripping off my head and waited for the serpent to show his face.

As I sat there, I started to boil. Vella's problem wasn't just going to be about the Medusa or how he was a double dealer on The Seashell. His major problem was that I just didn't like him. Then I got to thinking about Mila. What she didn't seem to get was how bad things were going to be for her if I find out she's been lying to me. She might be afraid of Schmidt, but she would be sorry thinking I was a saint compared to him. There were two diablos on this island, if it came to a boss fight, and I had a serious amount of motivation to bury Schmidt more than just six feet under.

As I took another sip of my Coke, I clocked Vella, looking like he preferred to be well below the radar. And, as Mila had said, he went straight for the gents. I gave it few minutes and then made my entrance.

Pissing Willy was drinking Vella's offering and jerking off. It seemed a shame to disturb their casual ecstasy, but such is life. I grabbed Vella by the collar, pushed in the back of his knees and dragged him into a cubicle. I could hear Willy screaming like a girl but I wasn't going to waste time apologising.

Poor old Vella didn't know what had hit him, as I rammed his head down the toilet bowl and gave it a full flush. He was trying to kick out so I grabbed his pants and yanked them so hard, even I thought it was painful. I suppose he didn't know who it was behind him, so I got up close to his ear and said, 'Where the fuck is it, you slimy little fucking cocksucker!'

Then, without giving him a chance to answer, I pushed his head down into the bowl and made him drink it.

I pulled his head back and he managed to say, 'Stop... stop... please... stop...'

As much as I hated him, it was going to be his lucky day.

I wasn't going to kill him, partly because I needed to know everything he knew and partly because I didn't want to get locked up for a real murder – just yet. Still, that didn't mean

181

I wasn't going to carry on being nasty. I stuck his head back down so all he could do was stare at the toilet bowl.

'Where is it?' I said, holding his head.

He mumbled something into the bowl, which sounded like an echo chamber.

'What was that?' I said, bringing him up for a little bit of fresh air.

'I don't have the deeds,' he said, whimpering away.

'Oh, don't worry about them. I mean the artefact, the Medusa. Who did Schmidt sell it to?'

'Please stop,' he said, crying like a baby. 'I cannot help you like this.'

'Wrong, Vella. The only way you can help me is with your head down where it belongs and you coughing up what I need to know.'

'Please, Steven, Mr Mason, you must understand, I am not a man who controls these things.'

'Well, I think I'll stick with the messenger boy for today, and that just happens to be you and not Schmidt.'

'You must understand my position,' he begged.

'I do, your position is right where I've put you. And you ain't going nowhere until you tell me what I need to know.'

'I am innocent!' he shouted.

'No, you're not, you useless fucking fanny fart!'

And I pushed his head back down and gave it another good flush.

Then, out of the side of my eye, I caught Pissing Willy looking in on all the commotion.

'Fuck off!' I told him.

'He hasn't paid me,' he said.

'Haven't you heard of invoicing.'

'Get real, Steven.'

I yanked Vella up so he was on his knees looking up at Pissing Willy.

'You need to pay your debts,' I said.

Vella was shaking, disorientated.

Pissing Willy reached down and pulled out Vella's wallet from his inside jacket pocket and removed all the cash.

'Right,' I said, 'now fuck off… so I can finish my private conversation.'

But Pissing Willy had a little piece of advice for Vella: 'If I were you, I would tell him the truth… oh… and that's the whole truth and nothing but the truth.' And then to me, he said, 'Sorry but I always wanted to say that.'

'Great,' I said. 'Now you've got that off your bucket list, Vella has something he would like to tell me, haven't you?'

Vella looked sorry for himself as Pissing Willy waved goodbye.

'Right,' I said, propping him up on the toilet seat. 'What have you got to tell me?'

'It's that bitch!' he said, spitting out all the toilet flush.

'What bitch?'

'That Mila… she's the one you need to talk to… she's the one you need to be doing this to – not me!'

'But I have talked to her and that's why I'm talking to you.'

'She has taken you in.'

'Yeah, why's that then?'

'Because it is her, or it, or whatever he/she thinks she is. It's her and Schmidt behind this.'

'How?'

He took a deep breath.

'You don't know much, do you,' he said, gulping enough air so he could start laughing at me.

That was it, I thought. I was being nice and all he does is laugh at me.

I slapped him.

Then I slapped him again.

He didn't seem to care.

So I grabbed his collar and was ready to flush his head down the toilet when he said, 'Please, enough... I will talk... but enough of this.'

'Then talk to me, Vella, and don't talk to me as if I'm a fucking idiot.'

I gave him a few seconds to pull himself together.

'She has you fooled,' he said. 'She has been going there, to the palace, asking for this, asking for that – impossible things.'

'You mean, she's been trying to sell the Medusa? Is that to Grech?'

He shrugged, so I guessed it was.

'How much did Grech pay?'

'He has paid is all I can say, but there is no value in that piece of crap.'

'The Medusa?'

'Yes, it is a useless piece of junk that has no value. It is made from plaster and clay, cooked in an oven – just like any other tourist trinket. Instead, you must think of the Medusa as the real messenger.'

'What does that mean?'

'A message is inscribed on the base of this so-called artefact. It is a code. It is the code that someone like Grech needs to purchase, and it is the code that has caused so much distrust, conspiracy, violence and murder.'

For once, I believed Vella.

'OK, so what is this code for?'

'Oh, it is not for treasure, or gold coins. No, it is a different type of commodity, one for this age, one which has greater value than precious metals or bank notes. It is access to information, data and knowledge of transactions.'

'What kind of transactions?'

'Financial.'

'So, you mean this code gives you access to financial information? Is this about all the land being bought up here on the island?'

'In part, but it is far greater.'

'Yeah, so how big is this information?'

Vella stretched out his hands like he had caught the biggest fish ever.

'All right, so how does this code work?'

'It is a password which gives you access to a server.'

'What's the address of the server?'

Vella didn't want to say, but he didn't have a lot of choice.

'It is very simple: Gorgon portal dot com, forward slash, dot login. Once you get into the server with the passcode, you will have all the information.'

'You mean, all the corruption?'

'If that is what you want to call it.'

'You mean, business that businessmen don't want anybody to know about. Is that why they had the journalist killed, Garibaldi, because they were scared Schmidt was going to sell it to him?'

'Schmidt was never going to sell such a golden nugget for the amount Garibaldi was prepared to pay,' said Vella, who used his hand to comb his toilet hair back. 'Once Schmidt knew what he had, things were always going to be negotiated at the highest level.'

'But Schmidt was meant to deliver it to me?'

'I believe that would be a matter for you and your client – your boss. Perhaps it was cash on delivery. Or perhaps Schmidt just took the money and thought he would make a little bit more from Garibaldi. Then he thought he could make even more and just keeps hiding from people like you, until he gets the maximum of what it is worth from everybody.'

There was some sense in what Vella said, but Schmidt hadn't exactly been hiding from me.

Then Vella stood up. I think he thought he had said enough.

'Now, you must punish that bitch you are so fond of,' he said. 'It is with her you will find the depth of the lies and the lying.'

Vella tried to push past me.

'Heh, not so fast,' I said, stepping in front of him. 'You need to get rid of that repossession order on The Seashell.'

'That,' he said smiling, 'is the least of your problems.'

'Yeah?'

'Goodnight,' he said, all cocky, as he tried to push past me.

Whatever… I let him go.

After all, he was right. I needed to get back to Mila, and I needed to get Mila to take me to see Schmidt.

4

It was proper dark outside by the time I got back to Mila's. There were no lights, but that didn't mean she wasn't in there. I snuck around the back and dropped in over the wall, all ninja-like. The glass in the back door had been broken. I could tell it was a professional job. I pushed the door open and let it creak on its hinges. I waited, not wanting to get my head bashed in.

Then I got the invitation.

'The doors open, Steven.'

It wasn't Mila.

Well, there was no point in pretending I wasn't there and so I walked in, still expecting to be jumped. In the half light, I could see the guy sitting where I'd been sitting.

Then I looked down.

Mila was all messed up lying on the floor.

'She's dead,' they said.

It was Spiteri.

I stayed where I was, looking at Mila. Her face was all mutilated and she'd had her guts ripped out of her.

'Don't tell me wild animals did that,' I said, noticing there were bits of that stupid elephant gun lying around.

'No, you may never get to be a detective, Steven, but I believe even you can conclude from the evidence that Mila has died from an unfortunate accident.'

I wasn't going to argue.

'So,' I said, 'were you just popping in for a blow job?'

'Mila is not to my tastes. However, I continue to carry out our inquires, not that I need to justify my actions to you.'

'True… but you just did.'

I couldn't see Spiteri's face in the dull light but I could sense he wasn't laughing.

'And can you explain why you are entering the scene of a crime like a professional criminal?'

'Well, I think you've answered that one yourself.'

'So, what type of crime were you intending to commit? I do not believe it was robbery because Mila has nothing of value.'

'Are you sure about that?'

Spiteri kept quiet for a good few seconds, then said, 'You should sit down, Steven. It is time to have a full and frank conversation.'

'Aren't you going to call the calvary?'

'All in good time,' he said.

'That's OK, I can listen standing up.'

I wasn't going to get cosy with Spiteri. I wanted to stay by the back door for a quick exit.

'Very well, I appreciate that what I am about to say to you may come as a shock, but I also believe that a man like you, with an acute natural intelligence, will not be overly surprised with what I must tell you.'

'Thanks, you're almost making me think I should use a big word, but I'll stick to the simple ones.'

'And that is?'

'Oh, eh… fuck you!'

'Proof then, Steven, that a leopard can never change its spots.'

'Yeah, well, depends on the environment.'

That shut Spiteri up for a few seconds, then he got back to telling me all the things he wanted to tell me.

'I believe it is in your interests not to run off before I have fully conveyed to you all that you need to know. I believe bad news should always come before… less bad news, so you can get over the surprises and assimilate the texture and nuances related to these issues.'

Here it comes, I thought.

'You will be charged tomorrow morning with the murders of Tommaso Garibaldi and Joseph Borg. In addition, there are charges relating to public disorder and three counts of illegal trespass.'

'Yeah,' I said, not really that surprised. 'And you're sure it's me who is the unhinged psycho and not some other guy?'

'Yes, to meet the interests of all our stakeholders, we have decided it will be you. And if you were just another ordinary citizen, I would concede that you would be entitled to feel these charges were to some extent… unjustified. But it is not the case, Steven, that you are just an ordinary person trying to mind your own business. In fact, it is your business which has led to this point in your life where accountability has caught up with you.'

'Well, I know my mum will be disappointed.'

'Forever the wit and sarcasm, which I do find to be an endearing quality, if also overtly obtuse.'

'Call it what you like but a leopard doesn't change its spots.'

'The plain fact is,' said Spiteri, sounding pissed, 'your time on this island is up.'

'You mean, this is just about showing me the door?'

'Yes, the door and the limited amount of time you have to find the exit.'

'Can I pack a suitcase?'

'Surely, your suitcase case is packed, seeing as you have the passports back in your possession?'

He had a point.

'And what about Schmidt?' I said, whilst calculating my options.

'Exactly!' said Spiteri, getting all excited. 'What to do about our German friend? I suspect the departed Mila was aiming at him and this has caused her to shuffle off this mortal coil.'

'Nicely put, for a health and safety issue.'

'Please, Steven, it would be easier if you sat down while I provide you with… the slightly less bad news.'

'No, you're all right, I've left enough DNA lying around here – you never know what people might think.'

'You do not have to touch her.'

I stood and stared.

'Fair enough, let us talk about Max Schmidt and our mutual interest.'

This sounded like a deal was coming my way, with no options.

'I am not sure how much you know and what you do not know. So, to save you explaining to me what you may or may not know, I will explain everything to you.'

'Listen,' I said, 'if you start with, once upon a time, and there is a happy ending, I'm all ears.'

'As you wish. Once upon a time, there was a man, who took it upon himself to extract all the information he could from his temporary employer and hide it away from everyone until he had the means to reveal it to the world. This man had good intentions because he believed that he would be able to expose all the corruption which underpins our vibrant global financial system. But, once word got out that he had such an asset, so it became rather toxic for him to be sitting and waiting for a solution to relieve him of this morally onerous task. And he was right to feel scared.

'Those people who were threatened by this highly confidential information, which I might add, he had effectively stolen, arranged by surreptitious methods to obtain the treasured passcode to the only server which could be unlocked, and the data decrypted and downloaded. This, I believe, is where the Medusa begins to play a role. Dressed up to be a rare artefact, it was to be etched with the passcode and to make its way back to the financial global hub in London, courtesy of the third-party arrangement, for which your boss – a grandfather or godfather I believe he is called – would ensure safe passage. However, the contractor believed the passcode was on its way to Garibaldi, such was the level of duplicity in this process. Unfortunately, the hiring of Max Schmidt as courier was the fatal mistake for all concerned.'

'You mean, he found out?'

'He did and liquidated the contractor.'

'I don't see that being a problem for the third party in London – they are going to be far more concerned that the Medusa was on its way to a nosey journalist.'

'True…'

'And I suppose there was information about Grech and all the property deals on the island?'

I could see Spiteri nod.

'So all you had to do was kill Garibaldi and Schmidt?'

'Not me personally, but we all have our paymasters and loyalties to contend with.'

'But Schmidt had sussed you out, and you've got Schmidt on the loose and he wants payback.'

Spiteri shrugged.

'And all that stuff with Mila and the Presidential Palace, that was her working for Schmidt to get the best price for the passcode?'

'A price worth paying. Everyone implicated in the treasure trove of data would benefit, including our own situation here and the need to contain a restless population.'

'But you're going to tell me that Schmidt hasn't been playing by the rules, or the way you guys like to write the rules, and he's taken the money, but you guys still don't have the Medusa?'

'If there are any rules in such matters, Schmidt is the one who likes to break them.'

'I think all he needs is some more customer service training, so I can get my parcel delivered.'

'Whether he delivers, or should I say communicates, the passcode to us or to London, I believe the outcome would have been mutually beneficial.'

'And do you think he's ever going to do that?'

'No, he will seek to trade it like a commodity but never deliver. It is fair to say we have all underestimated him and he is a person capable of anything. After all, Borg thought he would be better off dead, rather than be confronted by Schmidt with questions about the villa, the tenancy and the bomb.'

'Well, anyone would be pissed if you tried to blow them up.'

'The saying is to kill two birds with one stone.'

'Or one bomb.'

'Our constabulary training is second to none.'

'Nice… and I hope you know Borg killed himself then, even if you are going to charge me with his murder.'

'Eyes and ears, Steven, is our motto, which helps us determine the case.'

'Good to know justice is working. And I suppose it was you lot who gave me the rope to get me out of the cave?'

'No, that was Schmidt apparently. For some reason he wants to keep you alive, whilst at the same time feel you are close to death when six feet under. Perhaps he likes you.'

'Well, I don't like him.'

'Nobody does, Steven. We have had infrequent communications with Schmidt, some of which has been informative and entertaining, but mainly troublesome. Desperate times has meant risks taken, which have not paid off, and Schmidt is someone who has fooled us all.'

That's when the penny dropped. 'You want me to find him because he's ripped off Grech?'

'There is only so much murder that can be done by the forces of law and order. Now we must outsource. It would be in your interests – it will appease London and your boss, and it would certainly make all of us sleep far more easily in our beds. Which means you will escape from this island tonight because there will be international warrants out for your arrest in the morning. The quid pro quo is to utilise your skill set and your dysfunctional relationship with Schmidt – track and trace and liquidate him. If you do that, then all the charges will be dropped.'

'Listen, I would be more than happy to stick his head in a blender, but you can't expect me to just disappear overnight.'

'But we do, Steven. You will not be seeking the Medusa,

but just the man who carries with him a passcode which only he has – we hope. We need to see that passcode buried with the body.'

'Do you want me to send you pictures?'

'Eyes and ears, Steven. We will know when it is done.'

'But you do know I've never seen the guy?'

'True, which is why you can take those children with you. Was that not the deal, so they could identify Schmidt on the island?'

'Zammit…' I said under my breath.

'That's brothers for you, always falling in and out.'

'You must have some ID on Schmidt?'

'Not really…'

'But you know where he's gone?'

'He is on his way to the mainland via Sicily – a lovely place, especially at this time of the year. We believe he will seek to obtain another passport when he gets there, before he hops over to Italy proper. That will be your window of opportunity. We think you will have the connections and the ability to find out who does this type of work, and that is how you will trap him. And with the experience of the children who know Schmidt, I believe you will find him.'

'You must think these kids will sniff him out?'

'They have been very close to him.'

'What about this flat? Mila must have a photo of him?'

'Be my guest,' he said, 'but you are missing the point. It is the presence of the man, his aura, which will enable you to detect him. So, I would use what time you have left more wisely.'

'OK, OK…' I said, trying to get my head around what I had to do. 'Just tell me: why did Schmidt get involved with trafficking that family?'

'Money, maybe. He had no guarantee that anything would work in his favour once he got back. Always an opportunist, he must have thought it was an easy win, with little or no cost to himself.'

I looked down at Mila's fucked-up body, trying my hardest to think.

'I will leave you to get on with things,' said Spiteri standing up. 'He is on his way now, crossing the sea by boat. If we were to apprehend him, he will spill the beans all over the world. You, on the other hand, can prevent this from happening, intercept and exterminate, so to speak. Think of yourself as the back-door abortionist – an unofficial solution to a problem that everyone needs resolved.'

'Are you sure you can't use a proper nurse?'

'We believe in you, Steven. You are a man of many talents. If you survive, you should reflect on this. Perhaps then you will find the peace you are looking for.'

Spiteri headed to the front door and then stopped.

'Oh, and by the way, we have a saying on this island: if you don't like it here, there's always a boat in the morning.'

'To be honest with you, it would be nice to fly for once.'

Spiteri hesitated, then said, 'I understand Mrs Cini has a boat. Goodbye and good luck.'

5

Time was against me. I grabbed a taxi and got up to Cini's place. She had people round so I phoned her and got her to meet me outside her main gate.

It didn't look like she wanted to talk and then she just laid into me about the whole riot thing as if it was my fault. She said it gave Grech the excuse to use extra powers to keep a lid on things. It was a simple equation: the people who were raising questions about democracy and corruption had a radical agenda, and he was the one to bring peace and reconciliation. I laughed. Why would anyone believe him now any more than they ever did? Cini said I had a lot to learn about politics. Maybe I did, maybe I didn't, but I had some intel for her, if she was interested.

So I told her as much as I could about Garibaldi, Schmidt, the Medusa and the passcode, and the server with a stack of info on all the corruption, which would show what Grech and his buddies were up to. It turns out, I told her, that Schmidt was trying to get money from Garibaldi when the villa was blown up by the police. Plus, Schmidt had probably already been paid by my London connection and had screwed Grech over for a load more money. But the key thing was, nobody had managed to get hold of the Medusa, the bullshit artefact that had the passcode for the server etched on it.

'We knew from Garibaldi,' she said, looking back at her house to make sure no one came running over, 'that there had been some release of data from a file. Not much, just a taster, so Tommaso had said. He was part of a consortium of international journalists which shared this kind of information. But Tommaso couldn't wait. He wanted to use what he could to start exposing the corruption, and that's what got him noticed by everyone.'

'You mean, he should have waited?'

'You cannot tell a journalist like Tommaso to wait.

Whatever he had, he would run with it. Had he got access to the server he would have fed it all back to the consortium. He should have listened to wiser heads and waited, then he might be alive today. But the truth, Steven, is that the murder of Tommaso was not just about cutting off a link or a connection. It was to send a message. This kind of thing would have been sanctioned at the highest level, above the head of Grech, because so much global power and wealth would be implicated. And the message is a simple one: if the server is accessed and the information is released, there will be consequences.'

'Sounds like it's not worth it then.'

She didn't like that.

'Have you no moral compass? Is everything just about how you survive and make a living?'

'It is for most people.'

'Not if you are someone who knows better.'

'I thought I was just some nasty English gangster.'

'You are,' she said, turning away, ready to go back into her house and her guests.

'Hang on!'

She stopped but didn't look back at me.

'I can get the passcode for you,' I said, 'but I need a bit of help.'

She slowly turned around to face me again.

'I need a boat... your boat... to track down Schmidt.'

'Do you think I'm a fool, Steven? Lawyers talk, and on a small island like this, the few lawyers we have know everything there is to know about arrest warrants, trials, convictions and acquittals. In your case, there will be an international arrest warrant for murders you probably did not

197

commit. And in exchange, you will try to hunt down this Schmidt and eradicate the last remaining evidence of corruption and injustice. You do not need my help to save your own skin and help people who are powerful, greedy and corrupt.'

She had a point.

'Well, I ain't going to lie because the truth is, I don't know what I'm going to do when I find him. But you should know, I am trying to do some good. You see, there's these two kids, orphans really, and they're British and they need my help. They're going to come with me and I'm going to get them a better life because they deserve it. And if I don't do it, they're going to end up being left to rot, with no hope, just a number for some report that nobody reads because nobody really gives a shit.'

Cini smiled.

'See,' she said, 'I knew you had it in you. I know about the children. They should not be punished for what their parents did.'

If that's what it took, I thought, so be it.

'I will assume you know something about boats?' she asked.

'I know they float,' I said, with a cheeky grin.

'Steven, the Mediterranean is not a pond in the park. You need to be prepared for unpredictability, and it is the season for sudden, violent storms.'

She was right, but it was hardly going to stop me.

'How long does it take to get across to Sicily?'

'A day, but plan for a few days. The winds are notorious so you must be able to navigate. Are you sure you are capable? You could be sending these children to their deaths.'

'They know what that's like.'

'Death?'

'Yeah.'

'And they are now to benefit from your moral compass having turned slightly in the right direction?'

'Something like that.'

She didn't believe me of course.

'You will find my boat moored in the marina. It is easy to find because it is named after my husband.'

'Is it called Bob?'

'No, unsurprisingly, it is named after me and my husband: The Cini. Wait here and I will get the keys for the motor.'

'Have you ever sailed it across the Med?'

'Yes, but you cannot do it on your own, you will need help to sail her. Let me know if you make it and where it is landed.'

'And what about the passcode, do you want it?'

'I will leave that up to you. I understand that the world is not black and white and you will have choices to make. Perhaps a small miracle is the best you can hope for.'

'You think I need to pray?'

'If you don't, I will.'

'I'll take that.'

While Cini walked back up to the house to get the keys for me, I got straight onto the phone with Tony and then called a taxi. Cini came back, kissed me on the cheek and told me that responsible adults always put their children first.

'You do know they're not my kids?'

'Of course, but they don't know that.'

And then she left me.

If I had more time, I would have had another drink with her, a long conversation, and promised to make love and not just have sex. But time, like a few other things, wasn't on my side.

I waited at the crossroads, looking for a neon taxi banner blazing above the stone walls of the lanes. I wasn't sorry about leaving the island, after spending six months here, but the plan had been to stay low and off the radar for a good couple of years. It meant I couldn't go back home, even if I did manage to get myself out of the shit I was in. So, I gave myself a destination, once I'd handed over the kids in Berlin. I'd always fancied Amsterdam, for the culture.

I spotted the taxi, its yellow sign dipping up and down and then doing a sharp turn in front of me. I jumped in the back and told the guy to drop me off at the marina. I thought that was simple enough but the taxi wasn't moving.

So I had to check: 'You know the marina?'

'Yes, I know,' he said, looking at me in his rear-view mirror. 'Sorry, but I remember you.'

'Yeah well, trust me, I ain't famous and I ain't rich.'

'You were with that crazy Arab guy, Zammit. You had your family with you and you ran up the hill. He beat me, you know, for nothing.'

'Well, they've locked him up, if that helps.'

'He broke two ribs and he busted my face. Why? Because he thinks he owns the road, because he thinks he owns everything, when he owns nothing.'

What could I say?

'Do you know,' he said, which meant he was going to make sure I knew, 'I lost a week of money because of him. And what does he do? Does he come to see me in the hospital? Does he come to see me to say sorry? No, instead he takes my routes. That's what he does. You know, my friend, he is like all the other Arabs here… they have got big in their heads… they like to think that they are always right and we are always wrong. They cause hell all over the world because of this. Arabs are dirty scum. We need to think, get rid of the Arab and the world is a better place again. Amen.'

'Look,' I said, leaning into the front seat so I could see his ugly beaten-up face, 'you're not the first taxi driver to tell me that all we need to do is wipe out a chunk of people, but all I want is for you to get to the marina.'

I then gave him my grievous look.

That was enough for him.

'And on the way,' I said, leaning back, 'you must think only good things about people and believe silence is the way to inner peace. Amen.'

And if he said amen back to me again, I was going to punch him in the head. I didn't hear a squeak out of him for the next ten minutes.

'Right,' I said, as we drove through the old town, 'pull up outside in front of Crazy Prices. There's five hundred to help me load up and unload at the marina.'

He shrugged, like he didn't think he had a choice, and he was right.

The shop was open twenty-four seven, with different generations of one family keeping the shelves stacked, keeping the lights on and making up the crazy prices. Night-time was for the young brothers; early morning, the grandparents; and in the afternoons, the mum, the dad and the kids.

I shot straight to the back of the shop and pulled apart the plastic partition to the stockroom. There was loads of stuff sitting on the shelves.

I shouted out, 'I need the boxes of tinned tuna, the cans of baked beans, the bags of pasta, bottled water and those boxes of chocolate bars.'

The two brothers moved swiftly, as the amen taxi driver wandered in.

'Stick it in his cab,' I said, as I put a load of cash down and went back outside.

I crossed the road over to the other side of the street so I was looking across the bay at the old fortifications, all lit up for the tourists.

I had to phone my mum.

Her phone kept ringing but I wasn't giving up, as I watched the provisions being loaded.

Then she answered.

'It's me,' I said.

'What do you want, Steven?'

'I need a favour.'

'That's wrong, Steven. You can't be asking me for favours. You know you can't do that.'

I ignored her.

'I need your help. You need to let your family know I'm coming to see them. I've got a boat, The Cini. I'm leaving tomorrow and I'll be there in a day. Give them this number. And I'm bringing two kids with me.'

'What are you talking about, Steven? You don't have kids.'

'Well, I do now.'

'Don't be funny with me. You can't phone up out of the blue and expect favours that I can't give.'

'Look, I'm only asking.'

'Steven, they don't know you from Adam.'

'No, but you're not foreign to them – you're blood.'

'Don't talk to me about blood, Steven. You're lucky I'm even talking to you.'

'I know.'

I waited to see what she said.

'There's no guarantees,' she said.

'OK, and there's one other thing.'

'There shouldn't be another thing, Steven.'

I waited again.

'What is it?'

'Is Greg dead?'

'Why d'you ask?'

'Because I need to know.'

'Of course he's dead. You killed him.'

'Good, I just wanted to make sure.'

'Why wouldn't he be? Have you forgotten you killed your own brother?'

'No.'

'Then you'd better go, Steven, before I forget you're the only thing I've got left.'

'If that's how you want it…'

'It's not what I want, Steven, it's what has to be.'

It was my turn to say nothing, then I said, 'You know, with Greg, he gave me no choice.'

'Steven, it's done.'

If only…

'I've got to go,' I said.

'Steven…'

'What?'

'I won't tell him what you're up to if that helps.'

'You mean Grandad?'

'Yeah.'

'OK, thanks.'

'Stay safe.'

'Yeah, no problem…'

Half an hour later I was down by the marina.

It was a small inlet with a dozen or so boats and a couple of super yachts. The marina – if you could call it that – was surrounded on two sides by upmarket flats, topped off with a few penthouses. It wasn't exactly Monaco but neither was it Burnham-on-Crouch, which has a lot of boats going up and down a dirty old river.

I did my best to look like a casual deckhand. I found The Cini easy enough, a nice-looking forty-foot sailboat and a small motor for cruising. The rest of the boats were all quiet, like they'd gone into hibernation. I couldn't have asked for anything more really. The Cini was a better boat than the one I'd arrived in, having sneaked my way onto the island six months ago. There was a good-sized cabin, a couple of bunks, some provisions left over and a nice clean deck, for slipping and sliding on the sea water. The only thing that got me worried was all the modern navigation – I didn't have an effing clue! I pulled out a bunch of charts. I was starting to panic when I found a navigation that took a line across the sea and a port into Sicily. The port didn't matter, we just needed to be near the beach.

Well, if things went Pete Tong, there was always Google Maps or phone a friend.

Fuck it! I had a compass and a direction.

What could go wrong?

I got the amen taxi driver to earn the rest of his euros by loading the food boxes. I then told the amen taxi driver to eff off and keep his mouth shut and stood at the end of the marina as Tony and the kids turned up.

I thought Sonia and Zain would be grumpy, but Tony had done a good job in getting them ready. They were both excited because they were going to Germany.

I led them down to the boat and told them to sort themselves out in the cabin.

That left Tony standing on the marina.

'Do you know where you're going?' he said, like I didn't know what I was doing.

'Sicily,' I said.

'Yeah... and then what?'

'We'll see,' I said. Then I told him, 'And you're coming with me.'

'What?'

'Afraid so,' I said, knowing how much this was going to push Tony out of his comfort zone.

'You're kidding, mate. I can't go with you.'

'Look, Tony, I know you think you can't go with me because of Grandad and for a load of other reasons. But it's like this: I can't sail this boat on my own across the Med. And if I can't do this, then I go to jail, or I get a bomb shoved up my arse, and the kids end up with the authorities and pretty much what Grandad has invested here will be taken off him.'

'Hang on!' said Tony, putting his hand on his head hoping it would help him think. 'You said nothing to me about this on the phone, and I've got nothing with me.'

'I needed to tell you when you were here or else you wouldn't have come.'

'No, Steven, this ain't right. None of its right. This is like…'

'Emotional blackmail,' I said, so he knew that I knew I was guilty.

'Yeah, too effing right. You know, Steven, this is getting out of control. And it ain't just about me coming with yer. You ain't thinking about these kids, what you're doing with them.'

'Which is another reason for you to come with me.'

Tony took a step back, like he was checking over a dodgy second-hand car sale.

'It's a proper boat,' I said, 'but it needs at least two of us to sail. It will only take a day and then you can come back here and get Grandad up to speed with things.'

'It's Schmidt, isn't it?' he said, like he thought he'd worked me out. 'You're after that German bastard because he's been messing with your head.'

'No, Tony, I've told you everything – something that you haven't done.'

'What's that mean?'

'You know what I mean. We both know Grandad never does things straight. There are always angles, more to it, and this is just the way he operates. But it's survival time for me, for these kids, and it's a bit of a survival time for you.'

'Piss off! I've got a family, my own kids. I should just be doing messages.'

'Yeah but have you, Tony?'

'No way have I lied to you, mate.'

'I don't doubt it, Tony, but is that because you haven't had to lie to me yet?'

He breathed in deep. 'Jesus effing Christ!'

'I thought you'd you say that. Look, trust me, Tony, if I could get on a plane, a ferry, a bus, I would.'

'I can't swim,' said Tony, blurting it out.

'We're not swimming across the bloody ocean – that's what the boat is for.'

'Eff sake! I hear those seas are choppy out there. This ain't like a day trip to France.'

'Look, I'll teach you everything you need to know. You're a good learner aren't you. I thought you sounded like a Greek professor when you first got here – all that stuff you picked up off a video. It's just the same. Ten minutes and you'll be like Sir Francis fucking Drake.'

'Who's he?'

'Don't matter. The point is, there isn't a no in what I'm asking.'

Then from behind me, in the boat, was Sonia: 'Please…'

Tony put his hand to his face and rubbed his bristle.

'The kids want you,' I said. 'I want you. Can't you feel the love?'

'Is that what it is?'

'I love you,' said Sonia, like she meant it.

'There you go,' I said, jumping down onto the boat. 'That's what I call a no brainer.'

Tony shook his head.

'Listen,' he said, 'when I'm seasick, just stand in front of me.'

'Aye, aye, captain!'

And as Tony jumped down, both Sonia and Zain hugged him.

It was a relief for me.

I was taking a risk, a massive risk, but I didn't see how I had a choice, whatever Tony said.

Dust To Dust

1

Once we'd cast off and slipped out of the marina, I had Tony bed down the kids in the cabin. I sat the boat just outside the bay so it looked like we were floating tourists admiring the view of the island's fortifications.

Tony came back up top. He was happy with our little excursion and said that if the rest of the journey was as smooth as that, his stomach will stay close to where it is meant to be. As we rocked gently back and forth, I should have told him that out at sea, you go up and down a lot, unless you're on a fully loaded tanker. Instead, I told him to get a bit of shut eye before the sun came up.

I perched on the bow, doing a Titanic thing, pushing myself out over the railings, feeling the sea breeze and sticking my tongue out to taste the salt. It was a strange kind of freedom I had now – free and not free, just like most of my dreams, running to be free rather than having made it to freedom. I am always in transit, with a lead weight tied to my leg and a mission objective the SAS would struggle to achieve.

I wanted to sleep but the adrenaline was pumping around my body again. So I propped myself up against the front of the cabin and then spread out next to the mast. I looked all the way up the pole, the lines clanking against the metal, ringing out a rhythmic one-note tune. I knew the sea was like one vast watery desert. We would be trekking across a bottomless pit of fluid, which drains and drenches for laughs, pierces your skin like thin cuts of paper and smashes you over the head if it is feeling moody. It was like a psychotic relative who would lunge at you with the kitchen knife then give you treats as if nothing had happened.

The thing is, you didn't need to believe in God, but sometimes you needed to believe in the ocean gods – Poseidon – if you wanted to live through a storm. Perhaps the children of Medusa would prove a lucky omen or pull us down into the belly of the deepest trenches. But if it came to praying, I would be doing all things Greek to get us over to the other side of the sea.

After that thought, I must have dozed, before I felt the warm rays of the sun wake me. I had to get Tony and the little cherubs up sharpish because no way was I going to start the crossing without them knowing something about sailing and what they must do to make the boat go in the right direction. There were things that they would all need to do.

Somehow, I had to turn my little crew into sailors.

I grabbed hold of the bell by the wheel and gave it a good old tug. That got them up, Sonia first, then Tony, but no Zain.

Well, there was no point in giving little Zain the sailing lesson so I press-ganged the other two to stand in front of me on the deck. I was going to be a bit like the air steward on a plane, only it was about sailing and learning how not to die.

'Right, you have both had a bit of a sleep, I haven't had much but we're not doing the crossing until you have learnt what you need to do on this boat. I will teach you enough, so we can get through a day's sailing. And this is all about you doing a few things that helps me deal with the sea and the wind.'

Tony let one rip.

Sonia giggled.

'And what comes out of your arse, Tony, is not the kind of wind that is going to get us across the Med.'

'Fair enough,' he said, winking at Sonia.

'Right, so let's start with the basics. Behind you is a great big pole and that is called the mast, and the long pole attached to the bottom of the mast, which stretches across the boat, is called the boom. So, when we pull the sails up the mast to catch the wind, we use the boom to get the sails to trap the wind, to blow us along.'

'Simples,' said Tony.

'And underneath the boat is a fin, called a keel, to keep the boat steady, and another fin at the back here, which is used to turn the boat.'

'Where's the anchor?' asked Tony.

'That's at the front, also called the bow. I have dropped the anchor so we don't drift off, and if we lose the anchor, we can always use you, Tony.'

'I didn't have to come…'

'Wrong.'

'It's fun!' said Sonia.

'Good, because you are both going to have jobs to do.'

'Are you the captain?' she asked.

'Oh, he's the captain all right,' said Tony.

211

'That's right, and you know what happens to crew who don't do what they're told?'

'They walk the plank,' said Sonia, all excited.

'There you go, Tony.'

'Where is it?' he said, ready to jump ship.

'I'll wrap it around your head if you don't listen.'

'Is Uncle Tony being naughty?'

'Yes, very. Right, back to the wind – and I don't mean Tony's arse. We need the sails up to catch the wind or else we ain't going nowhere – we just sit here. Now, I don't want to get technical, but when the wind blows across the boat, we need to turn it to what's called the windward side. We need to get the sail looking like it's being pushed out and that will push us along. We also get a lift from the leeward side of the wind, but you don't have to worry about that as long as you, Tony, do what I tell you to do with the sails and the boom.'

Sonia stuck her hand up like she was back at school.

'What if the wind is going the wrong way?'

'Good question, Sonia,' I said, looking at Tony because he wasn't paying attention.

Tony saluted.

'We need to catch the wind first, and we do that by using the weathervane. You see that thing up there?'

I pointed.

'That will tell us where the wind is so we can catch it in the sail. It's only if there is no wind that we can't move, and then we drift. But most of the time, if we have caught the wind, we can always go forwards in the direction we want to go. But to do that we must keep moving the boom. You remember that don't you, Tony?'

'Yeah.'

'OK,' I said, ready to slap Tony for not listening. 'So, we use the ropes to get the sails in the right place. And that means we need the boom about forty-five degrees to the oncoming wind.'

'Fuck me!' said Tony. 'I didn't bring me protractor!'

'Don't worry, I will tell you what to do and when to do it.'

'Look, Steven, this don't sound so simple.'

'It is, once you get the hang of it. Just do what I tell you and we'll be all right.'

Tony shook his head.

'Now, Sonia, you are going to help me steer the boat. Would you like that?'

'Yes!'

'I thought you would. Behind you is the cockpit, a bit like an aeroplane, and there is the steering wheel.'

They both looked up to where the wheel was above the cabin door.

'That wheel turns the rudder at the back of the boat, but you can only turn the wheel once the boat is moving. I will show you what direction we need to keep going in because we never go in a straight line, we zig zag about.'

Sonia nodded, taking onboard her duties.

'Which means,' I said, looking back at Tony, 'that we need to be moving the boom so it catches that wind of yours...'

'I thought you said we didn't need my arse.'

'And what we will be doing a lot of is called tacking. And that's when you get hit on the head.'

Tony replied by letting another one rip.

'Because,' I said, 'that boom can come flying across the

213

boat as we tack. So when I say duck, don't look up thinking there's a bird in the sky. You need to duck down or else you will get knocked out cold.'

'I like that idea,' said Tony. 'Out cold for a whole week.'

'That's all right, Tony. When we do jibing, you will be knocked for six.'

'I thought we did tacking?'

'It's the same kind of thing, but riskier.'

'You know,' said Tony, looking up into the sky, 'all you effing birds up there don't know how effing lucky you are. Steven, there's a reason why we have legs and not fins, or wings, and I wish you'd thought this one out.'

'Shut up, Tony! You're pissing me off. I haven't had any sleep and you're sounding like a fucking old woman.'

Sonia looked a bit scared.

'Sorry,' I said.

'Heh,' said Tony, hugging Sonia, 'don't you worry. Uncle Tony is just getting his bearings and we'll be all right.'

'Are you sure?'

'Yeah…'

'Right,' I said, opening the benches until I found what I was looking for and pulled out the lifejackets.

'On deck,' I said, 'we wear these all the time. And we need to lather up because we'll get sandblasted by the wind and the sun.'

Sonia put her hand up again.

'Yeah?'

'How do we stop?' she asked.

'We move the sails out until they lose the wind.'

I could tell it didn't make sense to Sonia, or Tony, but I was tired of explaining.

214

'I need some shut eye,' I said, 'and then we need to do some practicing.'

I turned around and headed straight down into the cabin.

I had stashed all our supplies where I could and there were chocolate wrappers on the table, which must have been breakfast. Zain was lying on one of the bunk beds and sat up sharpish, so I smiled and put my arm around him.

'You all right, little man?'

He nodded.

'That's good. I've been talking to Uncle Tony and your sister about the jobs they need to do on the boat. Now, would you like to do something?'

He wasn't sure.

'OK, I tell you what, I'll tell you what I think you could do and then you let me know what you think.'

Not that I thought this would get him talking.

'This boat,' I said, 'is not like the one you went on with the Russian captain. This is a lot smaller and is a sailing boat. That means we can go a lot faster if we catch the wind. When me and Tony put the sails out it will feel like we're flying across the sea.'

Zain seemed to like what I was saying.

'But the thing is, me and Tony, and your sister, might be a bit busy with things up there on deck. So what I need is to have someone who can be a lookout.'

I don't think he knew what I meant.

'What you've got to do,' I said, putting my hand along the top of my head and pretending to be a scout, 'is to be looking at what's around in the sea, because what we don't want to be doing is crashing into any of those big ships that you were on. So when we're rocking on top of them waves, you just need to ring that bell to let us know you've seen something. And it can be anything, all right?'

Zain blinked and then nodded.

'I think that means yes for you, doesn't it?'

This time he did nod.

'OK, that's good.'

I stretched over to the other side of the cabin and rolled onto the bunk. I shut my eyes and then felt the warm body of Zain cuddle up next to me.

And for the first time in my life, I felt connected to somebody who I think deserved it.

2

I had Sonia on the wheel following the compass direction and the little man Zain keeping watch, and I had Tony on the lines, which was another word he hated because it meant the ropes. He had to pull on the lines to get the sail right, which I also told him was called a sheet. When I said he needed to get the mainsheet up, he started effing and blinding.

'Lock the mainsheet!' I shouted at Tony, as the sail pushed out with the wind inside it.

'How do I do that!' he shouted back at me, holding the lines in his hands.

'Use the cleat on the block!'

'Are you being dirty?'

'No! The cleat, on the pulley, it locks the mainsheet in place.'

We were picking up pace and Tony was looking at me like

his arms were going to be ripped off.

I jumped over and locked the line.

'I don't know what the eff you're talking about, mate,' he said, taking a rest.

'Listen,' I said, 'it's like the Army – you just take orders to make things work. Do, do and do. Don't think and it will work.'

'Yeah, and when were you in the Army? In fact, mate, when were you in the fucking navy?'

'Right,' I said, checking the wind direction and looking at the mainsheet. 'We need to trim.'

'That's not a haircut then?'

'No, Tony, it's fucking crash course so we can survive when we head out to sea.'

There was a lot of hate in Tony's eyes as I jumped up to Sonia and checked on our direction.

'Heh, that's good, Sonia. You all right with that wheel?'

She nodded, not wanting to speak because she was nicely focused.

'Zain, all good out there?'

He gave me the thumbs up.

'Tony, you need to let the mainsheet out. Let the wind push against the boom. Get it at forty-five degrees. We need the right point of sail.'

Tony looked at me to say he didn't know what the eff I was talking about again.

I jumped back down and let the boom swing out, feeling the wind pushing against my face.

'You see that,' I said to him. 'Forty-five degrees.'

'Listen, mate, I was shit at maths.'

'Yeah, well there's something else you're shit at.'

I got back up next to Sonia and we had good amount of sail, with the mainsheet out and the boat rocking along nicely. We kept this up for about ten minutes, following the coastline.

It was working… just.

'Hang on,' I said to Sonia, grabbing the wheel, 'we're going into the wind, the no-go.'

The sail collapsed, went luff and flapped in the wind.

'We're in irons,' I said to Tony, who didn't seem that bothered about the mainsheet. 'Heh! We lost the angle.'

'What angle?'

'Forty-five degrees.'

Tony shrugged, like he had given up.

'Come on,' I said to him, getting down by his side. 'We managed a bit of sailing, which was close-hauled and we didn't tip over.'

'Look, mate,' said Tony. 'I don't know where you got all this sailing lingo from but it's doing my head in. All I know is left and right, ropes and bedsheets. That's me, and all this other stuff is confusing dot com.'

'Tony,' I said, releasing the cleat and pulling on the line, 'it's half a dozen words, that's all. I'll let the mainsheet out and then we can trim. Just watch me.'

Tony sat down on a bench and I shouted to Sonia to keep it on the wheel in the same direction.

'Right,' I said to Tony, 'I'm letting the mainsheet out so it's starting to flutter… flap about a bit. Now I'm going to trim so we get a nice fat bubble in the sail. Now, I'm going to bring it back in again until it stops.'

I pulled and eased on the line as we began to pick up wind and speed.

'Now,' I said, 'we're sailing into the wind again, kind of, but if the wind was behind us, that's called running, but it could make us all feel a bit seasick.'

'I feel queasy already, mate.'

'Christ, Tony!'

'It's you who wanted me.'

'No,' said Sonia, who looked down on the struggling Tony. 'I asked you.'

'For eff sake, that's all I need, two bloody captains given me jip.'

'Tony... focus...' I said, 'and try and forget about the up and down. There's one more thing I need to show you and then we can practise for the rest of the day, before we set off.'

'OK,' said Tony, who wasn't interested.

'Tacking,' I said. 'It's making sure we catch the wind because the wind moves about and we must catch it with the sails. And if you don't watch and listen, you're going to get your head chopped off by the boom as it swings around.'

'Mate, I like that idea.'

I ignored him.

'So, when we hit a no-go zone, the sail has gone, no wind, and we need to tack, windward side to leeward side, left and right, right and left kind of thing.'

Tony put his thumbs up.

'So, here, I'm going to tack.'

I also shouted to Zain to keep his head down. The sail fluttered and the boom rattled its way towards the centre of the boat. The wind then caught the mainsheet and I checked the sail trim. I jumped up to the wheel and gave Sonia a new course.

'There you go, Tony,' I said, looking at a man who had

219

decided life was too difficult. 'That's all we need to do for the rest of the day. Practise this and then we head out.'

'I ain't moving,' said Tony.

I looked at him as if he were effing useless.

I let the mainsheet luff and the boat slow.

'Heh, kids,' I said, as I sat next to Tony. 'Why don't you make us a bit of food?'

'Chocolate and pasta!' said Sonia, all excited, as she helped Zain down from his little perch on the top deck.

'Sounds good,' I said.

The kids dropped down into the cabin and as soon as they were gone, Tony piped up. 'This ain't going to work.'

'Well, you ain't helping,' I said. 'And as I told you, we haven't got a choice.'

'Are you sure about that?'

'Yeah, I'm dead effing sure. This is the only way.'

'I don't get it,' said Tony, who slid himself away from me on the bench. 'Why not just get on some ferry and you'd be across the water in half a day? Leave the kids with me. I'll look after them and I'll look after things for Grandad. You chase this Schmidt guy down and sort it all out.'

'Look, I told you what's happening and this is the way we're going to do it. You know, I can do it with you or without you now. I've got the kids believing in me and that's enough to get across.'

Tony started shaking his head.

'What is it, Tony? There's something going on and you ain't telling me.'

'Yeah, well, it's what you said last night, and it's been preying on me mind.'

'Is it about Grandad, because if you're going to tell me

he's trying to fuck me over, that ain't no surprise.'

'I dunno, Steven. I mean, he's your real dad and all, but you two have got some weird thing going on.'

'That means you know something. What is it?'

'All right, I'm gonna tell yer, to set things straight, before we go on this mad effing journey.'

'I'm all ears, Tony.'

'Right…'

'And?'

'The Medusa…'

'Yeah?'

'It ain't legit.'

'I know that.'

'I mean, it's a pile of crap.'

'I know that.'

'Yeah, well, there's something I didn't tell yer.'

'And?'

'I knew it was not the Medusa that meant anything, money wise. It was what was meant to be on it, the passcode.'

'Yeah, and I know about that.'

'I know you know.'

'So, Tony, are you just trying to tell me what we both know?'

'No, there's another bit.'

'What's that?'

'I knew about the whole thing, right from the start. Grandad told me. He said he'd been given money by some bankers in the city – like, a lot of money. They didn't want the passcode flying around the place all electronic. They thought if it was in the ether, it would be easy to hack.'

'So they went back to basics?'

221

'Yeah, right back, not even paper, just a few scratches on a bit of plaster of Paris – the Medusa. Anyway, that's what this contractor guy thought he was doing – getting his stolen data out to that journalist – when all along he was being fooled by Grandad. And this German fuck, Schmidt, all he was meant to do was pick it up and bring it back to you and the journo would never have seen the Medusa. Then I'd take it home and end of.'

'But why not get Schmidt to just memorise the code?'

'I wish. I suppose the risk is, Schmidt keeps it and trades it on the market.'

'Which is what has happened anyway.'

'Well, yeah, but you know what Grandad's like, he's got to see things physical, doesn't trust nobody.'

I breathed in, deep.

'To be honest with you, Tony, it's good to hear it from you, but that's nothing I didn't really already know.'

'Well, I just wanted to get it all off my chest,' he said, 'before we go on this effing journey, you know, just in case anything happens. I want things to be straight between us because it's going to be about trust, ain't it?'

'Yeah, you're right there.'

'So, do you trust me now?'

'I always did, Tony, even if you didn't tell me everything. It's Schmidt that's done the damage.'

'Yeah, he's the spanner in the works.'

'And he's got the Medusa, and he's got a shed load of cash.'

'So, do you think you've got a chance of finding him?'

'Maybe… I don't know. One step at a time.'

'Good way to think.'

Tony looked a bit better but there was still something eating away at him.

So, I had to ask. 'What is it, Tony?'

'I'm not a coward,' he said, as if I had hurt his pride.

'Yeah, I know that.'

'It's just… I've got a funny feeling.'

'In your elbow?'

'No, mate, here, in me stomach.'

'You're seasick?'

'No, I mean about things… I want you to promise, if anything goes wrong, that you see the wife and kids are all right.'

'Tony, we're only crossing the Med, we're not sailing around the effing world.'

'I want you to promise.'

I looked at Tony.

For the first time, I had to respect that he was serious.

'OK,' I said. 'I promise that I will look after your family if you…'

'Don't make it.'

'Yeah…'

There was a bang.

It was the cabin door sliding open and up popped Sonia with Zain behind her.

Good timing, I thought to myself.

They were both holding plates.

'We've made lunch,' she said.

'Yeah, what you made then?'

'Pasta and chocolate!'

We both looked at the plates.

Underneath a pile of chocolate chunks was a small

223

mountain of dried pasta.

'Good job!' said Tony, who said the right thing.

Well, I thought to myself, if the sea doesn't do some damage, there was a good chance dried pasta and chocolate will have us all puking.

We spent the rest of the day going up and down along the coastline, getting a lot of things wrong and a few things right. We were all knackered: Tony pulling on the lines, tacking and mainly close-hauling; Sonia holding the wheel; Zain falling asleep on watch; and me running around on deck, giving orders every ten seconds. I was Captain Pain-in-the-arse but I was happy with how things had gone. And by the time we dropped anchor, I felt sure we could now sail.

As we all sat together in the stern, I explained again there was the bow, which meant the front of the boat, starboard, which meant the right, and port, which meant the left side.

Tony told me to give it a rest.

I was just trying to sound as technical as I could to make everyone think I knew what I was doing. But there were big gaps in some of my sailing knowledge. I was just going to have to hope the ocean gods would smile on me if we got into any kind of trouble.

The lights in the harbour and the bay area of the island looked back at us. You could just make out the old fortifications, the car lights moving like little bees and the tourist hotels shining light down on the ripples of the sea. As we rocked gently on the surface, it was quiet and breezy and our last chance to look at land before we hit the waves. Perhaps that was what made us all keep our thoughts to ourselves, saying nothing to each other because there wasn't anything to say.

First thing in the morning, we were sailing, but even I was surprised how rough it turned out to be, and that was with little or no wind. However, the routines I had drilled into them the day before meant we could handle it. And I wasn't getting any more jip from Tony, which helped. I did have to take over the wheel from Sonia – it got too heavy for her to turn. She went and sat with Zain and loved it up top. They would point at something, like a boat or cargo ship, wave their hands about, and we would tack, zigzag and avoid an effing disaster.

With the sea spray, the wind and the sun, it kind of made you feel alive. It was blood pumping stuff, skipping across the crest of a wave, dipping down and back up again. The curly sea was like going out with a wild party animal – you just hoped you'd come out of the evening in one piece, without too much damage and shame. But I think Tony was the kind of guy who would have wanted to have stayed at home gaming. He hated every splash of water, foam and salt on his face and body.

The sky was almost sky blue, only thin wisps of white cloud, and Sonia and Zain got obsessed with pointing at every sea bird when it flew over. But it was good for them, with a load of sunlight on their faces. It was like life had been breathed back into them. From the belly of sadness, they had come up for air and caught the chance that maybe there really was something better. Maybe it doesn't have to be all faith, war, fear and guns. Maybe they might get to be like kids again.

There wasn't much not to like really about sailing The Cini for all she was worth, after all the craziness of the last few weeks. I didn't want to think too much about Mila, Vella, Grech, Borg, Zammit or even Cini – they were history. But I couldn't get Schmidt out of mind. Tony was right, he had got under my skin. There was not much I couldn't deal with, but one way or another, Schmidt did seem on another level – a guy who was way off the Richter scale. I always thought there had to be a reason for why people did things, however bad it was, but Schmidt seemed to be on some crazy trip, which was all about torment, torture and power.

For the rest of the morning, the sea rocked us up and down, sliding us along. I was doing my best on the navigation chart but I was also guessing. I was happier being on the wheel, sailing at about five or six knots, with the air always full of salt.

Later in the day, we had the wind behind us. We were running but it was not something I was keen on, not with my little crew and Tony about as bright as a rusty spark plug. The mainsheet was out at ninety degrees and the wind and the waves were turning the boat from side to side. Sonia and Zain were moaning about upset tummy, so I told them to get down below and lie on the bunks.

Tony, on the other hand, was doing all right. However, what you should never do is tell someone that they are doing good job because as soon as you say that, they don't do a good job.

I was at the wheel and felt the wind shift a bit, but I wasn't too sure if we needed to tack. Then I saw the sail catch the leeward side of the wind. I knew what was likely to happen, as I saw the boom swing across the cockpit.

'Duck!' I shouted at Tony.

'What?'

Too effing late.

It hit Tony right between the eyes.

'Jesus!' I said, as I let the mainsheet luff.

He was lucky it didn't knock him overboard, but he was out cold.

I dragged him down and checked his pulse.

He was still breathing.

I did my first aid routine.

'Tony!' I shouted. 'Tony! You useless effing turd. Come on, you ain't dead!'

I slapped him.

That felt better – for me, that is.

'Come on, Tony, you need to wake up!'

There was a stirring, like a great big fat hippo who had spent way too long in the swamp.

'You took a whack.'

'Eh! From you… you mean…' he managed to say.

'Well, Tony, when I say duck, you're meant to look down, not up.'

'What hit me?'

'The boom,' I said, without telling him I should have noticed it a bit earlier.

'Christ, my head,' he said, putting his hand to his forehead.

I heard the cabin door open and Sonia poked her head out.

'He's all right,' I said, just in case she burst into tears and thought the wrong thing.

She jumped over to Tony.

'Heh! Not on top of me,' he said.

'He got hit by the boom. So watch the boom,' I said to Sonia.

'Are you dead?' she asked.

'No, he's not dead,' I said, jumping up to the wheel to check on the course and what was ahead.

'I feel dead,' said Tony.

Then it was Zain's turn to take a butcher's.

'Uncle Tony got hit on the head,' said Sonia to Zain, who looked just as worried. 'But he's not dead.'

'OK, enough with the dead thing,' I said, pointing at Sonia to take the wheel.

'Christ,' said Tony, 'I think I'm concussed.'

'How many fingers?'

Tony thought about it.

'Two.'

'OK, you're concussed,' I said.

Zain smiled at him.

I cursed.

We were going to lose the rest of the day's sailing because Tony was away with the fairies.

By the evening, and once he had eaten a load of dry pasta and chocolate, he looked a lot more with it.

We all sat outside, gently rocking, when Sonia asked Tony for a story before they went to bed.

Now this, I had to hear.

'OK,' he said, clearing his throat. 'Once upon a time there was a girl in a red dress and a red hoodie. She lived with her mum and every Sunday she would go with her mummy to visit her granny, who lived on the other side of the park.

However, this Sunday, when she was meant to go to visit her granny, her mummy wasn't feeling too good. But Red Riding Hood, that was her name, still wanted to go there because she had baked some cookies and they were yummy. So her mum said she could go, if she stuck to the path and was back before it got dark. So off went Little Red Riding Hood through the park, with a basket full of chocolate cookies for her granny.'

Tony stopped because Sonia's hand had shot up like she was back at school.

'Did the cookies have brown chocolate in them or white chocolate?'

'Brown,' said Tony. 'What do you like then, brown or white chocolate?'

'Brown, I haven't had white chocolate.'

'OK, so yeah, that's the best chocolate for cookies, and she knew Granny would really like them. So she was like, out the house…'

'Was it a big house?'

'No, a small house because it was only her and her mum. So, anyway, off she goes, across the park, sticking to the path like her mum told her to.'

Sonia stuck her hand up again.

'Did the park have swings?'

'Yeah, the park had swings and a roundabout.'

'And did she go on them?'

'Eh, yeah she did, and that's where she met the wolf.'

'The wolf?'

'Yeah, the wolf.'

'What's a wolf?'

'A wolf… a wolf is like a great big dog that lives in the forest.'

'Why is there a wolf in the park?'

'It's looking for some dinner!'

'Is the wolf hungry?'

'Yes, very, and that's why he would like to eat up Little Red Riding Hood.'

'Oh, why doesn't she give him the cookies?'

'Because the cookies are for Granny.'

'Oh…'

I laughed at Tony.

'I tell you what, kids, Uncle Tony might need to lie down.'

'Does your head hurt?' asked Sonia.

'Yeah,' said Tony, who knew what kids were like, but was struggling.

Tony promised to finish the story later and I let him and my little crew sleep the rest of the night whilst I kept watch on a calm and cool, breezy night. I was shattered by the end of it and left my crew on the top deck as the sun rose, then crashed out, desperate for some sleep.

I think it was well into the morning when I got up and saw the sailing gods had felt sorry for me and at last decided to give me a bit of a hand. There was Tony, controlling the lines, Sonia at the wheel and Zain in sunglasses doing lookout, with The Cini cutting through the waves like nobody's business. They all looked chuffed with themselves. And for the first time since we had left the bay area, I put my feet up.

Miracles can happen, I thought to myself, as I lay back, put my hands behind my head and felt the sun soak in and warm my body. Five minutes later, I felt the warm body of Zain next me.

I opened one eye.

'Aren't you meant to be keeping a lookout?' I said, as I

watched his little head.

He shrugged.

'Well, if we crash into some great big container, then I'll know who to blame.'

He gave me that half-smile, the half-smile that meant he knew what I was saying, but he didn't see how he was going to solve it. Yeah, there's nothing like feeling cosy and safe, something that the poor kid probably craved. I still didn't know why he didn't talk, but I guessed it was to do with all the trauma: guns, bombs, war and all the shit that comes with it. All I ever did was run away from my old man and my big brother so I didn't get too much of a beating. With my eyes shut, I could almost hear those grasses again I used to hide in, down by the river. I remember crying, feeling lonely, feeling like the world was a bad and evil place, wishing one of them children's stories could be true and I would end up being looked after, living on some sugar mountain with sweets for breakfast, lunch and dinner.

If only the kid could talk. But perhaps he doesn't need to say anything. It was all there, written on his face – the wide, scared rabbit eyes full of shock and confusion. And the worst thing about it, I wasn't even sure if I was supposed to care. I was a gangster, a villain, not a bleeding refugee worker. I wasn't here to save the effing children; I was here to save my own effing skin. Sure, thinking about it, I cared. If I could do something for them I would. But as Tony would say, was I doing any of this for myself or for them? The only good answer, I think, was a bit of both.

I carried on hugging little old Zain and soon regretted having done all that relaxing and laying in the sun. I was like a red balloon because I'd forgot to lather up. And Tony didn't help by just laughing and calling me Captain Baboon Arse. The only thing that kept my mind off the sunburn was getting back to sailing.

I was beginning to think that we were doing all right getting across the Med. We'd kept away from all the big ships, waved at the odd ferry and a few other yachts, and the weather had been good to us. Only now and then had the waves whipped up a bit and made our stomachs churn. Touchwood, and I really didn't want to say it, but things were going way better than I ever thought they would because, hand on heart, I thought we'd end up being bottom feeders.

I was standing at the wheel, helping Sonia keep us on track, watching Tony leaning back on the rails and at last enjoying the sea spray soak his body, and Zain was up top like a little crow's nest.

Then Zain started jumping up and down and was pointing. There were no boats, but he carried on pointing.

Then Sonia shouted, 'Look, dolphins!'

Tony eased himself off the rails.

'That's unusual,' he said, as he stood with me and Sonia.

'What do you mean?' I said, as we watched the fins of the pod dip in and out, as if they were following us.

'There ain't meant to be dolphins around in the Med.'

'And how do you know?'

'I watched a video.'

'Really?'

'Yeah, mate, you should know by now, there's a lot you can learn from videos.'

4

I was keeping quiet but I was beginning to shit myself. A trip that should have only taken us a day had bled into two days now. It meant we were either seriously off course, or we hadn't been too good with the sailing or made the best use of the wind. But based on the time being out at sea, I was pretty sure we weren't too far from the coastline. Also, I'd had a message from Sicily saying they were tracking me – not bad for a bunch of wine and olive growers!

I stayed at the wheel while I let the others get some shut eye. It was getting dark and the wind had dropped to almost nothing. There was a strange peace to the night. For whatever reason, it didn't feel right. The clouds above my head were thick and there was hardly any light from the moon and the stars. I was getting twitchy, drifting like we were.

My plan had always been to get as close to the coastline as we could – use the motor, drop anchor, with a little swim to the beach. But my navigation was proving to be piss-poor, and there was no coastline where I thought it was meant to be. That's the problem, when you think all you need to do is keep the boat in a straight line and eventually you'll hit something. But that something could be a great big beast of a ship.

That's when Tony poked his head out of the cabin.

'You all right, mate?'

'Yeah,' I said, keeping my eyes front and centre.

Tony jumped up into the cockpit and stood beside me on the wheel.

'A bit dark out there,' he said.

'Yeah…'

'You look spooked,' he said.

'Yeah…' was all I could say, because I was, but I didn't know why.

'I don't suppose you know where we are then?'

'In the sea,' I said.

'Does that mean we're lost?'

I didn't say anything.

'Don't these boats have satnav?'

'This one has got charts,' I said, lying. 'But the thing is, Tony, I'm not sure where we are.'

'Well, are we going forwards or backwards?'

'I reckon we might be going round and round in circles.'

'Eff sake! You said it would take a day. Then you make out you're sailor of the effing year, with all this tick-tick tock-tock bullshit, but what you're really telling me is you don't know shit about where we are!'

'Listen, I taught you to sail, that's not BS.'

'We're drifting around in circles lost at sea!'

'Not lost, just looking… for the coastline.'

'What if we bump into something?'

I didn't say anything, probably because that was what I was getting spooked about. Plus I needed Tony to be quiet – I needed to listen. I just knew there was something out there. I could feel it, almost hear it. It wasn't moving, no motor, perhaps not even a ship.

'Use the spotlight,' I said to Tony. 'Shine it over there… starboard.'

'That's left, isn't it?'

'No, right side.'

Tony cursed.

Seven out of ten for trying.

He turned the spotlight on, straight into my eyes.

'For fuck's sake!'

I couldn't see a damn thing, and Tony was spraying the light around like some effing lightshow.

'Keep it in the water,' I said, blind as a bat.

'Like this?'

'Is it in the water?'

'Yeah, it's in the water.'

'Right, keep it low, on the sea.'

'What's the difference between sea and water?'

'One you drink and the other you sail on.'

I turned to starboard. I had the bulb of the spotlight still imprinted on my optics but I started scanning.

'There ain't nothing,' said Tony, who was keeping the light moving.

'We need to be quiet,' I said.

'I don't hear nothing.'

'That's because you're not quiet.'

Tony went quiet.

We watched and waited.

There was the sound of the sea, lapping against the side of the boat. Then we both heard something odd, like the sound of metal being hit. Tony was about to spray the spotlight but I told him to hold it where it was, pointing into the sea.

'And keep quiet,' I said.

We listened again. There was nothing for a bit and then we heard the clanking of the metal again.

Tony whispered, 'What do you think?'

'Just listen… it sounds like a pipe being hit.'

235

Again, we heard nothing for a bit, and then there was the metal pipe sound.

'Do you think it's a plumber?' said Tony.

'Well, if it is,' I said, 'we know where all the water is.'

Tony was going to laugh when the sound of the clanking metal pipework cut through to us again.

'There's got to be someone out there,' said Tony.

'No kidding...'

'And it ain't Mario.'

'Turn the light off.'

The spotlight went and the deck went dark.

I think we could both feel it, the presence of something. Then the metal pipe went *clank*. It was closer. Then another *clank*. It was there; whatever it was, we could feel it, like whoever was hitting the pipework was right next to us. And that's when we saw the weirdest, strangest thing run along the side of us.

At first there were eyes, bright, wide, popping-out eyes, loads of them, and all human, all staring and looking back at us. And the eyes looked like they were piled on top of each other. Then we could both see what looked like the side of a small cargo ship. There were people everywhere. Wherever we looked, there were people hanging on to things, so that the side of the ship was just a mass of people. And the people were made up of black faces, arms, chests and legs, all holding on to every bit of space there was on the ship. And there were not just men, but women and children.

Then the cogs started to move. A ship like that shouldn't be drifting – it would have a large propellor. Had it broken down? And a ship like that shouldn't be overloaded. And where was the captain and crew? And I kept saying to myself:

236

why are they all like that, just staring at us?

Then the penny dropped.

They'd been abandoned.

And as that thought came rushing to front of my head, I saw a guy try to reach across and grab the side of our boat.

'Tony!' I shouted, as I turned the ignition to start the engine.

'What the…'

He was dazed, trying to work things out.

'Push them back!'

The effing engine wasn't starting.

'You what?'

'I said, push them back!'

I could see other hands trying to reach out.

There was no way we could do it.

There was no way we could help.

Effing engine!

'Tony! Smash their fucking hands!'

'Are you crazy?'

'Tony! We can't help! Do it!'

There was a hand just below me.

I stamped on it.

There was a scream, and then all the silence broke. It was like a load of birds had woken up and were squawking at the same time. All the people on the boat knew what they had to do to survive – they needed to get off their own boat and onto The Cini.

I tried the ignition again.

Thank fuck…

As the engine started, I could hear people jumping into the sea.

'Tony!'

He got the message. He didn't like it, but he'd got the message.

I didn't waste time looking back. I pulled the boat sharp, portside, desperate to get away from desperate people. As I turned around to see how Tony was doing, I couldn't see any more hands but there were still people, men, jumping off the cargo ship. They weren't going to make it, not to The Cini, and not back onto the boat they'd come from.

I steered, keeping The Cini on a difficult turn. Then Tony was back up beside me. He was looking at me like I was Hannibal Lecter. There was no point in saying anything. If he didn't get it then he was a dumbass.

'Check the bow, will yer,' I said.

'For what?'

'Mermaids…'

'At least they can swim.'

I didn't give a shit. I kept the angle of the turn and looked behind me.

The faces were gone.

I straightened up the boat.

I shouted again. 'Tony!'

Nothing.

'Fuck!'

I turned on the spotlight and pointed it towards the bow.

Tony was being held in a headlock, with this big guy looking back at me.

I needed a weapon.

I looked around and grabbed a torchlight. There was only one way to deal with this type of thing.

I pulled myself along the side of the boat. The big guy was

238

trying to back off, but there was nowhere for him to go. Within a few seconds, I was right in front of him. I smiled so he didn't know what to think. Then I whacked him across the head.

He was stunned. He lost his hold and Tony dropped. The guy was wobbling, but not enough for me. I hit him again, hard as I could on the side of his head, and he fell forward on top of Tony.

The torch was busted so I threw it into the sea.

'You all right down there,' I said to Tony, checking the big guy's pulse.

'Will you get this fucker off me!'

'I dunno, I think you make a nice couple.'

'Is that supposed to be funny?'

'Yeah.'

I rolled the guy off him.

'Come on,' I said, 'let's tie him up.'

'Why don't we just drown him,' said Tony, who was being all moral with me.

'If that's what you want.'

'I thought that's what you wanted.'

'For fuck's sake, Tony, you're turning into right effing Mother Theresa.'

He said nothing as he pulled himself up.

He went silent on me as we dragged the big guy and dropped him down onto the deck.

That's when Sonia poked her head out of the cabin door. She couldn't work it out.

'Don't worry,' I said, 'Uncle Tony went fishing and look what he caught.'

I think she was going to tell us that the big guy was not a

239

fish, when Tony said, 'We found him in the sea.'

Sonia was still thinking about it as I tied the big guy's wrists behind his back and then propped him up so he was like an oversized teddy bear sitting on his bottom.

'Don't touch,' I said, as Sonia got up close to him.

'Is he asleep?'

'Yeah, he must have been swimming a lot. That makes you tired.'

'Does he like chocolate?'

'Yeah, everyone likes chocolate.'

'Shall I get him some?'

'Later, maybe, but I think we'll let him sleep for a bit.'

Sonia carried on staring at him.

Then I looked around for Tony. He'd gone.

Weird.

I jumped up by the wheel.

He was out on the bow, sticking his tongue out.

'What's up?' I shouted.

He stayed there as I noticed his shirt catching the wind, like a strong breeze had just come from nowhere.

Sailing time, I thought to myself.

Tony wedged his way back along the railings.

He was looking confused.

'What?'

'There's something up,' he said.

'There's nothing wrong with the wind,' I said. 'We need it.'

'It's not that.'

'What then?'

I heard Sonia shout something.

I turned around and she was sticking her tongue out.

240

'It's dust,' she said, licking her hands.

'No, mate,' said Tony, in my ear. 'It's sand.'

'That's good,' I said. 'It must mean we're near the beach.'

Then Tony looked at me the way I'd been looking at him for the last couple of days.

It meant he knew something wasn't right.

And we were about to find out what was coming our way.

5

'It's a sandstorm,' said Tony.

'What are you talking about? We're at sea – we're not in the bloody desert.'

'March 2014, south westerly winds sent a cloud of Saharan dust out of Egypt and across the eastern Mediterranean Sea. I watched it on a video.'

'No shit!'

'What about him?' said Tony, nodding at the big guy tied up on the deck.

'Leave him… he's not going to do anything.'

'True…'

'Let's get the mainsheet up, see if we can't catch some of that wind.'

'Is that what you're supposed to do in a sandstorm?'

'Look, who's the effing captain here? Anyway, whatever your video tells you, I reckon it's just Saharan sand blowing across. If there's a storm, we can bring the mainsheet down.'

Sonia was still looking at the big guy all unconscious.

'Go and wake your brother,' I said, 'and get those life

jackets on. But stay down there, don't come up.'

Sonia disappeared like she knew something was up.

'Tony,' I said, 'release the cleat and pull on the line, then let the mainsheet out and then we can trim.'

Tony also did what he was told.

The mainsheet fluttered and flapped around a bit, but I could tell the wind was getting up fast.

'You need to trim, Tony!' I shouted, keeping hold of the wheel.

The sail bubbled out, then Tony brought it back in again, until it stopped. We began to pick up wind and speed, which was what I wanted, but what I didn't like was the way the wind seemed to be quickly changing direction. I told Tony to tack and the boom can come flying across the boat.

We kept this up for a good two or three hours, sailing into the wind, sometimes with the wind behind us. Tony would have a good puke when we were running, and Sonia kept sticking her head up wanting to know if everything was all right. In the end, I told her to stay sitting on the steps and keep an eye on the big guy, who kept stirring.

It was getting tiring, for both me and Tony, with the wind whipping up the sea, the spray from the waves, and the rain soaking us and making us frozen. I think I'd also lost all sense of direction, not that I had any sense of direction before, but I now definitely had no idea if we were going straight towards Sicily or being blown way off course. But north or south, east or west, I was not thinking about which way the boat was going because the wind was now a storm.

I helped Tony with the sail and we carried on downwind, under bare poles – no sail at all – running before the wind. I was getting worried – we were going too fast, even without the sail. I could see the boat come down a large wave and bury the bow in the back of the wave in front. It was getting scary. The wind was howling and the waves were huge. I had to think, but I couldn't think. Everything was getting out of control. Nature was taking over. The sea was a raging beast, a bastard of an unforgiving soul. A hateful, vengeful ocean god was coming out to eat us up in the dead of night. We were going up and down, round and round, like being stuck in an effing washing machine, riding along on an everlasting rollercoaster. The foam was spraying all around and there was constant water coming over the top of the boat. The blowing spray and foam was making it almost impossible to see.

I told Tony to get back into the cockpit before he got blown overboard.

'But we're getting hit!' he shouted back at me.

I knew what he meant.

We had nothing tied down.

I shouted at Sonia, 'Where's Zain?'

He poked his head out from underneath Sonia's legs.

'Keep holding those rails,' I said, as they clung on to the ladder.

With all the commotion and the water flooding the deck, the big guy was coming round. He was dulled but looked scared as hell. He was saying something to me; it sounded French.

'What's he saying?' I said to everyone else.

'His hands,' said Sonia. 'I think he means his hands.'

'We need to untie him,' said Tony, who at the same time took a big gulp of water, which drenched his face and body.

'Not yet,' I said.

Not unless we were sinking.

But we were going up and down, thirty feet plus, and the ups and downs were followed by lots of jerks, as waves on the swells pushed the boat around. Every movement was tiring. We would fall down a wave and at the bottom of the trough, the wind would feel a lot less strong, but as we came up to the top of the crest, the wind would be howling again in our ears and screaming in our faces. I felt like I was falling off into a halfway place, part awake and part zombie. I think I was so exhausted, I was starting to not care, as I watched the seawater keep draining away from the drenching over the deck and over the cockpit, and all my strength seemed to be draining away with it too.

'How long is this going to go on for?' asked Tony, holding on as I kept my frozen fingers stuck to the wheel.

'Didn't it tell you in the video?'

'Oh yeah, I remember now – we're all going to die!'

That didn't help as the wind and spray kept coming and the waves kept crashing across the side of the boat.

Then there was a loud *clunk*.

I looked at the mast. That was OK.

Then the *clunk* sounded again.

'What's that?' said Tony.

Clunk!

'Check the anchor,' I said. 'It might have dropped. If it is, it's hitting the hull.'

'And that's not good?'

'See if it is first – we don't want the anchor punching a hole in the boat.'

It meant Tony holding on to the rails as he slid along the side of the boat towards the bow. I looked down at the big guy. He deserved better. I cut the rope so his hands were free and told him to stay there.

I tried my best to keep an eye on Tony as the boat surfed the next wave then plunged back down. The Cini pitched like a cartwheel. We came back up. Then we bounced and skidded down the surface of another huge wave, the wind from behind pushing the boat down the face, then at the bottom of the wave, we hit no wind, as if we were in a deep depression.

We stalled and then a wave roared up from behind us, picking up the boat and throwing it down the next wave. I was not in control. We were in the hands of the sea god Poseidon. And if the sea wants you, it will take you – there is not much else you can do about it.

Then all was black.

The power of the next wave turned us upside down. I could feel myself rolling over as The Cini capsized.

Round and round the laundromat I spun. Cold water pouring through my lungs. Saltwater filling up. The force taking away my breath. Drowning. Spinning like a spinning top. Bumping into things. Things bumping into me. Wondering where I was. The noise of the water whooshing, cleansing for a moment, suspended in the deep blue sea, in the world of nothing.

Zeus, Poseidon, Hades, have you been waiting too long to get your hands on the English gangster? You can have me if you want. I am ready. You have stuck me in too many holes, played me like a sucker. And now you soak me in your sodding sea, filling up my lungs with freezing water, blanking out my sight and blinding me, bringing down the curtain on my useless effing journey.

That's if you want me?

Then I was rising, being lifted, a large hand gifting me the chance of life again, if I wanted it. I rose and swam and rose again, seeking light, seeking air, looking to breathe once more, desperate to find oxygen.

And I hit the surface.

Coughing, spluttering, my ears stuffed with thick cotton wool.

In a moment, I started to think. I was no longer drowning. I was being gently looked after, cradled like a baby, lofted up high so I could say fuck you to the world around me, falling down into the pit of the rocking water, where all the rage above my head had gone away.

I rode another wave and then came back down.

That's when out of nowhere, I saw Sonia rise from beneath me, as if she had been there by my side all that time I had been under the water. In the murky foam and spray, she floated over to me. Her lifejacket, like mine, had saved her.

'Hold on to me!' I shouted.

Spitting and chuffing, she grabbed hold of my neck.

Then we went down again, as we rode the wave to the bottom of the sea. In the strange silence that lived down there, Sonia spoke: 'Where's Zain?'

'Don't worry,' I said, waiting for the wave to carry us back up again to the crest.

But I was worried, shit scared that we were the only ones left.

I felt a hard crunch into the side of my chest. It was blue and white. A box. A blue and white floating plastic box. I held on to it and could feel it had buoyancy. This was going to help. Now all we had to do was look into the raging sea for

246

Zain and Tony, and for anything else that came our way.

Again, we rode a wave and sunk back down.

'I can't see him,' said Sonia, whose body was starting to shake from the cold and the shock.

'We need to keep looking,' I said, as I let the plastic box take our weight and rise again to the top of the wave.

'Zain!' shouted Sonia. 'Zain!'

Then as we hit the top of the wave, we both saw The Cini upside down in the water, no more than twenty or thirty feet away. That was our chance, our chance to live. I pushed the plastic box out of the way and started swimming towards the upturned hull, with Sonia's arms still wrapped around my shoulders.

As soon as I got hold of the side of the boat, I pulled us both around to the stern. The keel had been snapped off but the rudder gave us grip to climb up.

Balancing on the upturned boat, it didn't feel like the storm was raging as bad. I let Sonia rest, lying on her stomach, and stood, crouched, looking around for signs of life. Then Sonia shouted out Zain's name, not like she was looking for him but had found him. I swivelled my head around and there was a body in the water, bobbing up and down. I couldn't tell who it was, if it was Zain or Tony.

Sonia was up, like me, on the curve of the hull, and she kept shouting out Zain's name. That's when I felt the upturned boat was floating towards them. And Sonia kept shouting, like she was sure it was Zain. Then the body started coming a bit closer. One body, swimming towards us. Then I could tell. It was the big guy and it was Zain, holding on.

'Stay there,' I said to Sonia.

I dived right in. And for the first time, and I don't know

247

why, I felt the cold really get to me. My muscles were tight. It was a struggle to move, to turn over my arms, to get closer. I was making things worse. I wasn't saving anybody in this state. I started treading water. I waited. They were close.

But where was Tony?

They came up close to me. The big guy swimming with all the energy he had in his heart.

'You see,' he said, 'I save your little man.'

I nodded to say thanks and swam back to the hull, helping both to get on top.

Sonia was hugging Zain.

Then the big guy looked at me funny, like he was sorry for something. He didn't have to be – he had saved Zain. But he used his eyes to tell me I should look back out to sea.

And that's when I knew.

That's when I saw Tony's body floating in the water, drifting away from the upturned hull of The Cini.

'What's wrong with Uncle Tony?' asked Sonia, who was holding Zain tightly.

'He's waving,' I said.

'Why is he waving?'

'He's just saying goodbye.'

'Is he going to drown?'

'No, he's going to swim back to the island.'

'Will he make it?'

'Yeah, no problem, he swam the English Channel once.'

'Did he?'

'Yeah, he's a champion swimmer is Uncle Tony.'

Sonia stood up.

She started waving madly.

'Bye bye, Uncle Tony, bye bye!'

And I said nothing, as we all watched Tony float away.

6

It seemed like the storm had done its worst, taking Tony away, that was until we started seeing other things in the water. Sonia was keen on grabbing stuff but I told her to leave it.

At first, it was all the flotsam from The Cini that had floated out from inside the cabin. Anything with air in it made it to the surface, like sealed packets of pasta.

But then came the bodies.

It was the beginning of the death parade, the marching bloated flash mob, sipping away at the salty sea waves that bobbed them up and down. One or two at first, face down, half bodies, stripped of clothes or just a shirt or a dress hanging off them. I suppose the hope was that someone might have lived, as the big guy – who told us his name was Pierre, which is like me saying my name is John Smith – looked for a body that might rise and wave for help. And this time, yes, they would be allowed on the boat, in our upside-down world of fucked-up-ness.

'You see,' said Pierre, 'I have to come on your boat.'

What he meant was, the people drowned in the water were from the abandoned cargo ship. I felt like saying that we had capsized as well, so it was the same difference. But I just nodded. After all, I had whacked him over the head and left him tied up and unconscious, and he was now in credit because he'd done the right thing by saving Zain.

Still, the whole morbid death thing kept floating our way. One body after another, then in clumps, like drifting seaweed. It was only when the youngsters, the children, were spotted that I told Sonia and Zain to stop looking, but there was nowhere else to look. It felt like death had been haunting me for the last few weeks on the island and now it was just passing me by on a conveyor belt, the hell of it all, a blank, meaningless reminder that death was a throwaway thing. Perhaps there was enough of us in the world to not really bother about thousands that get poured down the drain, or are blown up and shot up, through no fault of their own. The lava flow of human rubbish, packed like sardines on a rusty old crate, would be pecked, nibbled and gobbled before floating onto some beach to be tagged and then disposed of. The Med was like this watery drain of desperation, a border control based on survival of the fittest, a castle moat designed by nature to keep the savages out.

As we drifted on through the night, drifting away from all things nasty and hopeless, we watched the grey clouds in the dark sky above us begin to reveal some moonlight. The dead bodies would go away, the morning was going to come, and the sun would rise and warm us.

That was the hope, but shivering on top of the upturned hull, I was torn up about how I had led Tony down a path where he'd ended up dying. You could say it was an occupational hazard, but Tony was never the kind of villain who had gone out of his way to do anybody any damage. He didn't deserve it. I would just have to get the message back to Grandad that Tony's family had earned a good pension, and he had been a top servant to Grandad's cause of making money. Not much consolation to Tony's kids though. I was just glad I was more than likely going to be hundreds of miles away from all the fallout around this one. And seeing as I was some evil brother-killing bastard, they could all blame me back on the estate if they wanted.

When the morning did come, it was like nothing had happened, like nothing had gone wrong. The sea was a calm, happy child, even if we all knew it had been a psychotic bastard running around killing everyone. We watched and waited as the sun rose slowly, peering through the remaining cloud, giving us all hope. The wind was still there, not as strong, but like lizards we started to stretch out across the hull so we could get our human batteries up and running.

I must have dozed off by the time I felt something stabbing into the side of my stomach. I shot straight up, thinking I was about to be crushed by some effing container ship, when I saw little old Zain in front of me, doing his pointing thing out to sea.

That's when the word hope turned into reality: land, coastline, terra firma, where we belong. After all, we ain't fish, we ain't birds, we're stupid effing apes, and I was desperate to get back to where I belonged – climbing trees and stuffing myself with a cheeseburger and fries.

I slapped Pierre on the back and crawled over to Sonia to wake her.

'Come on,' I said, smiling. 'Fancy a swim?'

She wasn't with it. We were all exhausted, but there was no future on the hull of The Cini, drifting on top of the deep blue sea.

But that's when I realised I had to look at this guy Pierre and ask him for one more favour, one that he was probably well within in his rights to say no to. And it was in his eyes,

251

I could tell. He was thinking he owed me nothing. He was thinking he must fight for his own survival and that's why he was still alive.

'Can you take Zain?' I asked.

There was this blank look.

What could I say? I wasn't going to say sorry.

Then the guy suddenly leapt off the hull into the sea.

I thought that was it and I'd have Sonia and Zain to try and save, which would end up with us all dying.

But before I had time to stop him, Zain had jumped in as well.

'Zain!' I shouted, like an angry parent.

The kid came to the surface with the lifejacket keeping him up.

Pierre was treading water.

Perhaps all he did want was for me to say sorry.

'Wait!' I shouted.

But by this time, Sonia had slid down the hull and into the sea. Zain was already struggling with keeping afloat. I really needed Pierre to use his great big heart to help us.

I think that's when Sonia knew what was happening.

She just said one word: 'Please.'

He spat some water out. Did it matter to him who lived or died?

Then Pierre dived.

He was gone for five, ten seconds.

Zain screamed as he was pushed out of the water, as Pierre lifted him up on his shoulders.

Thank fuck!

The tension and relief made us all burst out laughing.

'You see,' shouted Pierre at me. 'I am human.'

I nodded, which was my way of saying thanks.

'On my back,' he said to Zain, 'my little man.'

So I jumped in, and the sea was freezing. That sun had been way too good to us and now it was going to bleach us.

Sonia was keen to try and swim on her own. I left her to it but the coastline looked a long way off and Sonia was struggling. And the cold of the sea felt a lot worse than it did last night. I was beginning to think this might be the hardest bit of the journey. I was getting sick of the seawater, sick of the sun beating down, sick of Sonia's hands around my neck, sick of the weight I was carrying, sick of swimming through treacle and fed up with everything.

Which was crazy. I should be thanking the ocean gods for having kept us alive. I should be writing a letter in my head to send to Tony's wife and kids. I should be on my knees kissing the feet of the big guy, Pierre, for saving little Zain. I should be doing a lot of things to say thanks and not moaning in my head about swimming these yards and lengths to get to the beach.

But it was getting to me. It was weird but I felt like giving up, as if it were enough that we had got this far.

Then I started telling myself I didn't care. I didn't care about the kids or anybody else. I was a heartless hard nut and the only way to survive was to look after number one and not waste time on things that don't give anything back.

What was I saying?

My stupid brain was saying stupid things.

I had to keep swimming.

And it wasn't far to go. Just keep pushing. Arms in and out. Legs in and legs out. Scissor kick. Don't drink the water. Scissor kick.

Don't strangle me, Sonia.

Not far to go.

But it was. That effing coastline. It wasn't getting nearer.

Perhaps we're going the wrong way.

I had to look back. I had to make sure.

No, we were going the right way.

Then the waves got up. The sea was breaking.

And Pierre was standing up.

And Zain was laughing.

And I put my feet down.

I could stand up.

And the coast, the beach, was under our feet – it was something we could walk on.

Sand.

And I threw myself down. I was fucked.

I tasted the sand.

I watched Sonia lie next to me. I watched Zain laughing. I watched Pierre running.

And a hand and another voice say something.

We were alive.

We had made it.

In Sure And Certain Hope

1

A coal black mountain with white streaks of snow was in the middle of a large window frame, with a thin river of blood-red orange flowing down from the top and disappearing. I couldn't work it out because I was sure I was lying in bed. Then I wondered if I was back in the villa and I was just dreaming one of those dreams that you think is real. All I knew was something had happened since we had landed on the beach, but all I could remember was the voice.

I shut my eyes. Best place to be sometimes is back in your dreams. I used to do that a lot, dreaming about being somewhere else, dreaming about living on an island and being at peace. Funny thing is, I ended up living on an island, but all the things I had run away from had caught up with me in the end: Grandad, crazy people, liars and bastards, scared people, angry people, jealous and greedy people.

Then I heard the voice from the beach.

'*Buongiorno.*'

I turned my head.

I opened one eye.

There was a kid, a teenager, all brown and silky skinned, with short jet-black hair and thin carved features.

He smiled at me.

I shut my eye and opened the other one.

He was standing in a doorway, still smiling at me.

I didn't move. I thought I was going to struggle to move, I felt so stiff and exhausted.

'Would you like some water?' he asked, in almost perfect English with an Italian accent.

I heard a jug of water clanking with some ice and the water beside me being poured into a glass.

'I found you,' said the kid. 'On the beach. We put a trace on your phone and tracked you when you were near to the coast. Then the storm comes, so I think your phone is at the bottom of the sea now.'

I rolled my head back and looked up at the ceiling.

'We had been looking for you, but then we knew the storm was bad, so we had other people look for you, but you swim all the way close to me.'

I tried to ask something but my mouth was like sandpaper.

'If it is hard for you to speak, I can tell you the children are safe.'

That was good, as my mind started putting things together. I now knew I was with my mum's family.

With a load of effort, I pulled myself up, so I was looking again at the black and white mountain through the window frame. I picked up the water and took a sip and noticed how there was little in the small room, apart from an old dark brown wardrobe and a table and chair.

The kid was back standing in the doorway.

'I would like to go to London,' he said, like it was

something I might be able to do for him.

I took another sip of water.

'What is London like?'

That was not what I was interested in, but I decided to try and answer to get the vocal cords working.

'Cold,' I said.

The kid looked disappointed, so I added, 'In the winter.'

'It can be cold here in the winter too,' he said, I suppose hoping this proved he could cope with the weather.

I needed more water.

As I drank, I kept looking at the weird black and white mountain through the window, which I was pretty sure was a volcano because it did have a lava thing going on.

'My family can look after you,' he said. 'And your family can look after me, if I go to London.'

I nodded but it was about as likely as me going on a foreign student exchange.

'Montebello,' he said, pointing to the window.

I moved my dry crusted mouth and managed to ask, 'Is that a volcano?'

'*Sì*, Montebello.'

'And is it active?'

'*Sì*,' he said, like it was not a problem.

'Does it ever go bang?' I said, using my hands to create an explosion.

'Of course.'

I then heard some shouting from below – a woman shouting in Italian.

'My mama,' he said, which I took to mean he had to go.

'One sec,' I said, lifting my hand. 'The children, the girl and the boy, are you sure they are OK – no injuries?'

'*Sì.*'

'And you know who I am?'

'*Sì,*' he said, like it was something I didn't have to say.

He was about to go, then he turned back.

'*Mio nonno, Il Padrino*, you will need to speak to him.'

And then he left.

Now that was one word I did know the meaning of: *Il Padrino* – his grandfather and The Godfather. My mum might be the most distant cousin ever related to the family, but there was always this Italian thing in the background. The only problem, nothing was ever going to be for free, and once you start this kind of thing, it never ends. It just keeps on going until you would rather die than carry on.

So, no problem there then.

The thing is, we all used to watch *The Godfather* films when we were kids and just laugh at them. We all thought *Scarface* was way better – more drugs, more violence. I told Grandad this and he got all serious and told me to go back and watch all of *The Godfather* films again, and then come back and tell me what I had learnt. So I listened to that fat old bastard Brando droning on and then gave a miss on the other two and told Grandad this: never let your enemy know what you are thinking. He liked that and then told me I had to read a load of military stuff on strategy, and to play lots of board games like Risk and stay off the video games because they would rot my brain. I did none of that. But I did learn one thing: if you can, think first before you do.

I carried on sipping water and looking through the window at the big black and white mountain. Smoke and clouds were hovering around the top, and that stream of lava was going somewhere, but not this way. People must get used to it, living with a destructive piece of nature on their doorstep. It rumbles away in the background, gives off a load of stuff now and then, blows up and pours red-hot lava down the sides of the mountain. But it must always be just a matter of time before the big one does a load of damage. In fact, thinking about it, I'm not sure how you could live like that, farming, or whatever it is they do around here, probably olives and wine, and tarting up the house, knowing that it could all just be flattened by lava and ash.

Still, having believed in the ocean gods getting me across the sea, I had to wonder if the volcanic beast was going to be a good or a bad omen. There was all that weird, dreamy stuff I had when I was sleeping under the tarpaulin where Borg had jumped, and now it was like as real as anything. That's like a prediction, it means something when that happens. Only problem is, I just didn't know what was going to happen – it was all going to be dependent on what *Il Padrino* said.

My thinking was then broken by the sound of the kids. I had learnt one thing about them: you know how they walk, how they run, and that tells you where they are and when they are coming.

Sonia and Zain stamped their way to the doorway, and just like the Italian kid, stood there looking at me.

'Are you OK?' asked Sonia.

'Yeah. And what about you guys? Any cuts, bruises or scratches?'

'Some,' said Sonia, holding out her leg and then the other one.

'And what about you, Zain, you still in one piece?'

He nodded but didn't bother to show off his minor injuries.

'Can we sit on the bed?' asked Sonia.

'Yeah, no probs.'

They both climbed up so they were at the foot of the bed.

'There's an older boy here,' said Sonia. 'His name is Leonardo.'

'Oh right, like the painter.'

I could tell Sonia didn't know what I meant.

'He goes back a long way, hundreds of years,' I said. 'And there's a painting in Paris called the Mona Lisa, and that is meant to be the greatest painting in the world.'

'Why?'

'Who knows,' I said. 'But it's very small. So small it might fit in a very large pocket.'

'Are you going to steal it?'

I laughed.

'So, who else is here and what is this place like?' I asked.

Sonia had the intel. 'There's a lady and she gave us some food, and there is an old man I saw in a room and he was coughing, and there are other men outside and some of them have guns, but I think some of them are farmers because there are tractors and trucks and barns. There are also lots of steps that go up high and they have small trees on them.'

It sounded like a well-armed farmhouse and vineyard.

'OK, and do you remember what happened on the beach?'

'Yes,' said Sonia, all excited. 'There were people there and they said they knew we were coming. You were asleep but they put you, and then me and Zain, in the back of a truck. Then they took us here and said we would be safe.'

'And what about Pierre?'

'He ran away.'

That fitted.

'Can we ask you a question?' asked Sonia.

'Yeah.'

'Can Uncle Tony really swim all the way back to the island?'

'No, he wouldn't be able to do that. But what will happen is a ship will see him and pick him up.'

'Does he know we are staying here?'

'Why?'

'So we can tell him we are all right.'

'Yeah, of course, I'll let him know. But remember, we can't stay here long. I need to talk to that old man who was coughing. Once I've done that, we need to get some things because we lost everything when the boat capsized.'

Sonia was thinking. Then she said, 'Do you think they have chocolate?'

'I don't know. Why don't you go and ask the lady?'

'How do you ask for chocolate?'

'You mean in Italian?'

She nodded.

'Say: *cioccolato.*'

She said the word back to me a few times.

'That's it,' I said.

'OK, bye!'

And they both jumped off the bed and ran back down the stairs.

2

The next day I had the best breakfast ever. Leonardo's mama

just piled it on the plate. So I ate like a pig with my head in a trough, or like it was my last meal before the meat wagon took me off to a better place.

Sonia and Zain drunk some milk and then ran outside to play in the courtyard of the old farmhouse. Then Mama disappeared and Leonardo brought in an old man and sat him down at the head of the kitchen table. This had to be *Il Padrino,* whose sun-wrinkled skin and heavy brow made him look like a big grizzly bear.

I smiled and he nodded.

Leonardo stood by his side and started to translate.

'My grandfather likes to welcome you to our house.'

I thought there would be more but there wasn't, so I said, 'Thank you for helping me.'

Leonardo said this back and on we went.

'My grandfather says that you are a lucky man and hopes you can still have many more lives because he knows how dangerous life can be.'

'I hope so to,' I said.

'My grandfather says that your mother used to come to this house when she was a child, before she left to go and live in London. He says that he was surprised to hear about you because she has not spoken to our family for a very long time. Do you know why?'

'No, I'm surprised too,' I said, 'because she always spoke to me about her family here. I can only apologise because I believe in family and understand how important it is, for trust and loyalty.'

This seemed to go down well with *Il Padrino*, who then spoke about half a dozen sentences, which Leonardo had to work out so he could repeat it all back to me.

'*Sì, sì,*' he said. 'My grandfather would like you to know that although there has been a long time where no one has spoken, the blood is still pure and keeps us all connected. It is this blood, your blood, and your mother's blood, which is the same blood my grandfather has, and that means there will always be blood ties that make us family.'

I hoped that would be it about blood and family but then Leonardo seemed to have one more thing he had forgotten. 'And my grandfather also says that blood is like a river which runs down from Montebello, down to the sea and out into the oceans. We are like the red river, a fire which will always burn if there is life in us.'

I nodded like I was Harry Potter getting advice from a wizard.

Then *Il Padrino* spent a bit of time thinking before Leonardo gave me a load more translation.

'My grandfather thinks that the marriage between the man and the woman is a sacred thing, but he does not think that your mother married wisely. However, these mistakes can be corrected. My grandfather also knows that there has been some tragedy in your family and that your brother was more like your father, a violent man. He would like to know the reason why you killed him?'

Christ, this was car-crash reality TV!

'Not all blood is good blood,' I said, as my mind struggled with pictures of rampant vampires.

Il Padrino also had a short answer to that: 'It is better we fight other families than fight within the family.'

'Sure,' I said, 'but when it comes to my half-brother, I wouldn't be sitting here now if I hadn't done what I had to do.'

The wise old bird spent more time thinking, then talking, then Leonardo said, 'My grandfather wants you to know that what has passed between you and your brother will remain with you. If there is bad blood in the family, there is sometimes only one solution – to remove what is bad and to keep what is good. He wishes that your mother had been more careful in choosing her husband and perhaps things might have been better for you and your mother. Also, my grandfather asks what has happened to your mother's husband?'

'He's inside,' I said. 'Prison... behind bars.'

Il Padrino understood that as he put his hand up to stop Leonardo.

Then I waited for the next bit of Sicilian wisdom and smiled back at Leonardo. 'Your English is very good.'

'*Sì*, thank you,' he said, as he also listened to *Il Padrino*, then thought for a bit about how to say what he had to translate.

'My grandfather says that he understands you do not work for your own family but another family, and that this other family has a grandfather, like I have my grandfather.'

'Well, yes, I have a boss and his nickname is Grandad. But tell your grandfather it is not the same... well... tell your grandfather that there are strange family ties... so it is family... but it is just business.'

'I don't understand,' said Leonardo.

He had a point.

'OK, just say that I work for another family, but it is not the same as it is here – my boss is not like a *padrino*.'

I could see the old bear found this odd.

'My grandfather suggests that perhaps you should have

your own family when you go back to London. He thinks it would be a good idea and we should stay in touch.'

'Of course,' I said. 'I will make sure that our families are tied together and not kept apart.'

This seemed to give *Il Padrino* what he wanted.

'My grandfather understands and believes you,' said Leonardo, who must have thought he'd booked his flight out of here. 'Therefore, he would like to know what it is we can do for you now, to help you on your journey.'

I had a list.

'Can you tell your grandfather that we lost everything at sea. It means I need to get hold of new passports for me and the children.'

Leonardo did the usual, then looked a bit uneasy, as he said, 'Are you not going to sell the children?'

The thought hadn't crossed my mind.

'Tell your grandfather that I have made a promise to their mother and they are in my care until they get to where they want to be.'

'OK, *sì*, my grandfather understands.'

Then Leonardo listened and told me, 'We can arrange for you to have these passports – I can take the photos for you.'

'Thank your grandfather for this. And there is one more favour I need to ask him, if he will allow me to ask?'

'*Sì, prego*,' said the old bear.

'I am looking for someone. He would have travelled here in the last day or two, and like me, he will be looking for a passport. He is German and goes by the name of Max Schmidt. I would be in your debt if you were able to find anything out about him since he arrived here.'

Up to this point, *Il Padrino* had given nothing away, but

as soon as I mentioned Schmidt, the bushy eyebrows raised and his eyes told me he knew the name.

Then Leonardo said, 'How do you know this Max Schmidt?'

I suppose this is where I should try and use the lesson about not letting your enemy know what you are thinking.

'We just need to have a chat,' I said, 'before I leave with the children – that's of course if he is still here?'

I waited and then Leonardo said, 'There are many German people who visit here, especially the Montebello. It would be difficult to find one man out of so many.'

'I know,' I said, 'but he would not be your usual tourist. I need to find him or know where he has gone.'

This time the old bear didn't waste time on Leonardo's translation – seems like he knew what I'd been saying since we started all of this.

'My grandfather says he will ask for you to be provided with any information on Max Schmidt. My grandfather says he must rest now.'

'Yeah, no problem.'

Leonardo then did his duty and helped *Il Padrino* to his feet.

I stood up.

As the old man left, he didn't look as strong as he did when he came in, as he coughed his way back to his coughing room.

After that, Sonia and Zain were keen to give me a tour of the place, like we had booked a cool farmhouse for a week's holiday in the sun. I checked out that there were two kinds of people who did two different things on the *Il Padrino's* property. There were the farm workers, who were looking after the grapes and the olives, and there were the guys walking around who looked bored – they had the guns strapped to their chests. Then there were a few outbuildings that had the farm workers going in and out. And all this was surrounded by an eight-foot-high brown stone wall and a large, thick wooden gate where the guards hung out. But one thing I couldn't keep my eye off was that brooding mountain volcano, Montebello.

Grandad had a farm back in Essex but that was all about cows and containers going off-piste. Really, what was missing back home, was a great big effing active volcano looking down on you, just to spice things up and get the cows crapping all over the place. I mean, Essex can make you depressed and feel like slashing your wrists, but out here, it was another type of mood – like a low current of fear plugged into the mains.

So I got it into my head that I should be ready for anything because I just didn't know what was going to happen. Not that any of this sort of thing touched Sonia and Zain, and there was no reason why it should. I was learning, I think, that kids just bounce back, like Duracell bunnies – no matter what gets thrown at them, all they want to do is play and have fun. And as Tony would have to said to me, that was bleeding obvious, poor bastard.

Leonardo got me a phone but I kept the messaging to just the people in Germany who owed me a favour. They were keen on taking the kids and hoped we had a safe journey. But there was no way I was going to tell Grandad anything or let Tony's wife know what had happened. I was a coward when it came to letting Tony's lot know, but it was also because I wanted to be seriously below the radar, because there was no one I could trust. I just had to hope in the next few days I got a sighting of Schmidt, or else I'd end up rotting in some eurozone police cell.

After a lot of lying in bed and looking at the smoking black and white Montebello, the aches and pains of being capsized and swimming half an ocean eased off a bit. My top half was browning, and Sonia and Zain had a rich golden tone to their skin and looked well-suited to living out here, but I didn't fancy their chances given *Il Padrino's* thinking on them.

Leonardo's mama spent all day in and around the farmhouse, cooking or sweeping or hanging out washing. And at night, we would hear the old man coughing his guts up, the constant chatter of insects and the odd shouting by the guards at something, who were at least more alert than they looked during the day. However, there was always some dog barking its head off, prowling around and yapping at anything and everything. It was either that dumb mutt or the night-time heat that made for restless nights, one after the other.

Well, either that or the thought of Schmidt.

As much as I needed time to heal, my patience was beginning to wear thin with *Il Padrino's* efforts to locate the elusive Schmidt. I was starting to suspect that he was a pale shadow of a man, not The Godfather he made himself out to be. After all, I'd had no sight of any other family members to meet or greet, or to be challenged or insulted. Either the family wanted to keep us well below the Sicilian radar, or some things were not what they seemed.

And so, on the seventh day, we got to go on a picnic.

3

Leonardo, being the good kid he was, carried the basket full of goodies. He led the way through a side gate behind the old farmhouse, which took us straight into long lines of olive trees. Above us were the terraced vines on the volcanic soil of Montebello, and the coal black lines and white stains of snow, reaching up into the sky.

We sat down on the sunburnt grass under the shade of an olive tree, with insects chirping away and the heat like a thick warm coat. Crusty bread, tomatoes, grapes, cheese and lemonade were laid out on a blanket and it all went down a treat. With our bellies full, we all sat quietly, which for the kids was a rare thing. I looked into the eyes of Sonia and Zain and reckoned there were two things going on in their heads: this moment, which made life seem easy, a life of being children, and a second thing, a darkness, a shadow, a shade of pain, hurt and chaos. I had no power to make it better for them. I couldn't make the world a better place. But I understood why they were quiet.

When I was a kid, I found out what it was like to feel the world was a violent and brutal place. I knew what it was like to know that no one cared, no one wanted to know, no one had time or space for a kid. I knew what it was like to have nightmares and bad dreams. I knew what it was like to live in fear and danger. I knew what it was like to know that nothing was the way it was meant to be, the way people lived on TV and in movies.

As I bit into another tomato, the best and juiciest ever,

Sonia wanted to ask Leonardo a question.

'*Sì, che cos'e?*'

Sonia wasn't sure.

'What would you like to know?' I said, taking on the role of translator.

'Why would your grandfather sell me and my brother?'

I coughed, spluttered and nearly choked.

Leonardo didn't seem that bothered. 'He will not sell you.'

'Don't worry,' I said, 'we're going to Germany.'

'My grandfather is old,' continued Leonardo, 'he says strange things.'

I wiped the tomato off my face and winked at Zain.

Then Leonardo sighed.

'My grandfather,' he said, 'worries a lot about things. He thinks our family will not live for much longer.'

'Is there a war?' asked Sonia, speaking from experience.

'*Sì, probabilmente.*'

'Families like to argue about things,' I said.

'*Faida*,' said Leonardo.

'What's… *faida*?'

Leonardo looked at me for an answer.

'I think it means blood feud,' I said, looking in the basket for any more food.

'*Sì…*'

But I could tell Sonia still wasn't sure what that meant.

'This is going on for a very long time – many, many years,' added Leonardo. 'The families always like to fight. They say you killed my cousin, my brother, my sister, my papa, my mama. All the families have died and now there is only Salvatore.'

'Who is Salva—' Sonia couldn't finish the name.

'Salvatore? He is the one and he has destroyed all the heads of the old families. I think he will now win because he is different, he is new. He drives fast cars and he has friends everywhere.'

'But there is still your grandfather,' I said to Leonardo. 'He doesn't sound to me like he has given up the fight.'

'I will help him,' he said. 'And my brothers and my cousins. But I think we will all end up working for Salvatore – *il capo dei capi*.'

'Would he sell us?' asked Sonia.

Leonardo laughed.

'I don't think anyone wants to sell you,' he said. 'I think you will all go to where you want to go.'

'Good, I'm glad because we have been sold before, by my mummy.'

Leonardo laughed again.

'Why would your mama sell you?'

'She did not sell me but she sold my brother to Schmidt.'

'She sold your brother, for what?'

I looked at Zain, his eyes looking down.

'For this,' she said, her eyes angry, making a circle with one hand and putting a finger in and out.

And that's when everything that was wrong, from the day I walked onto the Leninsky Komsomol, made an ugly kind of sense. Why else would Schmidt help this family? And why else did the kids accept their mum's death? For sure, you'd be sad, but to let that fuck-up have his way to pay for passage on a shitty Russian cargo ship – that is desperate stuff. And no wonder the kid didn't say jack shit! If I could turn into that effing volcano, I was going to start spewing giant boulders

271

down on every fucked-up human being, so bad was the rage building up inside me.

Then Leonardo pulled out his phone and said he had a message.

'They have found him,' he said. 'He will be collecting his new passport. We can do the same, for you, and cut his throat at the same time.

'You mean Schmidt?'

'*Sì*, but we will need to go now.'

I could tell that Sonia now thought she could meet her end of the bargain, going all the way back to the cargo ship and Spiteri's visit to the villa. But she had done enough, seen enough, and it was time I took this piece of shit on, face to face.

'Listen to me,' I said to Sonia, 'I want you to stay here with your brother.'

'Why?'

'Because I know what Schmidt looks like now.'

'How?'

'I've seen a photo of him, the police showed it to me.'

'Oh…'

'Yeah, so no worries. As far as I'm concerned, you've kept your side of the bargain, our deal.'

Sonia looked down at the floor, like she had been naughty.

'What is it?' I asked.

'I think I can tell you now.'

'Tell me what?'

'What he looks like.'

'You mean Schmidt?'

She nodded.

'And?'

'He looks like the devil.'

I smiled.

'That's OK,' I said. 'I know he's a scary man. But remember, that's all he is, just a man.'

'OK, but will you still help us?'

'Yeah, I'm going to go with Leonardo to get the passports and then I will sort out Schmidt.'

'What are you going to do to him?'

'Well, he has something that is mine, remember, so I need to get that back.'

'And then we will kill him,' said Leonardo.

The teenage Rambo wasn't helping.

'But what if you die?' she said.

'I won't die. And we won't be long. I will get the passports and I will teach Schmidt a lesson so he never ever does what he did to your brother ever again.'

'We will cut off his penis and put it in his mouth,' said Leonardo.

I gave up pretending. 'There you go…'

'*Sì*,' said Leonardo, who was packing up the remainder of the food and pulling up the picnic blanket.

'Now,' I said, pulling the two children together so they stood side by side, 'we have come through a lot together and this is just all part of the journey, which for you has been even longer than it has been for me. So, I want you to know you are the bravest, strongest kids ever, and I am going to get you to Germany, and I have some nice friends there who are going to take care of you. Their names are Ann and Texas and they told me they can't wait to see you.'

Sonia put up her hand.

'Yes?'

273

'Is Texas in America?'

'Yes, but he is not American, if that's what you're thinking. He has had do the same as you, to travel a long way to get to Europe, so he will understand everything you've been through.'

'And when are we going?'

'Today… as soon as I'm back we are going to leave here… OK?'

The two kids both nodded.

'Right, I want you to stay in the farmhouse. I don't want you to go outside once I have left.'

They both nodded again, as Leonardo led the way back through the side gate and into the courtyard.

I took Sonia and Zain back into the farmhouse.

I looked at them both. They had innocence and tragedy all over their faces, sunk deep into their eyes, plastered all over their memory.

I put my hand on Zain's shoulder.

'Now, you're the big man, OK.'

He was surprised by that but liked what I said and smiled.

'OK, now be good, and ask if Leonardo's mama needs any help with anything.'

They didn't move at first. I knew they were scared because I was leaving, but I had to go. I could hear *Il Padrino* coughing in his room, then mama walked in and that was my chance to get up and go, without looking back at them.

Outside, I heard an engine chugging away. I looked around the courtyard but there was no sign of a vehicle or the farmyard guards doing anything except looking more bored than usual.

I followed the noise of the engine and that's when I found

Leonardo in a barn sitting on a tractor.

'*Bellissimo*,' he said, like it was his own little beauty.

'What are you doing!' I shouted, standing in front of the long engine.

'I am going to kill Schmidt,' he said, like he wasn't sure why I didn't already know that.

I walked up to the side of the tractor, which was hooked up to a low-level trailer, and told him to turn off the engine.

'I think you need to speak to your grandfather about all of this.'

'*Sì*, he knows. I have killed before. Our family knows about this man.'

'How?'

He shrugged.

'How do you know?'

'My grandfather knows, that is all I can say.'

'Where are your brothers?' I said to Leonardo.

His face went all tense.

'Or your cousins?' I said, as he kept his face hard and stiff.

Then he said just one word to me: 'Salvatore.'

'What about him?'

'They have all gone… to Salvatore.'

'You mean, they've deserted your grandfather?'

'*Sì*.'

'So, there's just you?'

'*Sì*.'

'But what about the guards?'

He shook his head.

'We pay, but they will not come with me to do this.'

This is where I should have told him to get off the tractor and go back to the farmhouse and watch Al Pacino movies for the next twenty-four hours.

But my brain wasn't working.

Leonardo was right. All I wanted to do, and perhaps all he wanted to do, was kill Schmidt. It didn't matter how, all that mattered was to get that bastard's face in my face and squeeze the fucking life out of him.

'Let's go then,' I said.

The kid lit up, like it was his birthday or Christmas.

I pointed to the trailer.

'*Sì,*' said Leonardo, as he started up the old monster.

I jumped in and stood up behind him. The gears started to grind and then I got thrown back as he jolted forward.

'*Scusa!*'

I spat out the dust I'd swallowed as Leonardo drove out into the courtyard and up to the main gates. I decided to keep low in the trailer as he ordered the guards to open them. Outside the gates and out on a rutted track, I kept myself on the floor of the trailer until he had us out on the main road.

As I lay on the floor of the dust box, my body going up and down in a bumpy rhythm, the coal black and white-streaked Montebello was in my sights. As soon as I had seen it through the window on my first day here, I had not stopped thinking about what it might mean to me. It was personal, the dark beast. It did not come out of nowhere but from the pit of the past, from famine and extinction, searching for the dead souls who needed to be taken off to hell.

Was it angry, Montebello, because it had lost a soul? Did it want revenge for losing out on a sinner like me? If only it had a face, something to look at, something that was not blank and gave nothing away. It was so hard to read the black heart, the chuffing chimney, the blood-red vein. I just knew

276

it wanted to speak to me, to tell me the whole truth and nothing but the truth – the final judgement, the only trial that had any meaning. It was not just a mountain, not just a volcano, it had a mind, a brain, it had superpowers. I think, it knew more about me than I knew about myself. It had more power than any human being and could blast away without reason and destroy everything in a couple of seconds and have no need to give a reason why.

Then my body was thrown to one side as Leonardo took a sharp turn. We were going uphill, as the gears started grinding, as Montebello disappeared.

I hauled myself up and got up close to Leonardo's ear.

'Heh!'

Leonardo turned around and smiled.

'How far is it?' I shouted into his ear because the tractor engine was louder than a jumbo jet.

Leonardo just pointed to the top of the hill.

'Is that where we are going?'

He gave me a serious-looking nod.

As I looked back down the hill, I could see *Il Padrino's* farmhouse, with the olive grove behind the farm buildings and the vineyard growing up the terraces towards Montebello. In that moment, I hoped everything was all right with the kids.

Should I have left them alone?

The tractor ground its way up the hill. I did my best to keep my footing behind Leonardo in the trailer, realising again I had gone against my own rules and was doing things having not thought it through.

The last time, I told myself.

As we got to the top of the hill, Leonardo started waving

with his hand.

'*Sdraiarsi, sdraiarsi.*'

I crouched down.

'*Sdraiarsi,*' he said again.

I laid flat in the trailer so no one could see me.

'*Sì, sì, buono.*'

It meant I could only see the blue sky, but as we got to the crest of the hill, the tractor levelled out and the tops of old white buildings came into view. As he pulled up, I rolled over to the side of the trailer and could see through the wooden slats.

I had a bit of a flashback: a shitty wet island, looking through the wooden slats of an old shack, watching my half-brother Greg just before I killed him. But this time, no rain, no night, no wind or the cold sapping my energy as I looked forward to another slice of revenge and a bit of old-fashioned justice.

I think Leonardo had parked us up in the town square. I could make out a fountain, pretty buildings, flowers in hanging baskets over the fronts of shop windows. And it was quiet, no one about, which meant siesta time.

Leonardo got down and stood by the trailer where I was lying.

'I go see,' he said to me.

And before I had chance to stop him, he was off.

Fuck! What was I doing, letting this kid fight my battles? I would give him five minutes, or maybe just ten seconds. I watched him cross over the square and into a shop: *Copia e Stampa.* Then I saw in the window a large photocopier. So I could translate that for myself, and it made sense for the passports.

Maybe I would give him five minutes, but what the eff was he doing about Schmidt? There's no way the kid can deal with him. It was tough, just lying there like a useless lemon. What was Leonardo up to? Was he getting the passports and then we go somewhere else to catch Schmidt? What was I thinking?

That was it. I'd had enough. Less than a minute but I had to find out and get in there.

I hauled myself over the side of trailer and didn't care what anybody thought, not that I could see anyone about. And there was no point in being stealth-like –I just went straight in.

There was a doorbell.

One, two, Freddy's coming for you.

A reception desk and piles of A4 boxes.

Then I heard a loud thump and an Italian going ape shit.

Not good.

I leapt over the reception desk and through the doorway. There were stacks of shelfs and a few more photocopiers, and on the floor was Leonardo, holding his hands up to protect his face and a guy the size of an effing sumo pounding him.

He didn't see me coming.

I grabbed him from behind and threw the fucker against the side of the photocopier. He was a brute but I didn't have time to tell him he was an ugly bastard as I punched him in the stomach three or four times. He was winded but I wasn't having none of it. I grabbed him by his shirt, pulled his grizzly face close to mine, opened the photocopier lid and shoved him down on the glass so his head cracked it, then got hold of the lid and rammed it down hard: *uno, due, tre, quattro*… smash, smash, smash… smash.

At the same time, the copier started going crazy and prints started flying out the other end. I wasn't going to check on the quality as I hit him again with the lid, blood pouring out of the back of his head. I stood back and the great lump went flying backwards and hit the floor.

Out cold, or dead, I didn't give shit.

Then all I could hear was the kid crying. I got down beside him. His face was all mashed up.

'*Scusa, scusa,*' he kept saying, through his busted mouth.

'Heh, don't worry,' I said, wondering what I should do with him.

'Is he the passport guy?' I asked, nodding at the fat bastard.

'*Sì, sì…*'

'So, what's the fight about?'

That's when his crying got worse.

'What is it, Leonardo, what's going on?'

'Salvatore…'

'What d'you mean? Is he Salvatore?'

He shook his head, still blubbing like the teenage kid he was, having taken a nasty beating.

Then he started going back to saying sorry.

I didn't get it.

'Heh, Leonardo, just tell me what's happened. I can't help if you don't tell me.'

Then he composed himself.

'Diablo… he is there…'

'What, you mean Schmidt is here?' I said, thinking he'd got his words the wrong way round.

He shook his head again.

I tried to think: no passports, no Schmidt and Salvatore in

280

the mix.

Oh christ!

Oh fuck!

I knew what he meant and I jumped up.

Jesus effing Christ!

'You'll live,' I said to him.

But I didn't know if anyone else would.

I ran back over the reception desk, threw open the door and looked at the tractor.

That was no good.

I had to run.

Run like fuck, run like the fucking wind.

I had to get back to the farmhouse.

4

I ran like hell, running down the hill, my legs struggling to keep up with the speed I was going due to the gradient. But I wasn't going to stop the crazy pace I was going at and I wasn't going to look at that bloody Montebello. I was going to keep my eyes on the farmhouse in the distance, on the vineyard and the olive grove. I was going to look for signs of things happening and hope that things there were just as I had left them.

Then I reached the bottom of the hill and I could feel the pain in my legs from all that running. But next it was up hill and I had to keep going, I had to get back to the farmhouse because I knew, I just knew, things had seriously gone wrong. I should have seen it coming. I should have stuck to my way of doing things – think it through, think it through before doing anything. But I didn't and I just didn't see it coming. What a mug, what a dingus!

I was slowing down. There was no way I was going to keep it up. I put my hands on my knees and took in massive gulps of air. A few cars whizzed by. Who cares, I had to keep going. How far was it? Not too far. But my legs felt like lead, like running through treacle. But I had to keep going until I got there, huffing and puffing, until I got to the beginning of the track leading up to the farmhouse.

But no more running.

I had to be careful. I wasn't going straight up to the gate. I didn't want to be seen. I bent down in the burnt tall grass running along the crusty track. I got up to the side of the brown stone walls and crept around the side into the olive grove where we'd been eating the picnic.

The side gate was open.

I checked the courtyard.

The place was empty – no farmworkers, no guards, no nothing. I kept looking to make sure there were no surprises, then stepped out into the yard.

Again, I looked around, checking the large front gates, checking the few outbuildings. The place was deserted. That left only one more place to look: the farmhouse.

The door to the kitchen was open, but then it always was. I didn't rush in. I stood by the side of the wall, trying to get an angle to see in.

One body on the floor, face down, blood all over the place. It looked like Leonardo's grandfather, *Il Padrino*.

Then I heard a voice from inside: 'Please, no need to wait outside, come on in and make yourself comfortable.'

The accent was German. It had to be Schmidt.

'There is nothing to see out there,' it said. 'If you want to see, you must come indoors. No need to be afraid. There is only you and me, and then we can have some talk.'

I didn't have a choice. I was either going to be dead or I had a chance to live for however long he wanted me to.

So I went in.

And there, sitting at the end of the kitchen table, was Diablo.

'Take a seat,' he said. 'Sorry about the mess.'

I scanned the kitchen and saw Leonardo's mum in the doorway, bloodied and dead, but no sign of the kids. And as I stood, I looked straight into the eyes of the devil. What I thought was a red mask, like the one he had worn at The Sapori, was either glued to his face or it was his face. I squinted through the dull light and realised that there was no mask, there must have never been a mask – his face was surgically transformed into Diablo. Grinning from ear to ear, his skin might have been painted red, but his nose was a thick-edged bone, his eyes were flaming, his ears had arrow points at the top, his mouth had rubbery lips and his forehead was marked by two small goat head bumps.

But was it really Schmidt? For a second or two I wasn't sure. He – it – was beyond normal, outside of everything, a disgusting, distorted, vile and ugly gargoyle, a puss-ball of evil. And if it was Schmidt, which I suppose it had to be, he was this thing, a devil from hell, spewed out of Montebello to spread havoc, destruction, horror and pain. And he gloried in it, a man beyond the pale, beyond all reason. I knew then someone like this probably only goes when they are ready to go back to hell.

'Your passports are here,' he said, holding a shotgun balanced in front of him. 'I collected them for you.'

'How kind,' I said, wondering if I should sit or try and rush him.

The decision was made for me, as he moved the shotgun up to my chest height.

I sat down and said, 'Does that mean I can have them?'

He leaned back on his chair and sighed. 'We will have to see.'

That meant he wanted to talk. It meant he wanted something before he tried to kill me.

'Why the look… the devil thing?' I said, doing my best to size him up for weight and muscle. 'Must be a bit of problem at passport control.'

'Shut up!' he shouted.

Sensitive…

I waited.

He calmed down.

'If you must know, Steven Mason, and I am sure that useless whore Mila would have told you: I am an evil man obsessed with the devil. And on that point, and that point only, she is right.'

'Well, if that's all sorted, I'd like to know where my parcel is.'

'Oh, my sincerest apologies, but it got damaged during its long and arduous journey. It really is completely worthless. And unfortunately, there are no refunds available.'

'Then I'd like to make a formal complaint.'

'So would I, Steven Mason.'

'You mean you want to complain about yourself?'

That wound him up again as he thrust his finger down on

284

a small black pocketbook on the table.

'You know,' he said, trying to get his cool back, 'we are similar, you and me. We get asked to do things, dangerous things, I think. Then we find out that as we do these dangerous things, the people who expect us to put our lives on the line for them have been paying a tiny percentage of the real worth of the task assigned – I believe the "return on investment" to be the correct business term for this. The cost benefit is all risk on our part but without the commensurate reward for all the trials and tribulations we endure.'

I didn't say anything, as I tried to read upside down the title of his little black book, which was printed in gold lettering. He used my interest to lean forward in his chair, keeping his hand on the trigger, and flip open the black book.

'I have been thinking about you a lot, Steven Mason, and found something which I believe is true, for you and me:

> *'We're all in the same game*
> *Just different levels.*
> *Dealing with the same hell*
> *Just different devils.'*

'That's not from the bible then?'

'No, Dante!' he said, real angry.

'Just checking.'

'OK, enough, I think,' he said, pissed that I wasn't playing along with his fart-arse BS.

He leant back in his chair, his red beady eyes studying me, calculating what he wanted to say or do next.

'It is a shame you are not a literary man, but then you have far humbler origins than my own. But I know what burns

285

inside you, Steven, that keen sense of betrayal, the family ulcer. Like you, I have had this cruel burden, a biological tie which cannot be reconciled. So, both you and I know, families cannot be trusted.'

'What's that got to do with you murdering, pimping and ripping off everyone?'

'As a renaissance man, I only seek to offer you enlightenment.'

'Bollocks! Why put me in a hole six feet under?'

'That hole... this hole,' he said, like he knew I had slept under the tarpaulin and freaked out. 'To touch the ghosts of the past is a privilege very few of us get to experience. After all, I believe that to know hell is to know oneself.'

'I don't remember putting in a request for a visitor pass...'

'Are you sure you were just visiting?'

'The only thing I'm sure of, Schmidt, is you're not telling me the truth. Who's behind all of this? Who's paying you to fuck with my head?'

'The devil plays games, that's all I can tell you.'

Then he paused, like he might let me in on his psychotic thinking.

'What I can say, Steven, is I have enjoyed working with you and hope to see you in hell, sooner rather than later. What I have seen and heard, what I have observed, drew me to the conclusion that we have far more in common than any differences which temporarily have got in our way.'

'Why have you been playing games with me?'

'Sorry, Steven, you misunderstand if you think any of this is just a game.'

'Then what the fuck is it!'

'Think of it as a jigsaw, but one that can only be

completed without help from anybody else.'

I wanted to grab hold of the shot gun and stick it up his arse.

'You're a deviant fuck, aren't you, Schmidt?'

'Perhaps. Let's just say, for argument's sake: *the path to paradise begins in hell.* I'm just a naughty devil, waiting to be called back to hell.'

'Trust me,' I said, looking straight into his bulging red eyes, 'I don't give a shit about paradise or hell.'

'Such a shame because I think you have seen hell. But as Dante says, we have only three things left of paradise: *the stars, the flowers and the children.*'

'You like your riddles, don't you, Schmidt?'

'What else is there, once our lives become empty, except fun with poetry?'

'Insanity?'

'I may be many things, Steven,' he said, pushing his finger down again on the black book, 'but madness is not one of them. There is a logic to me. We must make sure that white is whiter than white. To keep things pure, we need to test ourselves in all that is despicable.'

'I think you mean despicable you, rather than despicable me.'

'Jihad, Steven, is not just for *them*, it is for our white race too. This means a white Jihad. We must do the most unthinkable things so we are prepared to commit the necessary acts to further our cause for the white race.'

I think he was trying to tell me he had some fucked-up higher calling, but it sounded like a racist ego-trip.

'And what about this mess in the kitchen,' I said, nodding at the blooded bodies of *Il Padrino* and Leonardo's mama.

287

'Is this just about money for you, doing the dirty work for the Salvatore family?'

'Exactly, it is only business – the devil needs to eat.'

'Haven't you got enough money after what Grech paid you?'

Schmidt burst out laughing, as if I'd made a big tit of myself.

'Why do you think I have to create this kind of chaos?' he said, waving the shotgun around the kitchen.

'Because you enjoy it…'

Schmidt sighed, clearly disappointed in me.

'I have only a few motivations,' he said, like it was not that big a deal to rape kids, murder and pillage. 'One of them is money, and if I had any of the money which Grech told you he paid me, I would not be doing Salvatore's dirty work for him – at, I might add, a hefty discount.'

'You're telling me no one's paid you for the password?'

He scoffed.

'Steven, you are a like man running wild in a field, trying to collect seed after the harvest has gone. They have arrest warrants out for you, and yet you want to do their dirty work for Grech, for next to nothing. They never paid me. No doubt they have not paid you, and yet I suspect they want you to kill me.'

'To be honest,' I said, cursing that I had let Spiteri trick me again, 'I don't need to be paid to kill you.'

'Ah… a man of virtue. Like all things Greek, virtue was a preoccupation with minimal return.'

'Then give me the password, or the Medusa, and get Grandad to pay you.'

'The thing is, Steven, the one thing I have learnt since I

travelled to retrieve this link to corruption is that those identified as corrupt are so corrupt they will never pay. They will use all the tools of the law, Steven, rather than pay what is due. But then, you have not even begun to scratch the surface of what it is going on in front of your very own eyes, and what is done by those big bosses of yours in your own country. Perhaps a little history lesson will help you understand.'

'Do I have a choice?'

'No,' he said firmly. 'We Germans know the British Empire is dead, but out of the ashes rose a secret second empire, a financial colossus, which spans the globe today. This is where real power is, hidden and managed through the language of a public school boy's and off-shore trusts and beneficiaries. You should know it all starts in the city of London, the money laundering capital of the world. This is where all the corruption, all the money from crime, is hidden by that innocuous term: financial services. Run by bankers and lawyers, they have their snouts in the trough. They are the real mafia. I find it rather amusing that the root of all evil is an accountant. But we don't belong to that kind of world, Steven. It is your boss who belongs, but not you. Like me, you are a little fishy in a very polluted pond.'

'You know what, Schmidt, it's not a revelation that most of us are getting fucked over.'

'I like your wisdom, Steven,' he said, pleased that I had been a good student and listened to him. 'Which is why I am prepared to negotiate a little with you, as a sign of good faith, before I seek an answer to a difficult question for you.'

'I can't wait…'

'I have concluded that I have only one option, one I should

have stuck to with Garibaldi, and handed over the Medusa
for him to reveal the corruption and slime that is done by all
those who rule. The password is simple, something only a
stony-faced mother would know. The Medusa, which turns
people to stone.'

'That's the password, the Medusa?' I said, kicking myself
for being so slow.

'Yes, so simple it is almost clever.'

'And why are you telling me now?'

'Because I think there is some virtue in you, Steven, and
a battle inside you, between good and evil. Unlike myself,
who has decided on a path of unadulterated evilness, yours, I
believe, is still unresolved. Therefore, I have given you the
power to decide who is most deserving of the password. It
will help you realise on whose side you belong.'

'But nothing is for free...'

Schmidt then touched his black book with his finger.

'*Never leave someone who touches your soul more than
your body.* So, Steven, where are the children of the
Medusa?'

Just as I was about to call him a sick bastard, we both
heard Sonia's voice.

'Take me,' she said, standing in the doorway, with Zain
behind her.

This caught Schmidt's attention, just long enough for me
to spot a long carving knife lying on the kitchen top.

'Well, if it isn't the bitch's daughter,' spat Schmidt.

Good, that's what I wanted, Schmidt focused on other
things.

'My mummy's dead,' said Sonia, who could see me ease
out of the chair and move closer to the knife.

'Well, as you can see, in my evil eyes, little bitch, there are no tears for your pimping mother.'

I felt the blade of the knife in the palm of my hand and flipped the handle.

'Why are you so cruel?' said Sonia, which was a better question than I could ever think of.

'You are too young to understand what makes a man what he is and why he must become what destiny has proscribed.'

'You need to leave us alone!' she shouted, ballsey as hell.

Schmidt stood up.

He pointed the gun at her.

She flinched.

I threw myself on the floor and rolled across to Schmidt, using the cover of the table. I looked up and could see the barrels coming towards me.

The only thing I could do was stab the side of his leg.

I plunged the knife in as deep as I could.

Then a loud screech, like a crazed wounded animal, came out of Schmidt's foul mouth.

It seemed to last forever, Schmidt's screaming, me holding the blade, making sure it was stuck right in. The screaming only stopped when I felt a massive whack on my head.

And I was out cold in a second.

5

I felt myself rocking backwards and forwards. I wanted it to stop but I kept being pushed and prodded.

Then there was the voice, which kept going: 'Wake up! Wake up!'

Why... why should I wake up? Can anyone tell me why I should wake up? Yes, you, the person pushing me – stop pushing me! There's no need to push. Look, I'm waking up.

But they kept banging on about waking up. Which I suppose I had to, even if my head was throbbing like a red-hot baboon's arse.

I opened my eyes.

There was Sonia, all angry. I put my hand where it hurt the most and felt a wetness – my head was seriously in need of some repair.

'You need to get up!'

I was doing my best as I looked at my fingers, which were covered in blood, which meant I was hit on the head by... Schmidt.

'Christ!'

'He's got Zain,' she said, her eyes all fiery.

'OK, OK,' I said, struggling to come around.

I think... I was concussed.

Then Sonia was pulling my arm. 'Come on, come on, we need to go.'

'Hang on, please, Sonia,' I said, touching the back of my head again to make sure there wasn't bits of skull and brain hanging out.

'But we need to catch him up.'

'Yes, I know,' I said. 'Just give me a minute. Tell me what happened.'

'He took Zain,' she said, which was no more than she'd already told me.

'OK, did you see where he went?'

She pointed with her arm out and stretched upwards.

I looked at her so she knew I needed a bit more explaining.

'He's on the mountain.'

'Are you sure?'

'Yes, I can see him. Come on, let's go,' she said, pulling on my arm again.

'All right,' I said, 'don't worry. He won't get far with a knife in his leg – trust me, I've seen it before.'

'He took the knife out.'

'Well, knife in or out, he's not going to get far.'

I grabbed hold of the kitchen table and pulled myself up. I was wobbling, trying to get the old gyroscope working.

'How long have I been out for?' I asked Sonia, who was now standing by the doorway.

She shrugged, eager to just get going.

Not long, I hoped, as I managed to keep myself steady and look around the courtyard. That's when Sonia pointed, beyond the vines that grew up the terraces, overlooked by the black fuming lump.

'I saw them there,' she said, her eyes bright with fury.

OK, no rush, no vehicle, I thought, and if we were lucky, there would be a blood trail from his leg.

'Was he limping?'

Sonia didn't care as she led the way through the side gate.

I stumbled along, doing my best to keep up, around the brown stone walls of the farmhouse and into the lines of the vines that led up the hill and onto a track running up Montebello.

As my brain got into gear, I couldn't figure what Schmidt was up to. He must have someone, or something, waiting for him. I mean, if I were a doing an execution, I would have a sure-fire way of exiting. But this didn't look like any kind of plan. Or perhaps his leg wound had scrambled his thinking.

We followed the track and there was a dip into a small cluster of lava-infested homes. We got to a wire fence, which looked like it had been put up to keep people out. There was a red and white sign that said:

ZONA RISERVATA

It was easy for Sonia to squeeze through under the fence. As I pulled my bulk through, I spotted a fresh stain of blood on a concrete post.

'They've come this way,' I said, looking up at the coal face of Montebello.

But I was worried we hadn't seen them since we had set off, and I was worried that Schmidt had made it to some rendezvous and had escaped.

But Sonia was all go.

'Just give me a minute,' I said, my head spinning, resting on a lump of concrete.

Schmidt had given me a severe headache, if not days of concussion. And that's when another thought popped into my head: why hadn't he killed me? Why spend all that time trying to convert me to his way of thinking? If it had been me, I would have pulled the trigger after saying hello. All of which reminded me of the last moments with Greg.

Anyway, Sonia was getting fed up with me sitting around doing nothing. She was right.

'Let's look around here,' I said, guessing Schmidt could have crashed out, given how bad that leg wound was.

'I will look,' she said, running into a broken stone house.

'Hang on,' I said, trying to keep my voice down. 'If they are here, we need to surprise them, not let Schmidt know we're coming.'

This made sense to Sonia, as I went ahead of her and looked inside the place. It had been abandoned in a hurry, with all the things that make up a family life left just as they were.

Sonia followed me in.

'I don't think they're here,' she said, loud enough to tell anyone else that we were.

But she was right.

'Let's just check the rest of the buildings,' I said, mainly because I couldn't think where else Schmidt could go.

As much as I hoped he could be hiding in one the houses, maybe half a dozen of them, I also felt he wasn't there. But what else did I have to go on? Just some blind instinct, some invisible thread that was leading us somewhere, perhaps to where Schmidt wanted us to go.

Back outside, the light had changed. The sun had gone down like a dead weight. It was dull, as if a blanket with holes had been covered over us. Gone was the heat of the day and we were wandering around in shadows. It was a strange feeling, an odd quietness, and I could see Sonia looking scared.

'Don't worry,' I said, 'we're going to find your brother.'

'But it's dark.'

'It's getting dark,' I said. 'I tell you what, let's look elsewhere.'

'Where?'

Christ, if only I knew. But there was only one place to keep looking, and that was above our heads.

'Let's just see what's on the other side of this place.'

We clambered over the mud and stone and then up to the ridge. Ahead of us was the burnt crust of another vineyard, scalded trees and black earth. We walked quietly through them, but we both noticed how silent everything was, like being in a bubble, keeping us alert and on our toes. And then I remembered what all this reminded me of, the grip of the silence playing with our heads. It was like walking through a graveyard when you were a kid, spooked out by the presence of gravestones and death.

There was nowhere else to go, either for Schmidt or for us, other than up and up towards the peak of Montebello. We stood with our feet on the fine, soft black gravel that had been spewed out of the guts of the mountain. Under our feet, it felt like we were walking on a rubbery kids' play area.

Sonia bent down and spread out her hands.

'It's warm,' she said, crunching the grains like it was sand.

That's when I didn't want to say we might have lost them.

And then she said the weirdest thing. 'Don't be afraid.'

'What's that?'

'Look!'

And she did her pointy thing and I followed her finger up the side of Montebello. And halfway up, we could see them. Schmidt limping and pulling Zain along. I didn't have chance to stop her. Sonia was off, running up Montebello like a swift little chimp. There was no point in shouting to tell her to slow down – she wasn't going to stop. And why should she? She wanted her brother back and we had them in our sights.

As much as my head felt like mush, I had to do the same thing and run, which was not as easy as it sounds. The incline and the black gravel made it feel like we were running up an escalator. But as we got closer, I was praying Sonia didn't shout out – I still needed to tackle Schmidt.

Not that I could see much in the poor light, but I didn't think he had the gun with him, or anything else. It was just him and Zain. And for whatever reason, he was just running to get to the top.

We ran and chased, stopped for breath, then ran some more, each time getting closer and then further away. Where was he going? What was he doing? There was nothing up there, just the cloud coming down and the dark moving over, with no escape.

Shattered as I was, we were getting closer. Near the peak, I looked back down and we had done some serious yards to keep up with him.

Then Schmidt stopped.

He was holding Zain tightly against his body.

He was waiting for us to catch up.

I stumbled, picked myself up, then got as close as I dared.

The cold was eating into me as the sweeping white clouds were rolling down and screening Schmidt and Zain. They would appear for a few seconds, then disappear again. Like barely visible ghosts, they moved in and out of sight, in and out, in and out. Or was it steam flowing down the mountainside? Was there heat on this bleak and empty mountain peak?

And why did I feel both calm and confusion?

'Where are they?' said Sonia. 'I can't see them.'

We peered and we looked, surrounded now by the swirling whiteness, with freezing ice forming on our faces.

'Zain! Zain!' shouted Sonia, just like she had on the

upturned hull of the capsized Cini.

Was Schmidt out there? Perhaps he was next to us. Perhaps he had disappeared back down the mountain.

But I was ready to give up. It was impossible to keep it together. We were risking our own lives. Montebello was beating us, keeping secrets with the devil, and the mountain would take us if we didn't head back down.

'Come on,' I said, 'I think we need to go.'

'No!' screamed Sonia back at me, with tears frozen onto her cheeks.

And just as I thought it was all over and I would have to carry her back down, we both saw Schmidt appear again through the cloud, no more than fifty yards ahead of us.

Sonia started to walk up to him, but I lunged forward and held her back.

'Wait,' I said, putting my hand on her shoulder.

Schmidt was trying to say something, breathless from the running and the wound.

'Zain!' she shouted, the poor kid looking scared and exhausted.

'You need to let him go!' I shouted to Schmidt.

That just made Schmidt hold Zain tighter against his body.

'Listen,' I said, across the swirling fog of cloud, 'there's no need for any of this. Just let the kid go.'

'Come and get him!' he shouted.

That's not what I wanted.

I noticed his leg was bleeding badly, but I didn't want to get too close to Schmidt in case he tried something.

But I took a few steps forward.

Then Sonia shot out from my grip and ran straight at Schmidt.

Shit!

I ran as well.

I was a few yards behind, just as Sonia got up close to Schmidt.

'Sonia!' I shouted.

But she wasn't going to stop.

Schmidt grabbed her as she tried to thump him with her fists.

I was there now. And I felt the rush of heat. The lava flow behind them.

Then Schmidt let go of Zain.

The kid ran at me and grabbed my leg. I was stuck for a second as Schmidt held on to Sonia.

He was not Schmidt, he was Diablo.

Then he said to me, 'Don't be afraid… of the end.'

That's when time stands still, when a thousand things could have been done in the time I had, but instead, I just stood there and watched… watched as the demented eyes of Diablo, the red flaring face, the insanity of an insane man and his twisted logic took hold, when fate – his fate, his destiny – dragged Sonia into the orange and red flowing river of lava below.

6

I cradled Zain in my arms and started running.

'Did you know,' I said, 'there were once three brothers. One of them was called Zeus and he was a sky god and chief head honcho of all the gods. And there was also a brother called Hades, who was god of the underworld. And there was another brother called Poseidon, and he was king of the sea, and the earth and horses. He also had a weapon, like a great big fork, you know, the kind we should eat with. But this fork was so big it had a special name called a trident. Anyway, I reckon he probably used it for a bit of fishing, or to deal with baddies. So, the point is, buddy, I think we've been lucky because I think Poseidon's been looking after us, especially when we were doing that sea crossing. Well, the other thing about Poseidon, he has to look after the earth, you know, because it can shake about a bit in some places and cracks up a lot and things seep out of the earth like lava. So, you see, he's been making sure we don't fall through the cracks in the earth. Now, your sister, Sonia, bless her, I think she might have fallen down a bit of a crack with that horrible man Schmidt. And if she has, we don't have to worry too much because I know Poseidon is the kind of god who would look after your sister. And with Schmidt, I think what Poseidon would do is he'd take his great big fork, the trident I told you about, and he would stick it right in him. Which is what he deserves after what he's done to you.

'But I promise you, Zain, I promise you more than anything that I am going to make sure you have a proper life after all of this. Don't you worry, we're going to get this all sorted. And you know, the other thing about Poseidon was he liked to make horses. Yeah, he loved horses, and he would make them with other women. One of them, and I don't mean anything bad about your mum, but one of them was called Medusa. Well, some say she had hair made of snakes but she was supposed to be very beautiful, and I know Poseidon fancied her a lot. But the thing about Medusa was that

Poseidon had fallen for someone who wasn't a god. Now, I don't think that was strictly legal in the god world, and for whatever reason, this Medusa ended up getting killed by another god called Perseus. It sounds all a bit sick, I know, but it's the only way to tell you the story because when he cut off her head, she gave birth to two sons. One was called Chrysaor and the other one was called Pegasus.

'Well, the story goes that the severed head of Medusa had the power of turning everything into stone if you looked at her. But Pegasus was a bit special because he was a winged horse, which meant he could fly. Wouldn't that be great, Zain, to be like Pegasus and be able to fly? In fact, some people, you know, like the gods and the Greeks, tried to use Pegasus because he was so special. One of them tried to get Pegasus to fly up to heaven but he fell off on the way up there. I think that's because Pegasus was the kind of horse that didn't want to do things that other people wanted him to do. Pegasus was only going to do what he wanted, however special he was.'

Then I stopped running.

I didn't really know where I was.

The dark had come down on us.

I sat down on the soft Montebello gravel, with Zain still in my arms. The poor kid was crying, just little tears for a little guy, his whole world smashed up.

'Heh,' I said, pointing up at the stars. 'You see that square of stars up there, and the other stars either side, did you know that's Pegasus up there? That's where he ended up, with the stars, and helping Zeus. So, you know, in the end, he's got to live forever, looking down on us.'

Zain looked up and we both just looked at the stars in the

sky.

I must admit, I didn't really know if it was the Pegasus constellation, but it was something that made us both calm down.

'Heh, we've been on a journey, that's for sure,' I said, 'but not much further to go. Yeah... not much further... I promise...'

The Resurrection To Eternal Life

1

People who do evil things never tell you really why they do it. That's part of the game they play, which isn't nice, but that's the way it is with the evil that gets into them. Once it starts, once you've crossed over into that evil state of mind, there's no stopping them, no going back, no normal, just madness.

Anyway, that's how I thought about Schmidt. I didn't get it – all the games, all the stuff, all the damage he wanted to cause, it was just all part of Schmidt's twisted brain. Had Schmidt abused Sonia? Who knows. He took her and everything else with him down into hell.

The injuries hurt, the mental and physical, that's for sure, like being punched a thousand times in the stomach and being told to stop complaining and just get on with it. But if there was any good to come out of it, I knew I had to get away forever from Grandad.

There was a bit of payback when I let Cini know the

password was Medusa. I thought it was a fair price for losing her boat at sea.

And me and Zain, we were like two peas in a pod, both lost, both just travelling to get from A to Z. I wasn't going to tell him that the world should be a better place. It wasn't. He'd just seen it all close up and personal, at its darkest, at its most honest, unforgiving and painful.

I always kept the kid with me as we made our way by train all the way into Germany. And once we'd got to Berlin, it was a case of setting things up. Then after a week or so, I had Zain scrub up and we headed off on the U-Bahn to the Museum Berggruen.

I'd told him as much as I could about the people he would be settling down with. He seemed OK with it, after I'd talked and talked about how wonderful these people were, but I was always having to just look into his eyes and work things out because he still wasn't saying anything.

Zain held my hand real tight as we walked down a long wide road of grand buildings with thick stone faces. There was a large dome with columns on top of the museum, but inside it was a modern art gallery. We found the seat where we needed to sit, in front of a painting by Picasso. It was called the Seated Harlequin – a clown who was mute.

I told Zain to look at the painting closely and to keep looking and not turn his head. I told him that he was such a special boy and like the gods I'd told him about, he was going to live forever, that all his family were stars in the night sky looking down on him and no one will ever, ever hurt him again. I then said a very tall black man was going to sit next to him and his name was Texas. Like Zain, he had travelled on a long journey to get to where he wanted to be and he was going to be the best dad ever.

I slid off the leather seat and nodded in Texas as I walked away.

I was gutted, torn up inside.

And I couldn't help it, but I was crying like an effing baby.

Enough, I told myself – get a grip.

And then, just as I was leaving the building, I spotted Ann, sitting by the entrance.

'Where are you going, Mr Steven?' she asked, her pale face looking a bit older since I'd last seen her in London.

'Where am I going?'

'Yes.'

'Where I've always been.'

'And where is that?'

'Hell…'

END

Postscript

If you want to know more about Steven Mason and how he ended up on a Mediterranean island, then please read *The Dead Hand of Dominique*. And if you read that, you won't have to wait too long for the third and final book, which will tell the story of Steven's final journey.

PRAISE FOR *THE DEAD HAND OF DOMINIQUE*

'Brilliant writing and plot... if you liked *Three Billboards*, *Seven Psychopaths* and *In Bruges*, you will love this book... five stars.'

'An enjoyable, fast-paced slice of Brit Grit taking place in the wilds of Essex and London... busy, violent, funny, dark, and quirky.'

'*The Dead Hand of Dominique* is an enjoyable romp through

the murky criminal underworld of Essex and London, in the company of some memorable characters.'

'This book was a wild ride. I really enjoyed the mystery of it all. I loved how I never knew who I could or couldn't trust and the ending was perfect.'

'Excellent book, couldn't put it down. Good twists throughout, but especially near the end. Highly recommended.'

'There is a great cast of characters. Unique, eccentric, villainous and murderous.'

'What a great cover and title! I started reading it and got totally sucked in.'